RUPERT OF HENTZAU

THE CHILDREN'S ILLUSTRATED CLASSICS

See page 198

'*There, man, I'm ready for you*'

Rupert of Hentzau

BEING THE SEQUEL TO A STORY BY THE SAME WRITER
ENTITLED 'THE PRISONER OF ZENDA'

By ANTHONY HOPE

With four colour plates and line drawings in the text by
MICHAEL GODFREY

LONDON: J. M. DENT & SONS LTD
NEW YORK: E. P. DUTTON & CO. INC.

'ANTHONY HOPE' (Sir Anthony Hope Hawkins, knighted for his services in the Ministry of Information, 1914–18), cousin of Kenneth Grahame, was born on 9th February 1863 in London, and died on 8th July 1933 at Walton-on-the-Hill, Surrey. After winning a brilliant First at Balliol College, Oxford, becoming President of the Union, and proving himself a fine all-round sportsman, he became a barrister. By the time he was thirty he could take his choice from law, politics and literature with a good chance of success in each.

His first five novels had scarcely done well enough to make him choose literature; but on 28th November 1893, as he was walking home after the conclusion of a successful case at the Bar, a new adventure story seemed suddenly to unroll before him, set in an imaginary country which he named Ruritania. He began to write that evening and had finished 'The Prisoner of Zenda' by the end of the year. It was published in April 1894 and made him famous almost overnight. 'The debonair chivalry of its hero, the vivid narration and the tenderness of the love story took more than the town by storm,' wrote A. E. W. Mason. It speedily gained a place among the few supreme examples of stories of sheer adventure—a place which it still holds unchallenged.

'The Prisoner of Zenda' and the society sketches of 'The Dolly Dialogues', published a month later, settled his future, and in July 1894 'Anthony Hope' gave up the Bar and devoted his whole time to writing. He wrote many novels with considerable success and several plays which were long popular: but he remains the inventor of Ruritania— one of the few authors who have added a new country to general acceptance and a new word to the language.

A sequel to 'The Prisoner of Zenda' appeared in 1898 as 'Rupert of Hentzau', and is one of the few examples of a continuation which does not fall short of its original. Much else of what he wrote is still worth reading, but his fame rests on these two books. Of the rest his only other book of Ruritanian adventures, 'The Heart of Princess Osra' (1896), is the most memorable—though his own favourite was 'The King's Mirror' (1899).

CONTENTS

ILLUSTRATIONS

COLOUR

BLACK AND WHITE

CHAPTER 1

The Queen's Goodbye

A MAN who has lived in the world, marking how every act, although in itself perhaps light and insignificant, may become the source of consequences that spread far and wide, and flow for years or centuries, could scarcely feel secure in reckoning that with the death of the Duke of Strelsau and the restoration of King Rudolf to liberty and his throne there would end, for good and all, the troubles born of Black Michael's daring conspiracy. The stakes had been high, the struggle keen; the edge of passion had been sharpened, and the seeds of enmity sown. Yet Michael, having struck for the crown, had paid for the blow with his life: should there not then be an end? Michael was dead, the princess her cousin's wife, the story in safe keeping, and Mr Rassendyll's face seen no more in Ruritania. Should there not then be an end? So said I to my friend the Constable of Zenda, as we talked by the bedside of Marshal Strakencz. The old man, already nearing the death that soon after robbed us of his aid and counsel, bowed his head in assent: in the aged and ailing the love of peace breeds hope of it. But Colonel Sapt tugged at his grey moustache and twisted his black cigar in his mouth, saying: 'You're very sanguine, friend Fritz. But is Rupert of Hentzau dead? I had not heard it.'

Well said, and like old Sapt! Yet the man is little without the opportunity, and Rupert by himself could hardly have troubled our repose. Hampered by his own guilt, he dared not set his foot in the kingdom from which by rare good luck he had escaped, but wandered to and fro over Europe, making a living by his wits, and, as some said, adding to his resources by gallantries for which he did not refuse substantial recompense. But he kept himself constantly before our eyes, and never ceased to contrive how he might gain permission to return and enjoy the estates to which his uncle's death had entitled him. The chief agent through whom he had the effrontery to approach the King was his relative, the Count of Luzau-Rischenheim, a young man of high rank and great wealth who was devoted to Rupert. The count fulfilled his mission well: acknowledging Rupert's heavy offences, he put forward on his behalf the pleas of youth and of the predominant influence which Duke Michael had exercised over his adherent, and promised, in words so significant as to betray Rupert's own dictation, a future fidelity no less discreet than hearty. 'Give me my price and I'll hold my tongue,' seemed to come in Rupert's off-hand accents through his cousin's deferential lips. As may be supposed, however, the King and those who advised him in the matter, knowing too well the manner of man the Count of Hentzau was, were not inclined to give ear to his ambassador's prayer. We kept firm hold on Master Rupert's revenues, and as good a watch as we could on his movements; for we were most firmly determined that he should never return to Ruritania. Perhaps we might have obtained his extradition and hanged him on the score of his crimes; but in these days every rogue who deserves no better than to be strung up to the nearest tree must have what they call a fair trial, and we feared that, if Rupert were handed over to our police and arraigned before the courts of Strelsau, the secret which we guarded so sedulously would become the gossip of all the city, aye, and of all Europe. So Rupert went unpunished except by banishment and the impounding of his rents.

Yet Sapt was in the right about him. Helpless as he seemed, he did not for an instant abandon the contest. He lived in the faith that his chance would come, and from day to day was ready for its coming. He schemed against us as we schemed to protect ourselves from him; if we watched him, he kept his eye on us. His ascendancy over Luzau-Rischenheim grew markedly greater after a visit which his cousin paid to him in Paris. From this time the young count began to supply him with resources. Thus armed, he gathered instruments around him, and organized a system of espionage that carried to his ears all our actions and the whole position of affairs at court. He knew, far more accurately than anyone else outside the royal circle, the measures taken for the government of the kingdom and the considerations that dictated the royal policy. More than this, he possessed himself of every detail concerning the King's health, although the utmost reticence was observed on this subject. Had his discoveries stopped here, they would have been vexatious and disquieting, but perhaps of little serious harm. They went further. Set on the track by his acquaintance with what had passed during Mr Rassendyll's tenure of the throne, he penetrated the secret which had been kept successfully from the King himself. In the knowledge of it he found the opportunity for which he had waited; in its bold use he discerned his chance. I cannot say whether he was influenced more strongly by his desire to re-establish his position in the kingdom, or by the grudge he bore against Mr Rassendyll. He loved power and money; dearly he loved revenge also. No doubt the motives worked together, and he was rejoiced to find that the weapon put into his hand had a double edge; with one he hoped to cut his own path clear, with the other to wound the man he hated through the woman whom that man loved. In fine, the Count of Hentzau, shrewdly discerning the feeling that existed between the Queen and Rudolf Rassendyll, set his spies to work, and was rewarded by discovering the object of my yearly meetings with Mr Rassendyll. At least he conjectured the nature of my errand: this was enough for him. Head and hand were soon busy in turning the knowledge to account; scruples of the heart never stood in Rupert's way.

The marriage which had set all Ruritania on fire with joy and formed in the people's eyes the visible triumph over Black Michael and his fellow conspirators was now three years old. For three years the Princess Flavia had been Queen. I am come by now to the age when a man should look out on life with an eye undimmed by the mists of passion. My love-making days are over; yet there is nothing for which I am more thankful to Almighty God than the gift of my wife's love. In storm it has been my anchor, and in clear skies my star. But we common folk are free to follow our hearts; am I an old fool for saying that he is a fool who follows anything else? Our liberty is not for princes. We need wait for no future world to balance the luck of men; even here there is an equipoise. From the highly placed a price is exacted for their state, their wealth and their honours, as heavy as these are great; to the poor what is to us mean and of no sweetness may appear decked in the robes of pleasure and delight. Well, if it were not so, who could sleep at nights? The burden laid on Queen Flavia I knew and know, so well as a man can know it. I think it needs a woman to know it fully; for even now my wife's eyes fill with tears when we speak of it. Yet she bore it, and if she failed in anything, I wonder that it was in so

For three years the Princess Flavia had been Queen

little. For it was not only that she had never loved the King and had loved another with all her heart. The King's health, shattered by the horror and rigours of his imprisonment in the Castle of Zenda, soon broke utterly. He lived indeed; nay, he shot and hunted, and kept in his hand some measure, at least, of government. But always from the day of his release he was a fretful invalid, different utterly from the gay and jovial prince whom Michael's villains had caught in the hunting-lodge. There was worse than this. As time went on, the first impulse of gratitude and admiration that he had felt towards Mr Rassendyll died away. He came to brood more and more on what had passed while he was a prisoner; he was possessed not only by a haunting dread of Rupert of Hentzau, at whose hands he had suffered so greatly, but also by a morbid half-mad jealousy of Mr Rassendyll. Rudolf had played the hero while he lay helpless. Rudolf's were the exploits for which his own people cheered him in his own capital. Rudolf's were the laurels that crowned his impatient brow. He had enough nobility to resent his borrowed credit, without the fortitude to endure it manfully. And the hateful comparison struck him nearer home. Sapt would tell him bluntly that Rudolf did this or that, set this precedent or that, laid down this or the other policy, and that the King could do no better than follow in Rudolf's steps. Mr Rassendyll's name seldom left his wife's lips, but when she spoke of him it was as one speaks of a great man who is dead, belittling all the living by the shadow of his name. I do not believe that the King discerned that truth which his wife spent her days in hiding from him; yet he was uneasy if Rudolf's name were mentioned by Sapt or myself, and and from the Queen's mouth he could not bear it. I have seen him fall into fits of passion on the mere sound of it; for he lost control of himself on what seemed slight provocation.

Moved by this disquieting jealousy, he sought continually to exact from the Queen proofs of love and care beyond what most husbands can boast of, or in my humble judgment make good their right to, always asking of her what in his heart he feared was not hers to give. Much she did in pity and in duty; but in some moments, being but human and herself a woman of high temper, she failed; then the slight rebuff or involuntary coldness was magnified by a sick man's fancy into great offence or studied insult, and nothing that she could do would atone for it. Thus they, who had never in truth come together, drifted yet further apart; he was alone in his sickness and suspicion, she in her sorrows and her memories. There was no child to bridge the gulf between them, and although she was his queen and his wife, she grew almost a stranger to him. So he seemed to will that it should be.

Thus, worse than widowed, she lived for three years; and once only in each year she sent three words to the man she loved, and received from him three words in answer. Then her strength failed her. A pitiful scene had occurred in which the King peevishly upbraided her in regard to some trivial matter—the occasion escapes my memory—speaking to her before others words that even alone she could not have listened to with dignity. I was there, and Sapt; the colonel's small eyes had gleamed in anger. 'I should like to shut his mouth for him,' I heard him mutter, for the King's waywardness had wellnigh worn out even his devotion.

The thing, of which I will say no more, happened a day or two before I was to set out to meet Mr Rassendyll. I was to seek him this time at Wintenberg, for I had been recognized the year before at Dresden, and Wintenberg, being a smaller place and less in the way of chance visitors, was deemed safer. I remember well how she was when she called me into her own room for a few hours after she had left the King. She stood by the table; the box was on it, and I knew that the red rose and the message were within. But there was more today. Without preface she broke into the subject of my errand.

'I must write to him,' she said. 'I can't bear it, I must write. My dear friend Fritz, you will carry it safely for me, won't you? And he must write to me. And you'll bring that safely, won't you? Ah, Fritz, I know I'm wrong, but I'm starved, starved, starved! And it's for the last time. For I know now that if I send anything, I must send more. So after this time I will not send at all. But I must say goodbye to him, I must have his goodbye to carry me through my life. This once, then, Fritz, do it for me.'

The tears rolled down her cheeks, which today were flushed out of their paleness to a stormy red; her eyes defied me even while they pleaded. I bent my head and kissed her hand.

'With God's help I'll carry it safely and bring his safely, my Queen,' said I.

'And tell me how he looks. Look at him closely, Fritz. See if he is well and seems strong. Oh, and make him merry and happy! Bring that smile to his lips, Fritz, and the merry twinkle to his eyes. When you speak of me, see if he—if he looks as if he still loved me.' But then she broke off, crying: 'But don't tell him I said that! He'd be grieved if I doubted his love. I don't doubt it—I don't indeed; but still tell me how he looks when you speak of me, won't you, Fritz? See, here's the letter.'

Taking it from her bosom, she kissed it before she gave it to

I bent my head and kissed her hand

me. Then she added a thousand cautions—how I was to carry her
letter, how I was to go and how return, and how I was to run no
danger, because my wife Helga loved me as well as she would
have loved her husband had Heaven been kinder.

'At least, almost as I should, Fritz,' she said, now between
smiles and tears. She would not believe that any woman could
love as she loved.

I left the Queen and went to prepare for my journey. I used to
take only one servant with me, and I had chosen a different man
each year. None of them had known that I met Mr Rassendyll,
but supposed that I was engaged on the private business which I
made my pretext for obtaining leave of absence from the King.
This time I had determined to take with me a Swiss youth, who
had entered my service only a few weeks before. His name was

Bauer; he seemed a stolid, somewhat stupid fellow, but as honest as the day and very obliging. He had come to me well recommended, and I did not hesitate to engage him. I chose him for my companion now, chiefly because he was a foreigner, and therefore less likely to gossip with the other servants when we returned. I do not pretend to much cleverness, but I confess that it vexes me to remember how that stout guileless-looking youth made a fool of me. For Rupert knew that I had met Mr Rassendyll the year before at Dresden; Rupert was keeping a watchful eye on all that passed in Strelsau; Rupert had procured the fellow his fine testimonials and sent him to me, in the hope that he would chance on something of advantage to his employer. My resolve to take him to Wintenberg may have been hoped for, but could scarcely have been counted on; it was the added luck that waits so often on the plans of a clever schemer.

Going to take leave of the King, I found him huddled over the fire. The day was not cold, but the damp chill of his dungeon seemed to have penetrated to the very core of his bones. He was annoyed at my going, and questioned me peevishly about the business that occasioned my journey. I parried his curiosity as I best could, but did not succeed in appeasing his ill humour. Half ashamed of his recent outburst, half anxious to justify it to himself, he cried fretfully:

'Business! Yes, any business is a good enough excuse for leaving me! By Heaven, I wonder if a king was ever served so badly as I am! Why did you trouble to get me out of Zenda? Nobody wants me, nobody cares whether I live or die.'

To reason with such a mood was impossible. I could only assure him that I would hasten my return by all possible means.

'Yes, pray do,' said he. 'I want somebody to look after me. Who knows what that villain Rupert may attempt against me? And I can't defend myself, can I? I'm not Rudolf Rassendyll, am I?'

Thus, with a mixture of plaintiveness and malice, he scolded me. At last I stood silent, waiting till he should be pleased to dismiss me. At any rate I was thankful that he entertained no suspicion as to my errand. Had I spoken a word of Mr Rassendyll he would not have let me go. He had fallen foul of me before on learning that I was in communication with Rudolf; so completely had jealousy destroyed gratitude in his breast. If he had known what I carried, I do not think that he could have hated his preserver more. Very likely some such feeling was natural enough; it was none the less painful to perceive.

On leaving the King's presence I sought out the Constable of Zenda. He knew my errand; and, sitting down beside him, I told him of the letter I carried, and arranged how to apprise him of my fortune surely and quickly. He was not in a good humour that day: the King had ruffled him also, and Colonel Sapt had no great reserve of patience.

'If we haven't cut one another's throats before then, we shall all be at Zenda by the time you arrive at Wintenberg,' he said. 'The court moves there tomorrow, and I shall be there as long as the King is.'

He paused, and then added: 'Destroy the letter if there's any danger.'

I nodded my head.

'And destroy yourself with it, if that's the only way,' he went on with a surly smile. 'Heaven knows why she must send such a silly message at all, but since she must she'd better have sent me with it.'

I knew that Sapt was in the way of jeering at all sentiment, and I took no notice of the terms that he applied to the Queen's farewell. I contented myself with answering the last part of what he said.

'No, it's better you should be here,' I urged. 'For if I should lose the letter—though there's little chance of it—you could prevent it coming to the King.'

'I could try,' he grinned. 'But on my life, to run the chance for a letter's sake! A letter's a poor thing to risk the peace of a kingdom for.'

'Unhappily', said I, 'it's the only thing that a messenger can well carry.'

'Off with you, then,' grumbled the colonel. 'Tell Rassendyll from me that he did well. But tell him to do something more. Let 'em say goodbye and have done with it. Good God, is he going to waste all his life thinking of a woman he never sees?' Sapt's air was full of indignation.

B

'What more is he to do?' I asked. 'Isn't his work here done?'

'Aye, it's done. Perhaps it's done,' he answered. 'At least he has given us back our good King!'

To lay on the King the full blame for what he was would have been rank injustice. Sapt was not guilty of it, but his disappointment was bitter that all our efforts had secured no better ruler for Ruritania. Sapt could serve, but he liked his master to be a man.

'Aye, I'm afraid the lad's work here is done,' he said, as I shook him by the hand. Then a sudden light came in his eyes. 'Perhaps not,' he muttered. 'Who knows?'

A man need not, I hope, be deemed uxorious for liking a quiet dinner alone with his wife before he starts on a long journey. Such, at least, was my fancy; and I was annoyed to find that Helga's cousin, Anton von Strofzin, had invited himself to share our meal and our farewell. He conversed with his usual airy emptiness on all the topics that were supplying Strelsau with gossip. There were rumours that the King was ill, that the Queen was angry at being carried off to Zenda, that the Archbishop meant to preach against low dresses, that the chancellor was to be dismissed, that his daughter was to be married, and so forth. I heard without listening. But the last bit of his budget caught my wandering attention.

'They were betting at the club', said Anton, 'that Rupert of Hentzau would be recalled. Have you heard anything about it, Fritz?'

If I had known anything, it is needless to say that I should not have confided it to Anton. But the suggested step was so utterly at variance with the King's intention that I made no difficulty about contradicting the report with an authoritative air. Anton heard me with a judicial wrinkle on his smooth brow.

'That's all very well,' said he, 'and I daresay you're bound to say so. All I know is that Rischenheim dropped a hint to Colonel Markel a day or two ago.'

'Rischenheim believes what he hopes,' said I.

'And where's he gone?' cried Anton exultantly. 'Why has he suddenly left Strelsau? I tell you he's gone to meet Rupert, and I'll bet you what you like he carried some proposal. Ah, you don't know everything, Fritz, my boy!'

It was indeed true that I did not know everything. I made haste to admit as much.

'I didn't even know that the count was gone, much less why he's gone,' said I.

'You see!' exclaimed Anton. And he added patronizingly: 'You should keep your ears open, my boy; then you might be worth what the King pays you.'

'No less, I trust,' said I, 'for he pays me nothing.' Indeed at this time I held no office save the honorary position of chamberlain to Her Majesty. Any advice the King needed from me was asked and given unofficially.

Anton went off, persuaded that he had scored a point against me. I could not see where. It was possible that the Count of Luzau-Rischenheim had gone to meet his cousin, equally possible that no such business claimed his care. At any rate the matter was not for me. I had a more pressing affair in hand. Dismissing the whole thing from my mind, I bade the butler tell Bauer to go forward with my luggage and to let my carriage be at the door in good time. Helga had busied herself, since our guest's departure, in preparing small comforts for my journey; now she came to me to say goodbye. Although she tried to hide all signs of it, I detected an uneasiness in her manner. She did not like these errands of mine, imagining dangers and risks of which I saw no likelihood. I would not give in to her mood, and, as I kissed her, I bade her expect me back in a few days' time. Not even to her did I speak of the new and more dangerous burden that I carried, although I was aware that she enjoyed a full measure of the Queen's confidence.

'My love to King Rudolf, the real King Rudolf,' said she. 'Though you carry what will make him think little of my love.'

'I have no desire he should think too much of it, sweet,' said I.

She caught me by the hands and looked up in my face.

'What a friend you are, aren't you, Fritz?' said she. 'You worship Mr Rassendyll. I know you think I should worship him, too, if he asked me. Well, I shouldn't. I am foolish enough to have my own idol.'

All my modesty did not let me doubt who her idol might be. Suddenly she drew near to me and whispered in my ear. I think that our own happiness brought to her a sudden keen sympathy with her mistress.

'Make him send her a loving message, Fritz,' she whispered, 'something that will comfort her. Her idol can't be with her as mine is with me.'

'Yes, he'll send something to comfort her,' I answered. 'And God keep you, my dear.'

For he would surely send an answer to the letter that I carried, and that answer I was sworn to bring safely to her. So I set out in good heart, bearing in the pocket of my coat the little box and the Queen's goodbye. And, as Colonel Sapt said to me, both I would destroy, if need were—aye, and myself with them. A man did not serve Queen Flavia with divided mind.

CHAPTER II

A Station without a Cab

THE arrangements for my meeting with Mr Rassendyll had been carefully made by correspondence before he left England. He was to be at the Golden Lion Hotel at eleven o'clock on the night of the 15th of October. I reckoned to arrive in the town between eight and nine on the same evening, to proceed to another hotel, and, on the pretence of taking a stroll, slip out and call on him at the appointed hour. I should then fulfil my commission, take his answer and enjoy the rare pleasure of a long talk with him. Early the next morning he would have left Wintenberg, and I should be on my way to Strelsau. I knew that he would not fail to keep his appointment, and I was perfectly confident of being able to carry out the programme punctually; I had, however, taken the precaution of obtaining a week's leave of absence in case any unforeseen accident should delay my return. Conscious of having done all I could to guard against misunderstanding or mishap, I got into the train in a tolerably peaceful frame of mind. The box was in my inner pocket, the letter in a *porte-monnaie*. I could feel them both with my hand. I was not in uniform, but I took my revolver. Although I had no reason to anticipate any difficulties, I did not forget that what I carried must be protected at all hazards and all costs.

The weary night journey wore itself away. Bauer came to me in the morning, performed his small services, repacked my handbag, procured me some coffee and left me. It was then about eight o'clock; we had arrived at a station of some importance and were not to stop again until midday. I saw Bauer enter the second-class compartment in which he was travelling, and settled down in my own coupé. I think it was at this moment that the thought of Rischenheim came again into my head, and I found myself wondering why he clung to the hopeless idea of compassing

Rupert's return, and what business had taken him from Strelsau. But I made little of the matter, and, drowsy from a broken night's rest, soon fell into a doze. I was alone in the carriage and could sleep without fear or danger. I was awakened by our noontide halt. Here I saw Bauer again. After taking a basin of soup I went to the telegraph bureau to send a message to my wife: the receipt of it would not merely set her mind at ease, but would also ensure word of my safe progress reaching the Queen. As I entered the bureau I met Bauer coming out of it. He seemed rather startled at our encounter, but told me readily enough that he had been telegraphing for rooms at Wintenberg, a very needless precaution, since there was no danger of the hotel being full. In fact I was annoyed, as I especially wished to avoid calling attention to my arrival. However, the mischief was done, and to rebuke my servant might have aggravated it by setting his wits at work to find out my motive for secrecy. So I said nothing, but passed by him with a nod. When the whole circumstances came to light, I had reason to suppose that, besides his message to the innkeeper, Bauer sent one of a character and to a quarter unsuspected by me.

We stopped once again before reaching Wintenberg. I put my head out of the window to look about me and saw Bauer standing near the luggage van. He ran to me eagerly, asking whether I required anything. I told him 'nothing', but instead of going away he began to talk to me. Growing weary of him, I returned to my seat and waited impatiently for the train to go on. There was a further delay of five minutes, and then we started.

'Thank goodness!' I exclaimed, leaning back comfortably in my seat and taking a cigar from my case.

But in a moment the cigar rolled unheeded on to the floor as I sprang eagerly to my feet and darted to the window. For, just as we were clearing the station, I saw being carried past the carriage on the shoulders of a porter a bag which looked very much like mine. Bauer had been in charge of my bag, and it had been put in the van under his directions. It seemed unlikely that it should be taken out now by any mistake. Yet the bag I saw was very like the bag I owned. But I was not sure, and could have done nothing had I been sure. We were not to stop again before Wintenberg, and,

with my luggage or without it, I myself must be in the town that
evening.

We arrived punctual to our appointed time. I sat in the carriage
a moment or two, expecting Bauer to open the door and relieve
me of my small baggage. He did not come, so I got out. It seemed
that I had few fellow passengers, and these were quickly dis-
appearing on foot or in the carriages and carts that waited outside
the station. I stood looking for my servant and my luggage. The
evening was mild; I was encumbered with my handbag and a
heavy fur coat. There were no signs either of Bauer or of baggage. I stayed where I was for five or six minutes. The guard of the
train had disappeared, but presently I observed the station-master:
he seemed to be taking a last glance round the premises. Going
up to him, I asked whether he had seen my servant; he could give
me no news of him. I had no luggage ticket, for mine had been in
Bauer's hands, but I prevailed on him to allow me to look at the
baggage which had arrived: my property was not among it. The
station-master was inclined, I think, to be a little sceptical as to
the existence both of bag and of servant. His only suggestion was
that the man must have been left behind accidentally. I pointed
out that in this case he would not have had the bag with him, but
that it would have come on in the train. The station-master
admitted the force of my argument; he shrugged his shoulders
and spread his hands out; he was evidently at the end of his
resources.

Now, for the first time and with sudden force, a doubt of
Bauer's fidelity thrust itself into my mind. I remembered how
little I knew of the fellow, and how great my charge was. Three
rapid movements of my hand assured me that letter, box and
revolver were in their respective places. If Bauer had gone hunting in the bag, he had drawn a blank. The station-master noticed
nothing; he was staring at the dim gas lamp that hung from the
roof. I turned to him.

'Well, tell him when he comes———' I began.

'He won't come tonight now,' interrupted the station-master,
none too politely. 'No other train arrives tonight.'

'Tell him when he does come to follow me to the Winten-
bergerhof. I'm going there immediately.' For time was short,

and I did not wish to keep Mr Rassendyll waiting. Besides, in my
new-born nervousness, I was anxious to accomplish my errand as
soon as might be. What had become of Bauer? The thought
returned, and now with it another, that seemed to connect
itself in some subtle way with my present position: why and
whither had the Count of Luzau-Rischenheim set out from
Strelsau a day before I started on my journey to Wintenberg?

'If he comes I'll tell him,' said the station-master, and as he
spoke he looked round the yard.

There was not a cab to be seen! I knew that the station lay on
the extreme outskirts of the town, for I had passed through
Wintenberg on my wedding journey nearly three years before.
The trouble involved in walking, and the further waste of time,
put the cap on my irritation.

'Why don't you have enough cabs?' I asked angrily.

'There are plenty generally, sir,' he answered more civilly,
with an apologetic air. 'There would be tonight but for an
accident.'

Another accident! This expedition of mine seemed doomed to
be the sport of chance.

'Just before your train arrived', he continued, 'a local came
in. As a rule hardly anybody comes by it, but tonight a number
of men—oh, twenty or five-and-twenty, I should think—got out.
I collected their tickets myself, and they all came from the first
station on the line. Well, that's not so strange, for there's a good
beer-garden there. But, curiously enough, every one of them
hired a separate cab and drove off, laughing and shouting to one
another as they went. That's how it happens that there were
only one or two cabs left when your train came in, and they were
snapped up at once.'

Taken alone, this occurrence was nothing; but I asked myself
whether the conspiracy that had robbed me of my servant had
deprived me of a vehicle also.

'What sort of men were they?' I asked.

'All sorts of men, sir,' answered the station-master, 'but most
of them were shabby-looking fellows. I wondered where some of
them had got the money for their ride.'

The vague feeling of uneasiness which had already attacked me

He directed me in a sympathetic tone

grew stronger. Although I fought against it, calling myself an old woman and a coward, I must confess to an impulse which almost made me beg the station-master's company on my walk; but, besides being ashamed to exhibit a timidity apparently groundless, I was reluctant to draw attention to myself in any way. I would not for the world have it supposed that I carried anything of value.

'Well, there's no help for it,' said I; and, buttoning my heavy coat about me, I took my handbag and stick in one hand, and asked my way to the hotel. My misfortunes had broken down the station-master's indifference, and he directed me in a sympathetic tone.

'Straight along the road, sir,' said he, 'between the poplars for hard on half a mile; then the houses begin, and your hotel is in the first square you come to on the right.'

I thanked him curtly (for I had not quite forgiven his earlier

incivility) and started on my walk, weighed down by my big coat
and the handbag. When I left the lighted station yard I realized
that the evening had fallen very dark, and the shade of the tall
lank trees intensified the gloom. I could hardly see my way, and
went timidly, with frequent stumbles over the uneven stones of
the road. The lamps were dim, few and widely separated; so far
as company was concerned, I might have been a thousand miles
from an inhabited house. In spite of myself, the thought of
danger persistently assailed my mind. I began to review every
circumstance of my journey, twisting the trivial into some
ominous shape, magnifying the significance of everything which
might justly seem suspicious, studying in the light of my new
apprehensions every expression of Bauer's face and every word
that had fallen from his lips. I could not persuade myself into
security. I carried the Queen's letter, and—well, I would have
given much to have old Sapt or Rudolf Rassendyll by my side.

Now when a man suspects danger, let him not spend his time
in asking whether there be really danger, or in upbraiding himself for timidity, but let him face his cowardice and act as though
the danger were real. If I had followed that rule and kept my
eyes about me, scanning the sides of the road and the ground in
front of my feet, instead of losing myself in a maze of reflection,
I might have had time to avoid the trap, or at least to get my hand
to my revolver and make a fight for it, or indeed, in the last
resort, to destroy what I carried before harm came to it. But my
mind was preoccupied, and the whole thing seemed to happen in
a minute. At the very moment that I had declared to myself the
vanity of my fears and determined to be resolute in banishing
them, I heard voices—a low strained whispering; I saw two or
three figures in the shadow of the poplars by the wayside. An
instant later a dart was made at me. While I could fly I would not
fight; with a sudden forward plunge I eluded the men who rushed
at me and started at a run towards the lights of the town and the
shapes of the houses, now distant about a quarter of a mile. Perhaps I ran twenty yards, perhaps fifty, I do not know. I heard the
steps behind me, quick as my own. Then I fell headlong on the
road—tripped up! I understood. They had stretched a rope across
my path; as I fell a man bounded up from either side, and I found

the rope slack under my body. There I lay on my face; a man
knelt on me, others held either hand; my face was pressed into
the mud of the road, and I was like to be stifled; my handbag had
whizzed away from me. Then a voice said:

'Turn him over.'

I knew the voice; it was a confirmation of the fears which I
had lately been at such pains to banish. It justified the forecast
of Anton von Strofzin, and explained the hint of the Count of
Luzau-Rischenheim. For it was Rischenheim's voice.

They caught hold of me and began to turn me on my back.
Here I saw a chance, and with a great heave of my body I flung
them from me. For a short instant I was free; my impetuous
attack seemed to have startled the enemy; I gathered myself up
on my knees. But my advantage was not to last long. Another
man, whom I had not seen, sprang suddenly on me, like a bullet
from a catapult. His fierce onset overthrew me, I was stretched
on the ground again, on my back now, and my throat was clutched
viciously in strong fingers. At the same moment my arms were
again seized and pinned. The face of the man on my chest bent
down towards mine; and through the darkness I discerned the
features of Rupert of Hentzau. He was panting from his sudden
exertion and the intense force with which he held me, but he was
smiling also, and when he saw by my eyes that I knew him, he
laughed softly in triumph.

Then came Rischenheim's voice again:

'Where's the bag he carried? It may be in the bag.'

'You fool, he'll have it about him,' said Rupert scornfully.
'Hold him fast while I search.'

On either side my hands were still pinned fast. Rupert's left
hand did not leave my throat, but his free right hand began to
dart about me, feeling, probing and rummaging. I lay quite helpless and in the bitterness of great consternation. Rupert found my
revolver, drew it out with a gibe and handed it to Rischenheim,
who was now standing beside him. Then he felt the box, he drew
it out, his eyes sparkled. He set his knee hard on my chest, so that
I could scarcely breathe; then he ventured to loose my throat, and
tore the box open eagerly.

'Bring a light here,' he cried. Another ruffian came with a dark lantern, whose glow he turned on the box. Rupert opened it, and when he saw what was inside he laughed again, and stowed it away in his pocket.

'Quick, quick!' urged Rischenheim. 'We've got what we wanted, and somebody may come at any moment.'

A brief hope comforted me. The loss of the box was a calamity, but I would pardon fortune if only the letter escaped capture. Rupert might have suspected that I carried some such token as the box held, but he could not know of the letter. Would he listen to Rischenheim? No. The Count of Hentzau did things thoroughly.

'We may as well overhaul him a bit more,' said he, and resumed his search. My hope vanished, for now he was bound to come upon the letter.

Another instant brought him to it. He snatched the *porte-monnaie* and, motioning impatiently to the man to hold the lantern nearer, began to examine the contents. I remember well the look of his face as the fierce white light threw it up against the darkness in its clear pallor and high-bred comeliness, with its curling lips and scornful eyes. He had the letter now, and a gleam of joy danced in his eyes as he tore it open. A hasty glance showed him what his prize was; then coolly and deliberately he settled himself to read, regarding neither Rischenheim's nervous hurry nor my desperate angry glance that glared up at him. He read leisurely, as though he had been in an armchair in his own house; the lips smiled and curled as he read the last words that the Queen had written to her lover. He had indeed come on more than he thought.

Rischenheim laid a hand on his shoulder.

'Quick, Rupert, quick!' he urged again, in a voice full of agitation.

'Let me alone, man. I haven't read anything so amusing for a long while,' answered Rupert. Then he burst into a laugh, crying, 'Look, look!' and pointing to the foot of the last page of the letter. I was mad with anger; my fury gave me new strength. In his enjoyment of what he read Rupert had grown careless; his knee pressed more lightly on me, and as he showed Rischenheim the passage in the letter that caused him so much amusement, he

turned his head away for an instant. My chance had come. With a
sudden movement I displaced him, and with a desperate wrench
I freed my right hand. Darting it out I snatched at the letter.
Rupert, alarmed for his treasure, sprang back and off me. I also
sprang up on my feet, hurling away the fellow who had gripped
my other hand. For a moment I stood facing Rupert; then I
darted on him. He was too quick for me: he dodged behind the
man with the lantern and hurled the fellow forward against me.
The lantern fell on the ground.

'Give me your stick,' I heard Rupert say. 'Where is it? That's
right!'

Then came Rischenheim's voice again, imploring and timid:
'Rupert, you promised not to kill him!'

The only answer was a short fierce laugh. I hurled away the
man who had been thrust into my arms, and sprang forward. I
saw Rupert of Hentzau: his hand was raised above his head and
held a stout club. I hardly know what followed: there came—
all in a confused blur of instant sequence—an oath from Rupert,
a rush from me, a scuffle as though someone sought to hold him
back; then he was on me; I felt a great thud on my forehead, and
I felt nothing more. Again I was on my back, with a terrible pain
in my head and a dull dreamy consciousness of a knot of men
standing over me, talking eagerly to one another.

I could not hear what they were saying; I had no great desire
to hear. I fancied, somehow, that they were talking about me;
they looked at me and moved their hands towards me now and
again. I heard Rupert's laugh, and saw his club poised over me;
then Rischenheim caught him by the wrist. I know now that
Rischenheim was reminding his cousin that he had promised not
to kill me, that Rupert's oath did not weigh a straw in the scales,
but that he was held back only by a doubt whether I alive or my
dead body would be the more inconvenient to dispose of. Yet
then I did not understand, but lay there listless. And presently
the talking forms seemed to cease their talking; they grew
blurred and dim, running into one another, and all mingling
together to form one great shapeless creature that seemed to
murmur and gibber over me, some such monster as a man sees in
his dreams. I hated to see it, and closed my eyes; its murmurings

and gibberings haunted my ears for awhile, making me restless and unhappy; then they died away. Their going made me happy; I sighed in contentment; and everything became as though it were not.

Yet I had one more vision, breaking suddenly across my unconsciousness. A bold rich voice rang out, 'By God, I will!' 'No, no!' cried another. Then, 'What's that?' There was a rush of feet, the cries of men who met in anger or excitement, the crack of a shot and of another quickly following, oaths and scuffling. Then came the sound of feet flying. I could not make it out; I grew weary with the puzzle of it. Would they not be quiet? Quiet was what I wanted. At last they grew quiet; I closed my eyes again. The pain was less now; they were quiet; I could sleep.

When a man looks back on the past, reviewing in his mind the chances Fortune has given and the calls she has made, he always torments himself by thinking that he could have done other and better than in fact he did. Even now I lie awake at night sometimes, making clever plans by which I could have thwarted Rupert's schemes. In these musings I am very acute; Anton von Strofzin's idle talk furnishes me with many a clue, and I draw inferences sure and swift as a detective in the story-books. Bauer is my tool: I am not his. I lay Rischenheim by the heels, send Rupert off howling with a ball in his arm, and carry my precious burden in triumph to Mr Rassendyll. By the time I have played the whole game I am indeed proud of myself. Yet in truth—in daylight truth—I fear that, unless Heaven sent me a fresh set of brains, I should be caught in much the same way again. Though not by that fellow Bauer, I swear! Well, there it was! They had made a fool of me. I lay on the road with a bloody head, and Rupert of Hentzau had the Queen's letter.

CHAPTER III

Again to Zenda

BY HEAVEN'S care, or—since a man may be over-apt to arrogate to himself a great share of such attention—by good luck, I had not to trust for my life to the slender thread of an oath sworn by Rupert of Hentzau. The visions of my dazed brain were transmutations of reality; the scuffle, the rush, the retreat were not all dream.

There is an honest fellow now living at Wintenberg comfortably at his ease, by reason that his wagon chanced to come lumbering along with three or four stout lads in it, at the moment when Rupert was meditating a second and murderous blow. Seeing the group of us, the good carrier and his boys leapt down and rushed on my assailants. One of the thieves, they said, was for fighting it out—I could guess who that was—and called on the rest to stand; but they, more prudent, laid hands on him, and in spite of his oaths hustled him off along the road towards the station. Open country lay there, and the promise of safety. My new friends set off in pursuit, but a couple of revolver-shots, heard by me but not understood, awoke their caution. Good Samaritans, but not men of war, they returned to where I lay senseless on the ground, congratulating themselves and me that an enemy so well armed should run and not stand his ground. They forced a drink of rough wine down my throat, and in a minute or two I opened my eyes. They were for carrying me to a hospital. I would have none of it. As soon as things grew clear to me again and I knew where I was, I did nothing but repeat in urgent tones: 'The Golden Lion, the Golden Lion! Twenty crowns to carry me to the Golden Lion!'

Perceiving that I knew my own business and where I wished to go, one picked up my handbag and the rest hoisted me into their wagon and set out for the hotel where Rudolf Rassendyll was.

The good carrier and his boys leapt down

The one thought my broken head held was to get to him as soon as might be, and tell him how I had been fool enough to let myself be robbed of the Queen's letter.

He was there. He stood on the threshold of the inn, waiting for me, as it seemed, although it was not yet the hour of my appointment. As they drew me up to the door I saw his tall straight figure and his red hair by the light of the hall lamps. By Heaven, I felt as a lost child must on sight of his mother! I stretched out my hand to him over the side of the wagon, murmuring, 'I've lost it.'

He started at the words, and sprang forward to me. Then he turned quickly to the carrier.

'This gentleman is my friend,' he said. 'Give him to me. I'll speak to you later.'

He waited while I was lifted down from the wagon into the arms that he held ready for me, and himself carried me across the threshold. I was quite clear in the head by now, and understood all that passed. There were one or two people in the hall, but

Mr Rassendyll took no heed of them. He bore me quickly up-stairs and into his sitting-room. There he set me down in an arm-chair and stood opposite to me. He was smiling, but anxiety was awake in his eyes.

'I've lost it,' I said again, looking up at him pitifully enough.

'That's all right,' said he, nodding. 'Will you wait, or can you tell me?'

'Yes; but give me some brandy,' said I.

Rudolf gave me a little brandy mixed in a great deal of water, and then I made shift to tell him. Though faint, I was not con-fused, and I gave my story in brief, hurried, yet sufficient words. He made no sign till I mentioned the letter. Then his face changed.

'A letter too?' he exclaimed, in a strange mixture of increased apprehension and unlooked-for joy.

'Yes, a letter too: she wrote a letter, and I carried that as well as the box. I've lost them both, Rudolf. God help me, I've lost them both! Rupert has the letter too.'

I think I must have been weak and unmanned from the blow I had received, for my composure broke down here. Rudolf stepped up to me and wrung me by the hand. I mastered myself again and looked in his face, as he stood in thought, his hand caressing the strong curve of his clean-shaven chin. Now that I was with him again it seemed as though I had never lost him, as though we were still together in Strelsau or at Tarlenheim, plan-ning how to hoodwink Black Michael, send Rupert of Hentzau to his own place and bring the King back to his throne. For Mr Rassendyll, as he stood before me now, was changed in nothing since our last meeting, nor indeed since he reigned in Strelsau, save that a few flecks of grey spotted his hair.

My battered head ached most consumedly. Mr Rassendyll rang the bell twice, and a short thickset man of middle age appeared; he wore a suit of tweed and had the air of smartness and respecta-bility which marks English servants.

'James,' said Rudolf, 'this gentleman has hurt his head. Look after it.'

James went out. In a few minutes he was back, with water, basin, towels and bandages. Bending over me, he began to wash and tend my wound very deftly. Rudolf was walking up and down.

c

'Done the head, James?' he asked, after a few moments.

'Yes, sir,' answered the servant, gathering together his appliances.

'Telegraph forms, then.'

James went out, and was back with the forms in an instant.

'Be ready when I ring,' said Rudolf. And he added, turning to me: 'Any easier, Fritz?'

'I can listen to you now,' I said.

'I see their game,' said he. 'One or other of them—Rupert or this Rischenheim—will try to get to the King with the letter.'

I sprang to my feet.

'They mustn't!' I cried; and I reeled back into my chair, with a feeling as if a red-hot poker were being run through my head.

'Much you can do to stop 'em, old fellow,' smiled Rudolf, pausing to press my hand as he went by. 'They won't trust the post, you know. One will go. Now which?' He stood facing me with a thoughtful frown on his face.

I did not know, but I thought that Rischenheim would go. It was a great risk for Rupert to trust himself in the kingdom, and he knew that the King would not easily be persuaded to receive him, however startling might be the business he professed as his errand. On the other hand, nothing was known against Rischenheim, while his rank would secure and indeed entitle him to an early audience. Therefore I concluded that Rischenheim would go with the letter, or, if Rupert would not let that out of his possession, with the news of the letter.

'Or a copy,' suggested Rudolf. 'Well, Rischenheim or Rupert will be on his way by tomorrow morning, or is on his way tonight.'

Again I tried to rise, for I was on fire to prevent the fatal consequences of my stupidity. Rudolf thrust me back in my chair, saying: 'No, no.' Then he sat down at the table and took up the telegraph forms.

'You and Sapt arranged a cipher, I suppose?' he asked.

'Yes. You write the message and I'll put it into the cipher.'

'This is what I have written: "Document lost. Let nobody see him if possible. Wire who asks." I don't like to make it plainer: most ciphers can be read, you know.'

'Not ours,' said I.

'Well, but will that do?' asked Rudolf with an unconvinced smile.

'Yes, I think he'll understand it.' And I wrote it again in the cipher; it was as much as I could do to hold the pen.

James

The bell was rung again, and James appeared in an instant.

'Send this,' said Rudolf.

'The offices will be shut, sir.'

'James, James!'

'Very good, sir; but it may take an hour to get one open.'

'I'll give you half an hour. Have you money?'

'Yes, sir.'

'And now,' added Rudolf, turning to me, 'you'd better go to bed.'

I do not recollect what I answered, for my faintness came upon

me again, and I remember only that Rudolf himself helped me
into his own bed. I slept, but I do not think he so much as lay
down on the sofa; chancing to awake once or twice, I heard him
pacing about. But towards morning I slept heavily, and I did not
know what he was doing then.

At eight o'clock James entered and roused me. He said that a
doctor was to be at the hotel in half an hour, but that Mr Rassendyll would like to see me for a few minutes if I felt equal to
business. I begged James to summon his master at once. Whether
I were equal or unequal, the business had to be done.

Rudolf came, calm and serene. Danger and the need for exertion acted on him like a draught of good wine on a seasoned
drinker. He was not only himself, but more than himself, his
excellences enhanced, the indolence that marred him in quiet
hours sloughed off. But today there was something more; I can
describe it only as a kind of radiance. I have seen it on the faces of
young sparks when the lady they love comes through the ball-
room door, and I have seen it glow more softly in a girl's eyes
when some fellow, who seemed to me nothing out of the
ordinary, asked her for a dance. That strange gleam was on
Rudolf's face as he stood by my bedside. I dare say it used to be on
mine when I went courting.

'Fritz, old friend,' said he, 'there's an answer from Sapt.
I'll lay the telegraph offices were stirred at Zenda as well as James
stirred them here in Wintenberg. And what do you think?
Rischenheim asked for an audience before he left Strelsau.'

I raised myself on my elbow in the bed.

'You understand?' he went on. 'He left on Monday. Today's
Wednesday. The King has granted him an audience at four on
Friday. Well, then——'

'They counted on success,' I cried, 'and Rischenheim takes
the letter!'

'A copy, if I know Rupert of Hentzau. Yes, it was well laid. I
like the men taking all the cabs. How much a head had they
now?'

I did not know that, though I had no more doubt than he that
Rupert's hand was in the business.

'Well,' he continued, 'I am going to wire to Sapt to put

Rischenheim off for twelve hours if he can—failing that, to get the King away from Zenda.'

'But Rischenheim must have his audience sooner or later,' I objected.

'Sooner or later—there's the world's difference between them!' cried Rudolf Rassendyll. He sat down on the bed by me, and went on in quick decisive words: 'You can't move for a day or two. Send my message to Sapt. Tell him to keep you informed of what happens. As soon as you can travel, go to Strelsau and let Sapt know directly you arrive. We shall want your help.'

'And what are you going to do?' I cried, staring at him.

He looked at me for a moment, and his face was crossed by conflicting feelings. I saw resolve there, obstinacy and the scorn of danger; fun, too, and merriment; and, lastly, that same radiance I spoke of. He had been smoking a cigarette; now he threw the end of it into the grate and rose from the bed where he had been sitting.

'I'm going to Zenda,' said he.

'To Zenda?' I cried, amazed.

'Yes,' said Rudolf, 'I'm going again to Zenda, Fritz, old fellow. By Jove, I knew it would come, and now it has come!'

'But to do what?'

'I shall overtake Rischenheim, or be hot on his heels. If he gets there first, Sapt will keep him waiting till I come; and if I come, he shall never see the King. Yes, if I come in time——' He broke into a sudden laugh. 'What?' he cried. 'Have I lost my likeness? Can't I still play the King? Yes, if I come in time, Rischenheim shall have his audience of the King at Zenda, and the King will be very gracious to him, and the King will take his copy of the letter from him. Oh, Rischenheim shall have an audience of King Rudolf in the Castle of Zenda, never fear!'

He stood, looking to see how I received his plan; but, amazed at the boldness of it, I could only lie back and gasp.

Rudolf's excitement left him as suddenly as it had come; he was again the cool, shrewd, nonchalant Englishman, as, lighting another cigarette, he proceeded:

'You see, there are two of them—Rupert and Rischenheim. Now, you can't move for a day or two, that's certain. But there

'But if you're seen—if you're found out?'

must be two of us there in Ruritania. Rischenheim is to try first; but, if he fails, Rupert will risk everything and break through to the King's presence. Give him five minutes with the King, and the mischief's done. Very well, then: Sapt must keep Rupert at bay, while I tackle Rischenheim. As soon as you can move, go to Strelsau and let Sapt know where you are.'

'But if you're seen—if you're found out?'

'Better I than the Queen's letter,' said he. Then he laid his hand on my arm and said quite quietly: 'If the letter gets to the King, I and I only can do what must be done.'

I did not know what he meant: perhaps it was that he would carry off the Queen sooner than leave her alone after her letter was known; but there was another possible meaning that I, a loyal subject, dared not inquire into. Yet I made no answer, for I was above all and first of all the Queen's servant. Still I cannot believe that he meant harm to the King.

'Come, Fritz,' he cried, 'don't look so glum. This is not so great an affair as the other, and we brought that through safe.' I suppose I still looked doubtful, for he added, with a sort of impatience: 'Well, I'm going, anyhow. Heavens, man, am I to sit here while that letter is carried to the King?'

I understood his feeling, and knew that he held life a light thing compared with the recovery of Queen Flavia's letter. I ceased to urge him. When I assented to his wishes, every shadow vanished from his face, and we began to discuss the details of the plan with business-like brevity.

'I shall leave James with you,' said Rudolf. 'He'll be very useful, and you can rely on him absolutely. Any message that you dare trust to no other conveyance give to him; he'll carry it. He can shoot too.' He rose as he spoke. 'I'll look in before I start,' he added, 'and hear what the doctor says about you.'

I lay there, thinking, as men sick and weary in body will, of the dangers and the desperate nature of the risk, rather than of the hope which its boldness would have inspired in a healthy active brain. I distrusted the rapid inference that Rudolf had drawn from Sapt's telegram, telling myself that it was based on too slender a foundation. Well, there I was wrong, and I am glad now to pay that tribute to his discernment. The first steps of Rupert's scheme were laid as Rudolf had conjectured: Rischenheim had started, even while I lay there, for Zenda, carrying on his person a copy of the Queen's farewell letter and armed for his enterprise by his right of audience with the King. So far we were right, then; for the rest we were in darkness, not knowing or being able even to guess where Rupert would choose to await the result of the first cast, or what precautions he had taken against the failure of his envoy. But although in total obscurity as to his future plans, I traced his past actions, and subsequent knowledge has shown that I was right. Bauer was his tool; a couple of florins apiece had hired the fellows who, conceiving that they were playing a part in some practical joke, had taken all the cabs at the station. Rupert had reckoned that I should linger looking for my servant and luggage, and thus miss my last chance of a vehicle. If, however, I had obtained one, the attack would still have been made, although of course under much greater difficulties.

Finally—and of this at the time I knew nothing—had I evaded them and got safe to port with my cargo, the plot would have been changed. Rupert's attention would then have been diverted from me to Rudolf; counting on love overcoming prudence, he reckoned that Mr Rassendyll would not at once destroy what the Queen sent, and had arranged to track his steps from Wintenberg till an opportunity offered of robbing him of his treasure. The full scheme, as I know it, was full of audacious cunning and required large resources; the former Rupert himself supplied, for the second he was indebted to his cousin and slave, the Count of Luzau-Rischenheim.

My meditations were interrupted by the arrival of the doctor. He hummed and ha'd over me, but, to my surprise, asked me no questions as to the cause of my misfortune, and did not, as I had feared, suggest that his efforts should be seconded by those of the police. On the contrary he appeared, from an unobtrusive hint or two, to be anxious that I should know that his discretion could be trusted.

'You must not think of moving for a couple of days,' he said; 'but then I think we can get you away without danger and quite quietly.'

I thanked him; he promised to look in again; I murmured something about his fee.

'Oh, thank you, that is all settled,' he said. 'Your friend Herr Schmidt has seen to it, and, my dear sir, most liberally.'

He was hardly gone when 'my friend Herr Schmidt'—*alias* Rudolf Rassendyll—was back. He laughed a little when I told him how discreet the doctor had been.

'You see', he explained, 'he thinks you've been very indiscreet. I was obliged, my dear Fritz, to take some liberties with your character. However, it's odds against the matter coming to your wife's ears.'

'But couldn't we have laid the others by the heels?'

'With the letter on Rupert? My dear fellow, you're very ill!'

I laughed at myself, and forgave Rudolf his trick, though I think that he might have made my fictitious *inamorata* something more than a baker's wife. It would have cost no more to make her a countess, and the doctor would have looked with more respect on me. However, Rudolf had said that the baker broke my head with his rolling-pin, and thus the story rests in the doctor's mind to this day.

'Well, I'm off,' said Rudolf.

'But where?'

'Why, to that same little station where two good friends parted from me once before. Fritz, where's Rupert gone?'

'I wish we knew!'

'I lay he won't be far off.'

'Are you armed?'

'The six-shooter. Well, yes, since you press me, a knife too; but only if he uses one. You'll let Sapt know when you come?'

'Yes; and I come the moment I can stand.'

'As if you need tell me that, old fellow!'

'Where do you go from the station?'

'To Zenda, through the forest,' he answered. 'I shall reach the station about nine tomorrow night, Thursday. Unless Rischen-heim has got the audience sooner than was arranged, I shall be in time.'

'How will you get hold of Sapt?'

'We must leave something to the minute.'

'God bless you, Rudolf!'

'The King shan't have the letter, Fritz.'

There was a moment's silence as we shook hands. Then that soft yet bright look came into his eyes again. He looked down at me, and caught me regarding him with a smile that I know was not unkind.

'I never thought I should see her again,' he said. 'I think I shall now, Fritz. To have a turn with that boy, and to see her again—it's worth something.'

'How will you see her?'

Rudolf laughed, and I laughed too. He caught my hand again. I think that he was anxious to infect me with his gaiety and confidence. But I could not answer to the appeal of his eyes. There was a motive in him that found no place in me—a great longing, the prospect or hope of whose sudden fulfilment dwarfed danger and banished despair. He saw that I detected its presence in him and perceived how it filled his mind.

'But the letter comes before all,' said he. 'I expected to die without seeing her; I will die without seeing her if I must, to save the letter.'

'I know you will,' said I.

He pressed my hand again. As he turned away, James came with his noiseless quick step into the room.

'The carriage is at the door, sir,' said he.

'Look after the count, James,' said Rudolf. 'Don't leave him till he sends you away.'

'Very well, sir.'

I raised myself in bed. 'Here's luck!' I cried, catching up the lemonade James had brought to me and taking a gulp of it.

'Please God,' said Rudolf, with a shrug.

And he was gone to his work and his reward, to save the Queen's letter and to see the Queen's face. Thus he went a second time to Zenda.

CHAPTER IV

An Eddy on the Moat

ON THE evening of Thursday, the sixteenth of October, the Constable of Zenda was very much out of humour; he has since confessed as much. To risk the peace of a palace for the sake of a lover's greeting had never been wisdom to his mind, and he had been sorely impatient with 'that fool Fritz's' yearly pilgrimage. The letter of farewell had been an added folly, pregnant with chances of disaster. Now disaster, or the danger of it, had come. The curt mysterious telegrams from Wintenberg, which told him so little, at least told him that. It ordered him—and he did not know even whose the order was—to delay Rischenheim's audience, or, if he could not, to get the King away from Zenda; why he was to act thus was not disclosed to him. But he knew as well as I that Rischenheim was completely in Rupert's hands, and he could not fail to guess that something had gone wrong at Wintenberg, and that Rischenheim came to tell the King some news that the King must not hear. His task sounded simple, but it was not so easy; for he did not know where Rischenheim was, and so could not prevent his coming. Besides, the King had been very pleased to learn of the count's approaching visit, since he desired to talk with him on the subject of a certain breed of dogs, which the count bred with great, His Majesty with only indifferent, success; therefore he had declared that nothing should interfere with his reception of Rischenheim. In vain Sapt told him that a large boar had been seen in the forest, and that a fine day's sport might be expected if he would hunt next day.

'I shouldn't be back in time to see Rischenheim,' said the King.

'Your Majesty would be back by nightfall,' suggested Sapt.

'I should be too tired to talk to him, and I've a great deal to discuss.'

'You could sleep at the hunting-lodge, sire, and ride back to receive the count next morning.'

'I am anxious to see him as soon as may be.' Then he looked up at Sapt with a sick man's quick suspicion. 'Why shouldn't I see him?' he asked.

'It's a pity to miss the boar, sire,' was all Sapt's plea. The King made light of it.

'Curse the boar!' said he. 'I want to know how he gets the dogs' coats so fine.'

As the King spoke a servant entered, carrying a telegram for Sapt. The colonel took it and put it in his pocket.

'Read it,' said the King. He had dined and was about to go to bed, it being nearly ten o'clock.

'It will keep, sire,' answered Sapt, who did not know but that it might be from Wintenberg.

'Read it,' insisted the King testily. 'It may be from Rischenheim. Perhaps he can get here sooner. I should like to know about those dogs. Read it, I beg.'

Sapt could do nothing but read it. He had taken to spectacles lately, and he spent a long while adjusting them and thinking what he should do if the message were not fit for the King's ear.

'Be quick, man; be quick!' urged the irritable King.

Sapt had got the envelope open at last; and relief, mingled with perplexity, showed in his face.

'Your Majesty guessed wonderfully well. Rischenheim can be here at eight tomorrow morning,' he said, looking up.

'Capital!' cried the King. 'He shall breakfast with me at nine, and I'll have a ride after the boar when we've done our business. Now are you satisfied?'

'Perfectly, sire,' said Sapt, biting his moustache.

The King rose with a yawn, and bade the colonel good night. 'He must have some trick I don't know with those dogs,' he remarked, as he went out; and——

'Damn the dogs!' cried Colonel Sapt the moment that the door was shut behind His Majesty.

But the colonel was not a man to accept defeat easily. The audience that he had been instructed to postpone was advanced; the King, whom he had been told to get away from Zenda, would not go till he had seen Rischenheim. Still, there are many ways of preventing a meeting. Some are by fraud, these it is no injustice to Sapt to say that he had tried; some are by force, and the colonel was being driven to the conclusion that one of these must be his resort.

'Though the King', he mused with a grin, 'will be furious if anything happens to Rischenheim before he's told him about the dogs.'

Yet he fell to racking his brains to find a means by which the count might be rendered incapable of performing the service so desired by the King and of carrying out his own purpose in seeking an audience. Nothing save assassination suggested itself to the Constable; a quarrel and a duel offered no security; and Sapt was not Black Michael, and had no band of ruffians to join him in an apparently unprovoked kidnapping of a distinguished nobleman.

'I can think of nothing,' muttered Sapt, rising from his chair and moving across towards the window, in search of the fresh air that a man so often thinks will give him a fresh idea. He was in his own quarters, that room of the new *château* which opens on to the moat immediately to the right of the drawbridge as you face the old castle; it was the room which Duke Michael had occupied, and almost opposite to the spot where the great pipe had connected the window of the King's dungeon with the waters of the moat. The bridge was down now, for peaceful days had come to Zenda; the pipe was gone, and the dungeon's window, though still barred, was uncovered. The night was clear and fine, and the still water gleamed fitfully as the moon, half full, escaped from or was hidden by passing clouds. Sapt stood staring out gloomily, beating his knuckles on the stone sill. The fresh air was there, but the fresh idea tarried.

Suddenly the Constable bent forward, craning his head out and down, far as he could stretch it, towards the water. What he had seen, or seemed dimly to see, is a sight common enough on the surface of water—large circular eddies, widening from a centre; a stone thrown in makes them, or a fish on the rise. But Sapt had thrown no stone, and the fish in the moat were few and not rising then. The light was behind Sapt, and threw his figure into bold relief. The royal apartments looked out the other way; there

From the moat right below him, a man's head emerged

were no lights in the windows this side the bridge, although
beyond it the guards' lodgings and the servants' offices still
showed a light here and there. Sapt waited till the eddies ceased.
Then he heard the faintest sound, as of a large body let very gently
into the water; a moment later, from the moat right below him,
a man's head emerged.

'Sapt!' said a voice, low but distinct.

The old colonel started, and, resting both hands on the sill,
bent farther out, till he seemed in danger of overbalancing.

'Quick—to the ledge on the other side. You know,' said the
voice, and the head turned; with quick, quiet strokes the man
crossed the moat till he was hidden in the triangle of deep shade

formed by the meeting of the drawbridge and the old castle wall. Sapt watched him go, almost stupefied by the sudden wonder of hearing that voice come to him out of the stillness of the night. For the King was abed; and who spoke in that voice save the King and one other?

Then, with a curse at himself for his delay, he turned and walked quickly across the room. Opening the door, he found himself in the passage. But here he ran right into the arms of young Bernenstein, the officer of the guard, who was going on his rounds. Sapt knew and trusted him, for he had been with us all through the siege of Zenda, when Michael kept the King a prisoner, and he bore marks given him by Rupert of Hentzau's ruffians. He now held a commission as lieutenant in the Cuirassiers of the King's Guard.

He noticed Sapt's bearing, for he cried out in a low voice:

'Anything wrong, sir?'

'Bernenstein, my boy, the Castle's all right about here. Go round to the front, and, hang you, stay there,' said Sapt.

The officer stared, as well he might. Sapt caught him by the arm.

'No, stay here. See, stand by the door there that leads to the royal apartments. Stand there, and let nobody pass. You understand?'

'Yes, sir.'

'And whatever you hear, don't look round.'

Bernenstein's bewilderment grew greater; but Sapt was Constable, and on Sapt's shoulders lay the responsibility for the safety of Zenda and all in it.

'Very well, sir,' he said with a submissive shrug, and he drew his sword and stood by the door: he could obey although he could not understand.

Sapt ran on. Opening the gate that led to the bridge, he sped across. Then stepping on one side and turning his face to the wall, he descended the steps that gave foothold down to the ledge running six or eight inches above the water. He also was now in the triangle of deep darkness, yet he knew that a man was there, who stood straight and tall, rising above his own height. And he felt his hand caught in a sudden grip. Rudolf Rassendyll was there, in his wet drawers and socks.

'Is it you?' he whispered.

'Yes,' answered Rudolf: 'I swam round from the other side and got here. Then I threw in a bit of mortar, but I wasn't sure I'd roused you, and I didn't dare shout, so I followed it myself. Lay hold of me a minute while I get on my breeches: I didn't want to get wet, so I carried my clothes in a bundle. Hold me tight— it's slippery.'

'In God's name, what brings you here?' whispered Sapt, catching Rudolf by the arm as he was directed.

'The Queen's service. When does Rischenheim come?'

'Tomorrow at eight.'

'The deuce! That's earlier than I thought. And the King?'

'Is here and determined to see him. It's impossible to move him from it.'

There was a moment's silence; Rudolf drew his shirt over his head and tucked it into his trousers. 'Give me the jacket and waistcoat,' he said. 'I feel deuced damp underneath, though.'

'You'll soon get dry,' grinned Sapt. 'You'll be kept moving, you see.'

'I've lost my hat.'

'Seems to me you've lost your head too.'

'You'll find me both, eh, Sapt?'

'As good as your own, anyhow,' growled the Constable.

'Now the boots, and I'm ready.' Then he asked quickly, 'Has the King seen or heard from Rischenheim?'

'Neither, except through me.'

'Then why is he so set on seeing him?'

'To find out what gives dogs smooth coats.'

'You're serious? Hang you, I can't see your face.'

'Absolutely.'

'All's well, then. Has he got a beard now?'

'Yes.'

'Confound him! Can't you take me anywhere to talk?'

'What the deuce are you here at all for?'

'To meet Rischenheim.'

'To meet——?'

'Yes. Sapt, he's got a copy of the Queen's letter.'

Sapt twirled his moustache.

'I've always said as much,' he remarked in tone of satisfaction. He need not have said it; he would have been more than human not to think it.

'Where can you take me to?' asked Rudolf impatiently.

'Any room with a door and a lock to it,' answered old Sapt. 'I command here, and when I say, "Stay out"—well, they don't come in.'

'Not the King?'

'The King is in bed. Come along,' and the Constable set his toe on the lowest step.

'Is there nobody about?' asked Rudolf, catching his arm.

'Bernenstein—but he will keep his back towards us.'

'Your discipline is still good, then, colonel?'

'Pretty well for these days, Your Majesty,' grunted Sapt, as he reached the level of the bridge.

Having crossed, they entered the *château*. The passage was empty save for Bernenstein, whose broad back barred the way from the royal apartments.

'In here,' whispered Sapt, laying his hand on the door of the room whence he had come.

'All right,' answered Rudolf. Bernenstein's hand twitched, but he did not look round. There was discipline in the Castle of Zenda.

But as Sapt was half way through the door and Rudolf about to follow him, the other door, that which Bernenstein guarded, was softly yet swiftly opened. Bernenstein's sword was in rest in an instant. A muttered oath from Sapt and Rudolf's quick snatch at his breath greeted the interruption. Bernenstein did not look round, but his sword fell to his side. In the doorway stood Queen Flavia, all in white; and now her face turned white as her dress. For her eyes had fallen on Rudolf Rassendyll. For a moment the four stood thus; then Rudolf passed Sapt, thrust Bernenstein's brawny shoulders (the young man had not looked round) out of the way, and falling on his knee before the Queen, seized her hand and kissed it. Bernenstein could see now without looking round, and if astonishment could kill, he would have been a dead man that instant. He fairly reeled and leant against the wall, his mouth hanging open. For the King was in bed, and had a beard;

D

yet here was the King, fully dressed and clean-shaven, and he was kissing the Queen's hand, while she gazed down on him in a struggle between amazement, fright and joy. A soldier should be prepared for anything, but I cannot be hard on young Bernenstein's bewilderment.

Yet there was in truth nothing strange in the Queen seeking to see old Sapt that night, nor in her guessing where he would most probably be found. For she had asked him three times whether news had come from Wintenberg, and each time he had put her off with excuses. Quick to forbode evil, and conscious of the pledge to fortune that she had given in her letter, she had determined to know from him whether there were really cause for alarm, and had stolen, undetected, from her apartments to seek him. What filled her at once with unbearable apprehension and incredulous joy was to find Rudolf present in actual flesh and blood, no longer in sad longing dreams or visions, and to feel his live lips on her hand.

Lovers count neither time nor danger; but Sapt counted both, and no more than a moment had passed before, with eager imperative gestures, he beckoned them to enter the room. The Queen obeyed, and Rudolf followed her.

'Let nobody in, and don't say a word to anybody,' whispered Sapt, as he entered, leaving Bernenstein outside. The young man was half dazed still, but he had sense to read the expression in the Constable's eyes and to learn from it that he must give his life sooner than let the door be opened. So with drawn sword he stood on guard.

It was eleven o'clock when the Queen came, and midnight had struck from the great clock of the Castle before the door opened again and Sapt came out. His sword was not drawn, but he had his revolver in his hand. He shut the door silently after him and began at once to talk in low, earnest, quick tones to Bernenstein. Bernenstein listened intently and without interrupting. Sapt's story ran on for eight or nine minutes. Then he paused, before asking:

'You understand now?'

'Yes, it is wonderful,' said the young man, drawing in his breath.

'Pooh!' said Sapt. 'Nothing is wonderful: some things are unusual.'

Bernenstein was not convinced, and shrugged his shoulders in protest.

'Well?' said the Constable, with a quick glance at him.

'I would die for the Queen, sir,' he answered, clicking his heels together as though on parade.

'Good,' said Sapt. 'Then listen.' And he began again to talk. Bernenstein nodded from time to time. 'You'll meet him at the gate,' said the Constable, 'and bring him straight here. He's not to go anywhere else, you understand me?'

'Perfectly, colonel,' smiled young Bernenstein.

'The King will be in this room—the King. You know who is the King?'

'Perfectly, colonel.'

'And when the interview is ended, and we go in to break-fast——'

'I know who will be the King then. Yes, colonel.'

'Good. But we do him no harm unless——'

'It is necessary.'

'Precisely.'

Sapt turned away with a little sigh. Bernenstein was an apt pupil, but the colonel was exhausted by so much explanation. He knocked softly at the door of the room. The Queen's voice bade him enter, and he passed in. Bernenstein was left alone again in the passage, pondering over what he had heard and rehearsing the part that it now fell to him to play. As he thought, he may well have raised his head proudly. The service seemed so great and the honour so high, that he almost wished he could die in the performing of his role. It would be a finer death than his soldier's dreams had dared to picture.

At one o'clock Colonel Sapt came out.

'Go to bed till six,' said he to Bernenstein.

'I am not sleepy.'

'No, but you will be at eight if you don't sleep now.'

'Is the Queen coming out, colonel?'

'In a minute, lieutenant.'

'I should like to kiss her hand.'

'Well, if you think it worth waiting a quarter of an hour for,' said Sapt, with a slight smile.

'You said in a minute, sir.'

'So did she,' answered the Constable.

Nevertheless it was a quarter of an hour before Rudolf Rassendyll opened the door and the Queen appeared on the threshold. She was very pale, and she had been crying, but her eyes were happy and her air firm. The moment he saw her young Bernenstein fell on his knees and raised her hand to his lips.

'To the death, madame,' said he in a trembling voice.

'I knew it, sir,' she answered graciously. Then she looked round on the three of them. 'Gentlemen,' said she, 'my servants and dear friends: with you, and with Fritz who lies wounded in Wintenberg, rest my honour and my life; for I will not live if the letter reaches the King.'

'The King shall not have it, madame,' said Colonel Sapt.

He took her hand in his and patted it with a clumsy gentleness; smiling, she extended it again to young Bernenstein, in mark of her favour. They two then stood at the salute, while Rudolf walked with her to the end of the passage. There for a moment she and he stood together; the others turned their eyes away and thus did not see her suddenly stoop and cover his hand with her kisses. He tried to draw it away, not thinking it fit that she should kiss his hand, but she seemed as though she could not let it go. Yet at last, still with her eyes on his, she passed backwards through the door, and he shut it after her.

'Now to business,' said Colonel Sapt drily; and Rudolf laughed a little.

Rudolf passed into the room. Sapt went to the King's apartments and asked the physician whether His Majesty were sleeping well. Receiving reassuring news of the royal slumbers, he proceeded to the quarters of the King's body-servant, knocked up the sleepy wretch and ordered breakfast for the King and the Count of Luzau-Rischenheim at nine o'clock precisely in the morning-room that looks out over the avenue leading to the entrance of the new *château*. This done, he returned to the room where Rudolf was, carried a chair into the passage, bade Rudolf lock the door, sat down, revolver in hand, and himself went to sleep. Young Bernenstein was in bed just now, taken faint, and the Constable himself was acting as his substitute: that was to be the story if a story were needed. Thus the hours from two to six passed that morning in the Castle of Zenda.

At six the Constable awoke and knocked at the door; Rudolf Rassendyll opened it.

'Slept well?' asked Sapt.

'Not a wink,' answered Rudolf cheerfully.

'I thought you had more nerve.'

'It wasn't want of nerve that kept me awake,' said Mr Rassendyll.

Sapt, with a pitying shrug, looked round. The curtains of the window were half drawn, the table was moved nearer to the wall, and the armchair by it was well in shadow, being quite close to the curtains.

'There's plenty of room for you behind,' said Rudolf; 'and when Rischenheim is seated in his chair opposite to mine, you can put your barrel against his head by just stretching out your hand. And of course I can do the same.'

'Yes, it looks well enough,' said Sapt, with an approving nod.

'What about the beard?'

'Bernenstein is to tell him you've shaved this morning.'

'Will he believe that?'

'Why not? For his own sake he'd better believe everything.'

'And if we have to kill him?'

'We must run for it. The King would be furious.'

'He's fond of him?'

'You forget. He wants to know about the dogs.'

'True. You'll be in your place in time?'

'Of course.'

Rudolf Rassendyll took a turn up and down the room. It was easy to see that the events of the night had disturbed him. Sapt's thoughts were running in a different channel.

'When we've done with this fellow we must find Rupert,' said he.

Rudolf started.

'Rupert? Rupert? True; I forgot. Of course we must,' said he confusedly.

Sapt looked scornful; he knew that his companion's mind had been occupied with the Queen. But his remarks—if he had meditated any—were interrupted by the clock striking seven.

'He'll be here in an hour,' said he.

'We're ready for him,' answered Rudolf Rassendyll. With the thought of action his eyes grew bright and his brow smooth again. He and old Sapt looked at one another, and they both smiled.

'Like old times, isn't it, Sapt?'

'Aye, sire, like the reign of good King Rudolf.'

Thus they made ready for the Count of Luzau-Rischenheim, while my cursed wound held me a prisoner at Wintenberg. It is still a sorrow to me that I know what passed that morning only by report, and had not the honour of bearing a part in it. Still Her Majesty did not forget me, but remembered that I would have taken my share, had fortune allowed. Indeed I would most eagerly.

CHAPTER V

An Audience of the King

HAVING come thus far in the story that I set out to tell, I have half a mind to lay down my pen, and leave untold how from the moment that Mr Rassendyll came again to Zenda a fury of chance seemed to catch us all in a whirlwind, carrying us whither we would not, and ever driving us onwards to fresh enterprises, breathing into us a recklessness that stood at no obstacle, and a devotion to the Queen and to the man she loved that swept away all other feelings. The ancients held there to be a Fate which would have its fill, though women wept and men died, and none could tell whose was the guilt nor who fell innocent. Thus did they blindly wrong God's Providence. Yet, save that we are taught to believe that all is ruled, we are as blind as they, and are still left wondering why all that is true and generous and love's own fruit must turn so often to woe and shame, exacting tears and blood. For myself I would leave the thing untold, lest a word of it should seem to stain her whom I serve; it is by her own command I write, that all may one day, in time's fulness, be truly known, and those condemn who are without sin, while they pity whose own hearts have fought the equal fight. So much for her and him; for us less needs be said. It was not ours to weigh her actions! We served her; him we had served. She was our Queen; we bore Heaven a grudge that he was not our King. The worst of what befell was not of our own planning, no, nor of our hoping. It came a thunderbolt from the hand of Rupert, flung carelessly between a curse and a laugh; its coming entangled us more tightly in the net of circumstances. Then there arose in us that strange and overpowering desire of which I must tell later, filling us with a zeal to accomplish our purpose, and to force Mr Rassendyll himself into the way we chose. Led by this star, we pressed on through the darkness, until at length the deeper darkness fell that stayed our steps. We also stand for judgment, even

47

as she and he. So I will write; but I will write plainly and briefly, setting down what I must and no more, yet seeking to give truly the picture of that time, and to preserve as long as may be the portrait of the man whose like I have not known. Yet the fear is always upon me that, failing to show him as he was, I may fail also in gaining an understanding of how he wrought on us, one and all, till his cause became in all things the right, and to seat him where he should be our highest duty and our nearest wish. For he said little, and that straight to the purpose; no high-flown words of his live in my memory. And he asked nothing for himself. Yet his speech and his eyes went straight to men's hearts and women's, so that they held their lives in an eager attendance on his bidding. Do I rave? Then Sapt was a raver too, for Sapt was foremost in the business.

At ten minutes to eight o'clock, young Bernenstein, very admirably and smartly accoutred, took his stand outside the main entrance of the Castle. He wore a confident air that became almost a swagger as he strolled to and fro past the motionless sentries. He had not long to wait. On the stroke of eight a gentleman, well horsed but entirely unattended, rode up the carriage drive. Bernenstein, crying, 'Ah, it is the count!' ran to meet him. Rischenheim dismounted, holding out his hand to the young officer.

'My dear Bernenstein!' said he, for they were acquainted with one another.

'You're punctual, my dear Rischenheim, and it's lucky, for the King awaits you most impatiently.'

'I didn't expect to find him up so soon,' remarked Rischenheim.

'Up! He's been up these two hours. Indeed we've had the devil of a time of it. Treat him carefully, my dear count; he's in one of his troublesome humours. For example—but I mustn't keep you waiting. Pray follow me.'

'No, but pray tell me. Otherwise I might say something unfortunate.'

'Well, he woke at six; and when the barber came to trim his beard there were—imagine it, count!—no less than seven grey hairs. The King fell into a passion. ''Take it off,'' he said. ''Take it off. I won't have a grey beard! Take it off!'' Well, what would you? A man is free to be shaved if he chooses, so much more a King. So it's taken off.'

'His beard!'

'His beard, my dear count. Then, after thanking heaven it was gone and declaring he looked ten years younger, he cried: ''The Count of Luzau-Rischenheim breakfasts with me today: what is there for breakfast?'' And he had the chef out of his bed and— but, by heavens, I shall get into trouble if I stop here chattering. He's waiting most eagerly for you. Come along.' And Bernenstein, passing his arm through the count's, walked him rapidly into the Castle.

The Count of Luzau-Rischenheim was a young man: he was no more versed in affairs of this kind than Bernenstein, and it cannot be said that he showed so much aptitude for them. He was decidedly pale this morning; his manner was uneasy, and his hands trembled. He did not lack courage, but that rarer virtue, coolness; and the importance—or perhaps the shame—of his mission upset the balance of his nerves. Hardly noting where he went, he allowed Bernenstein to lead him quickly and directly towards the room where Rudolf Rassendyll was, not doubting that he was being conducted to the King's presence.

'Breakfast is ordered for nine,' said Bernenstein, 'but he wants to see you before. He has something important to say; and you perhaps have the same?'

'I? Oh, no. A small matter; but—er—of a private nature.'

'Quite so, quite so. Oh, I don't ask any questions, my dear count.'

'Shall I find the King alone?' asked Rischenheim nervously.

'I don't think you'll find anybody with him: no, nobody, I think,' answered Bernenstein with a grave and reassuring air.

They had arrived now at the door. Here Bernenstein paused.

'I am ordered to wait outside till His Majesty summons me,' he said in a low voice, as though he feared that the irritable King would hear him. 'I'll open the door and announce you. Pray keep him in a good temper, for all our sakes.' And he flung the door open, saying: 'Sire, the Count of Luzau-Rischenheim has the honour to wait on Your Majesty.' With this he shut the door

promptly, and stood against it. Nor did he move, save once, and
then only to take out his revolver and inspect it carefully.

The count advanced, bowing low and striving to conceal a
visible agitation. He saw the King in his armchair; the King wore
a suit of brown tweeds (none the better for being crushed into a
bundle the night before); his face was in deep shadow, but
Rischenheim perceived that the beard was indeed gone. The
King held out his hand to Rischenheim, and motioned him to
sit in a chair just opposite to him and within a foot of the window-
curtains.

'I'm delighted to see you, my lord,' said the King.

Rischenheim looked up. Rudolf's voice had once been so like
the King's that no man could tell the difference, but in the last
year or two the King's had grown weaker, and Rischenheim
seemed to be struck by the vigour of the tones in which he was
addressed. As he looked up, there was a slight movement in the
curtains by him; it died away when the count gave no further
signs of suspicion, but Rudolf had noticed his surprise: the voice,
when it next spoke, was subdued.

'Most delighted,' pursued Mr Rassendyll. 'For I am pestered
beyond endurance about those dogs. I can't get the coats right.
I've tried everything, but they won't come as I wish. Now yours
are magnificent.'

'You are very good, sire. But I ventured to ask an audience in
order to——'

'Positively you must tell me about the dogs. And before Sapt
comes, for I want nobody to hear but myself.'

'Your Majesty expects Colonel Sapt?'

'In about twenty minutes,' said the King, with a glance at the
clock on the mantelpiece.

At this Rischenheim became all on fire to get his errand done
before Sapt appeared.

'The coats of your dogs,' pursued the King, 'grow so beauti-
fully——'

'A thousand pardons, sire, but——'

'Long and silky, that I despair of——'

'I have a most urgent and important matter,' persisted
Rischenheim in agony.

Rudolf threw himself back in his chair with a peevish air.

'Well, if you must, you must. What is this great affair, count? Let us have it over, and then you can tell me about the dogs.'

Rischenheim looked round the room. There was nobody; the curtains were still; the King's left hand caressed his beardless chin; the right was hidden from his visitor by the small table that stood between them.

'Sire, my cousin, the Count of Hentzau, has entrusted me with a message.'

Rudolf suddenly assumed a stern air.

'I can hold no communication, directly or indirectly, with the Count of Hentzau,' said he.

'Pardon me, sire, pardon me. A document has come into the count's hands which is of vital importance to Your Majesty.'

'The Count of Hentzau, my lord, has incurred my heaviest displeasure.'

'Sire, it is in the hopes of atoning for his offences that he has sent me here today. There is a conspiracy against Your Majesty's honour.'

'By whom, my lord?' asked Rudolf in cold and doubting tones.

'By those who are very near Your Majesty's person and very high in Your Majesty's love.'

'Name them.'

'Sire, I dare not. You would not believe me. But Your Majesty will believe written evidence.'

'Show it me, and quickly. We may be interrupted.'

'Sire, I have a copy——'

'Oh, a copy, my lord?' sneered Rudolf.

'My cousin has the original, and will forward it at Your Majesty's command. A copy of a letter of Her Majesty's.'

'Of the Queen's?'

'Yes, sire. It is addressed to——'

Rischenheim paused.

'Well, my lord, to whom?'

'To a Mr Rudolf Rassendyll.'

Now Rudolf played his part well. He did not feign indifference, but allowed his voice to tremble with emotion as he stretched out his hand and said in a hoarse whisper:

'Give it me, give it me.'

Rischenheim's eyes sparkled. His shot had told: the King's attention was his, the coats of the dogs were forgotten. Plainly he had stirred the suspicions and jealousy of the King.

'My cousin', he continued, 'conceives it his duty to lay the letter before Your Majesty. He obtained it——'

'A curse on how he got it! Give it me.'

Rischenheim unbuttoned his coat, then his waistcoat. The head of a revolver showed in a belt round his waist. He undid the flap of a pocket in the lining of his waistcoat, and began to draw out a sheet of paper. But Rudolf, great as his powers of self-control were, was but human. When he saw the paper, he leant forward, half rising from his chair. As a result, his face came beyond the shadow of the curtain, and the full morning light beat on it. As Richenheim took the paper out, he looked up. He saw the face that glared so eagerly at him; his eyes met Rassendyll's: a sudden suspicion seized him, for the face, though the King's face in every feature, bore a stern resolution and witnessed a vigour that were not the King's. In that instant the truth, or a hint of it, flashed across his mind. He gave a half-articulate cry; in one hand he crumpled up the paper, the other flew to his revolver. But he was too late. Rudolf's left hand encircled his hand and the paper in an iron grip; Rudolf's revolver was on his temple; and an arm was stretched out from behind the curtain, holding another barrel full before his eyes, while a dry voice said: 'You'd best take it quietly.' Then Sapt stepped out.

Rischenheim had no words to meet the sudden transformation of the interview. He seemed to be able to do nothing but stare at Rudolf Rassendyll. Sapt wasted no time. He snatched the count's revolver and stowed it in his own pocket.

'Now take the paper,' said he to Rudolf, and his barrel held Rischenheim motionless while Rudolf wrenched the precious document from his fingers. 'Look if it's the right one. No, don't read it through; just look. Is it right? That's good. Now put your revolver to his head again. I'm going to search him. Stand up, sir!'

They compelled the count to stand up, and Sapt subjected him to a search that made the concealment of another copy or of any other document impossible. Then they let him sit down again. His eyes seemed fascinated by Rudolf Rassendyll.

'Yet you've seen me before, I think,' smiled Rudolf. 'I seem to remember you as a boy in Strelsau when I was there. Now tell us, sir, where did you leave this cousin of yours?' For the plan was to find out from Rischenheim where Rupert was, and to set off in pursuit of Rupert as soon as they had disposed of Rischenheim.

But even as Rudolf spoke there was a violent knock at the door. Rudolf sprang to open it. Sapt and his revolver kept their places. Bernenstein was on the threshold, open-mouthed.

'The King's servant has just gone by. He's looking for Colonel Sapt. The King has been walking in the drive, and learnt from a sentry of Rischenheim's arrival. I told the man that you had taken the count for a stroll round the castle, and I did not know where you were. He says that the King may come himself at any moment.'

Sapt considered for one short instant; then he was back by the prisoner's side.

'We must talk again later on,' he said, in low quick tones. 'Now you're going to breakfast with the King. I shall be there, and Bernenstein. Remember, not a word of your errand, not a word of this gentleman! At a word, a sign, a hint, a gesture, a motion, as God lives, I'll put a bullet through your head, and a thousand kings shan't stop me. Rudolf, get behind the curtain. If there's an alarm you must jump through the window into the moat and swim for it.'

'All right,' said Rudolf Rassendyll. 'I can read my letter there.'

'Burn it, you fool!'

'When I've read it I'll eat it if you like, but not before.'

Bernenstein looked in again.

'Quick, quick! The man will be back,' he whispered.

'Bernenstein, did you hear what I said to the count?'

'Yes, I heard.'

'Then you know your part. Now, gentlemen, to the King.'

'Well,' said an angry voice outside. 'I wondered how long I was to be kept waiting.'

Rudolf Rassendyll skipped behind the curtain. Sapt's revolver slipped into a handy pocket. Rischenheim stood with arms dangling by his side and his waistcoat half unbuttoned. Young Bernenstein was bowing low on the threshold, and protesting that the King's servant had but just gone, and that they were on the point of waiting on His Majesty. Then the King walked in, pale and full-bearded.

'Ah, count,' said he, 'I'm glad to see you. If they had told me you were here, you shouldn't have waited a minute. You're very dark in here, Sapt. Why don't you draw back the curtains?' and the King moved towards the curtains behind which Rudolf was.

'Allow me, sire,' cried Sapt, darting past him and laying a hand on the curtain.

A malicious gleam of pleasure shot into Rischenheim's eyes.

'In truth, sire,' continued the Constable, his hand on the curtain, 'we were so interested in what the count was saying about his dogs——'

'By heaven, I forgot!' cried the King. 'Yes, yes, the dogs. Now tell me, count——'

'Your pardon, sire,' put in young Bernenstein, 'but breakfast waits.'

'Yes, yes. Well, then, we'll have them together—breakfast and the dogs. Come along, count.' The King passed his arm through Rischenheim's, adding to Bernenstein, 'Lead the way, lieutenant; and you, colonel, come with us.'

They went out. Sapt stopped and locked the door behind him.

'Why do you lock the door, colonel?' asked the King.

'There are some papers in my drawer there, sire.'

'But why not lock the drawer?'

'I have lost the key, sire, like the fool I am,' said the colonel.

The Count of Luzau-Rischenheim did not make a very good breakfast. He sat opposite to the King. Colonel Sapt placed himself at the back of the King's chair, and Rischenheim saw the muzzle of a revolver resting on the top of the chair just behind His Majesty's right ear. Bernenstein stood in soldierly rigidity by the door; Rischenheim looked round at him once, and met a most significant gaze.

'You're eating nothing,' said the King. 'I hope you're not indisposed?'

'I hope you're not indisposed?'

'I am a little upset, sire,' stammered Rischenheim, and truly enough.

'Well, tell me about the dogs while I eat; for I'm hungry.'

Rischenheim began to disclose his secret. His statement was decidedly wanting in clearness. The King grew impatient.

'I don't understand,' said he testily, and he pushed his chair back so quickly that Sapt skipped away, and hid the revolver behind his back.

'Sire——' cried Rischenheim, half rising. A cough from Lieutenant von Bernenstein interrupted him.

'Tell it me all over again,' said the King. Rischenheim did as he was bid.

'Ah, I understand a little better now. Do you see, Sapt?' and he turned his head round towards the Constable. Sapt had just time to whisk the revolver away. The count leant forward towards the King. Lieutenant von Bernenstein coughed. The count sank back again.

'Perfectly, sire,' said Colonel Sapt. 'I understand all the count wishes to convey to Your Majesty.'

'Well, I understand about half,' said the King with a laugh. 'But perhaps that'll be enough.'

'I think quite enough, sire,' answered Sapt with a smile.

The important matter of the dogs being thus disposed of, the King recollected that the count had asked for an audience on a matter of business.

'Now what did you wish to say to me?' he asked with a weary air. The dogs had been more interesting.

Rischenheim looked at Sapt. The revolver was in its place; Bernenstein coughed again. Yet he saw a chance.

'Your pardon, sire,' said he, 'but we are not alone.'

The King lifted his eyebrows.

'Is the business so private?' he asked.

'I should prefer to tell it to Your Majesty alone,' pleaded the count.

Now Sapt was resolved not to leave Rischenheim alone with the King, for although the count, being robbed of his evidence, could do little harm concerning the letter, he would doubtless tell the King that Rudolf Rassendyll was in the Castle. He leant now over the King's shoulder, and said with a sneer:

'Messages from Rupert of Hentzau are too exalted matters for my poor ears, it seems.'

The King flushed red.

'Is that your business, my lord?' he asked Rischenheim sternly.

'Your Majesty does not know what my cousin——'

'It is the old plea?' interrupted the King. 'He wants to come back? Is that all, or is there anything else?'

A moment's silence followed the King's words. Sapt looked full at Rischenheim, and smiled as he slightly raised his right hand and showed the revolver. Bernenstein coughed twice. Rischenheim sat twisting his fingers. He understood that, cost what it might, they would not let him declare his errand to the King or betray Mr Rassendyll's presence. He cleared his throat and opened his mouth as if to speak; but still he remained silent.

'Well, my lord, is it the old story or something new?' asked the King impatiently.

Again Rischenheim sat silent.

'Are you dumb, my lord?' cried the King most impatiently.

'It—it is—only what you call the old story, sire.'

'Then let me say that you have treated me very badly in obtaining an audience of me for any such purpose,' said the King. 'You knew my decision, and your cousin knows it.'

Thus speaking the King rose; Sapt's revolver slid into his pocket; but Lieutenant von Bernenstein drew his sword and stood at the salute; he also coughed.

'My dear Rischenheim,' pursued the King more kindly, 'I can allow for your natural affection. But, believe me, in this case it misleads you. Do me the favour not to open this subject again to me.'

Rischenheim, humiliated and angry, could do nothing but bow in acknowledgment of the King's rebuke.

'Colonel Sapt, see that the count is well entertained. My horse should be at the door by now. Farewell, count. Bernenstein, give me your arm.'

Bernenstein shot a rapid glance at the Constable. Sapt nodded reassuringly. Bernenstein sheathed his sword and gave his arm to the King. They passed through the door, and Bernenstein closed it with a backward push of his hand. But at this moment Rischenheim, goaded to fury and desperate at the trick played on him—seeing, moreover, that he had now only one man to deal with—made a sudden rush at the door. He reached it, and his hand was on the door-knob. But Sapt was upon him, and Sapt's revolver was at his ear.

In the passage the King stopped.

'What are they doing in there?' he asked, hearing the noise of the quick movements.

'I don't know, sire,' said Bernenstein, and he took a step forward.

'No, stop a minute, lieutenant: you're pulling me along!'

E

'A thousand pardons, sire.'

'I hear nothing more now.' And there was nothing to hear, for the two now stood dead silent inside the door.

'Nor I, sire. Will Your Majesty go on?' And Bernenstein took another step.

'You're determined I shall,' said the King with a laugh, and he let the young officer lead him away.

Inside the room Rischenheim stood with his back against the door. He was panting for breath, and his face was flushed and working with excitement. Opposite to him stood Sapt, revolver in hand.

'Till you get to heaven, my lord,' said the Constable, 'you'll never be nearer to it than you were in that moment. If you had opened the door, I'd have shot you through the head.'

As he spoke there came a knock at the door.

'Open it,' he said brusquely to Rischenheim. With a muttered curse the count obeyed him. A servant stood outside with a telegram on a salver. 'Take it,' whispered Sapt, and Rischenheim put out his hand.

'Your pardon, my lord, but this has arrived for you,' said the man respectfully.

'Take it,' whispered Sapt again.

'Give it me,' muttered Rischenheim confusedly; and he took the envelope.

The servant bowed and shut the door.

'Open it,' commanded Sapt.

'God's curse on you!' cried Rischenheim, in a voice that choked with passion.

'Eh? Oh, you can have no secrets from so good a friend as I am, my lord. Be quick and open it.'

The count began to open it.

'If you tear it up or crumple it, I'll shoot you,' said Sapt quietly. 'You know you can trust my word. Now read it.'

'By God, I won't read it!'

'Read it, I tell you, or say your prayers.'

The muzzle was within a foot of his head. He unfolded the telegram. Then he looked at Sapt.

'Read,' said the Constable.

'I don't understand what it means,' grumbled Rischenheim.

'Possibly I may be able to help you.'

'It's nothing but——'

'Read, my lord, read!'

Then he read, and this was the telegram:

'Holf, 19 Königstrasse.'

'A thousand thanks, my lord. And the place it's dispatched from?'

'Strelsau.'

'Just turn it so that I can see. Oh, I don't doubt you, but seeing is believing. Ah, thanks. It's as you say. You're puzzled what it means, count?'

'I don't know at all what it means.'

'How strange! Because I can guess so well.'

'You are very acute, sir.'

'It seems to me a simple thing to guess, my lord.'

'And pray,' said Rischenheim, endeavouring to assume an easy and sarcastic air, 'what does your wisdom tell you that the message means?'

'I think, my lord, that the message is an address.'

'An address! I never thought of that. But I know no Holf.'

'I don't think it's Holf's address.'

'Whose then?' asked Rischenheim, biting his nail, and looking furtively at the Constable.

'Why,' said Sapt, 'the present address of Count Rupert of Hentzau.'

As he spoke, he fixed his eyes on the eyes of Rischenheim. He gave a short sharp laugh, then put his revolver in his pocket and bowed to the count.

'In truth, you are very convenient, my dear count,' said he.

Chapter VI

The Task of the Queen's Servants

THE doctor who had attended me at Wintenberg was not only discreet, but also indulgent: perhaps he had the sense to see that little benefit would come to a sick man from fretting in helplessless on his back, when he was on fire to be afoot. I fear he thought the baker's rolling-pin was in my mind, but at any rate I extorted a consent from him, and was on my way home from Wintenberg not much more than twelve hours after Rudolf Rassendyll left me. Thus I arrived at my own house in Strelsau on the same Friday morning that witnessed the Count of Luzau-Rischenheim's twofold interview with the King at the Castle of Zenda. The moment I had arrived, I sent James, whose assistance had been, and continued to be, in all respects most valuable, to dispatch a message to the Constable, acquainting him with my whereabouts and putting myself entirely at his disposal. Sapt received this message while a council of war was being held, and the information it gave aided not a little in the arrangements that the Constable and Rudolf Rassendyll made. What these were I must now relate, although, I fear, at the risk of some tediousness.

Yet that council of war in Zenda was held under no common circumstances. Cowed as Rischenheim appeared, they dared not let him out of their sight; Rudolf could not leave the room into which Sapt had locked him; the King's absence was to be short, and before he came again Rudolf must be gone, Rischenheim safely disposed of and measures taken against the original letter reaching the hands for which the intercepted copy had been destined. The room was a large one. In the corner farthest from the door sat Rischenheim, disarmed, dispirited, to all seeming ready to throw up his dangerous game and acquiesce in any terms presented to him. Just inside the door, guarding it, if need should be, with their lives, were the other three—Bernenstein merry and triumphant, Sapt blunt and cool, Rudolf calm and clear-headed. The Queen awaited the result of their deliberations in her apartments, ready to act as they directed, but determined to see Rudolf before he left the Castle. They conversed together in low tones. Presently Sapt took paper and wrote. This first message was to me, and it bade me come to Zenda that afternoon; another head and another pair of hands were sadly needed. Then followed more deliberation; Rudolf took up the talking now, for his was the bold plan on which they consulted. Sapt twirled his moustache, smiling doubtfully.

'Yes, yes,' murmured young Bernenstein, his eyes alight with excitement.

'It's dangerous, but the best thing,' said Rudolf, carefully sinking his voice yet lower, lest the prisoner should catch the lightest word of what he said. 'It involves my staying here till the evening. Is that possible?'

'No; but you can leave here and hide in the forest till I join you,' said Sapt.

'Till we join you,' corrected Bernenstein eagerly.

'No,' said the Constable, 'you must look after our friend here. Come, lieutenant, it's all in the Queen's service.'

'Besides,' added Rudolf with a smile, 'neither the colonel nor I would let you have a chance at Rupert. He's our game, isn't he, Sapt?'

The colonel nodded. Rudolf in his turn took paper, and here is the message that he wrote:

'Holf, 19 Königstrasse, Strelsau. All well. He has what I had, but wishes to see what you have. He and I will be at the hunting-lodge at ten this evening. Bring it and meet us. The business is unsuspected.—L-R.'

Rudolf flung the paper across to Sapt; Bernenstein leant over the Constable's shoulder and read it eagerly.

'I doubt if it would bring me,' grinned old Sapt, throwing the paper down.

'It'll bring Rupert of Hentzau. Why not? He'll know that the King will wish to meet him unknown to the Queen, and also unknown to you, Sapt, since you were my friend: what place more likely for the King to choose than his hunting-lodge, where he is accustomed to go when he wishes to be alone? The message will bring him, depend on it. Why, man, Rupert would come even if he suspected; and why should he suspect?'

'They may have a cipher, he and Rischenheim,' objected Sapt.

'No, or Rupert would have sent the address in it,' retorted Rudolf quickly.

'Then—when he comes?' asked Bernenstein.

'He finds such a king as Rischenheim found, and Sapt here, at his elbow.'

'But he'll know you,' objected Bernenstein.

'Aye, I think he'll know me,' said Rudolf with a smile. 'Meanwhile we send for Fritz to come here and look after the King.'

'And Rischenheim?'

'That's your share, lieutenant. Sapt, is any one at Tarlenheim?'

'No. Count Stanislas has put it at Fritz's disposal.'

'Good; then Fritz's two friends, the Count of Luzau-Rischenheim and Lieutenant von Bernenstein, will ride over there today. The Constable of Zenda will give the lieutenant twenty-four hours' leave of absence, and the two gentlemen will pass the day and sleep at the *château*. They will pass the day side by side, Bernenstein, not losing sight of one another for an instant, and they will pass the night in the same room. And one of them will not close his eyes nor take his hand off the butt of his revolver.'

'Very good, sir,' said young Bernenstein.

'If he tries to escape or give any alarm, shoot him through the head, ride to the frontier, get to safe hiding and, if you can, let us know.'

'Yes,' said Bernenstein simply. Sapt had chosen well, and the young officer made nothing of the peril and ruin that Her Majesty's service might ask of him.

A restless movement and a weary sigh from Rischenheim attracted their attention. He had strained his ears to listen till his head ached, but the talkers had been careful and he had heard nothing that threw light on their deliberations. He had now given up his vain attempt, and sat in listless inattention, sunk in an apathy.

'I don't think he'll give you much trouble,' whispered Sapt to Bernenstein, with a jerk of his thumb towards the captive.

'Act as if he is likely to give you much,' urged Rudolf, laying his hand on the lieutenant's arm.

'Yes, that's a wise man's advice,' nodded the Constable approvingly. 'We were well governed, lieutenant, when this Rudolf was king.'

'Wasn't I also his loyal subject?' asked young Bernenstein.

'Yes, wounded in my service,' added Rudolf; for he remembered how the boy—he was little more then—had been fired upon in the park of Tarlenheim, being taken for Mr Rassendyll himself.

Thus their plans were laid. If they could defeat Rupert, they would have Rischenheim at their mercy. If they could keep Rischenheim out of the way while they used his name in their trick, they had a strong chance of deluding and killing Rupert. Yes, of killing him; for that and nothing less was their purpose, as the Constable of Zenda himself has told me.

'We would have stood on no ceremony,' he said. 'The Queen's honour was at stake, and the fellow himself an assassin.'

Bernenstein rose and went out. He was gone about half an hour, being employed in dispatching the telegrams to Strelsau. Rudolf and Sapt used the interval to explain to Rischenheim what they proposed to do with him. They asked no pledge, and he offered none. He heard what they said with a dull uninterested air. When asked if he would go without resistance, he laughed a bitter laugh.

'How can I resist?' he asked. 'I should have a bullet through my head.'

'Why, without doubt,' said Colonel Sapt. 'My lord, you are very sensible.'

'Let me advise you, my lord,' said Rudolf, looking down on him kindly enough, 'if you come safe through this affair, to add honour to your prudence, and chivalry to your honour. There is still time for you to become a gentleman.'

He turned away, followed by a glance of anger from the count and a grating chuckle from old Sapt.

A few moments later Bernenstein returned. His errand was

done, and horses for himself and Rischenheim were at the gate of the Castle. After a few final words and a clasp of the hand from Rudolf, the lieutenant motioned to his prisoner to accompany him, and they two walked out together, being to all appearance willing companions and in perfect friendliness with one another. The Queen herself watched them go from the windows of her apartment, and noticed that Bernenstein rode half a pace behind, and that his free hand rested on the revolver by his side.

It was now well on in the morning, and the risk of Rudolf's sojourn in the Castle grew greater with every moment. Yet he was resolved to see the Queen before he went. This interview presented no great difficulties, since Her Majesty was in the habit of coming to the Constable's room to take his advice or to consult with him. The hardest task was to contrive afterwards a free and unnoticed escape for Mr Rassendyll. To meet this necessity, the Constable issued orders that the company of Guards which garrisoned the Castle should parade at one o'clock in the park, and that the servants should all, after their dinner, be granted permission to watch the manœuvres. By this means he counted on drawing off any curious eyes and allowing Rudolf to reach the forest unobserved. They appointed a rendezvous in a handy and sheltered spot; the one thing which they were compelled to trust to fortune was Rudolf's success in evading chance encounters while he waited. Mr Rassendyll himself was confident of his ability to conceal his presence, or, if need were, so to hide his face that no strange tale of the King being seen wandering alone and beardless should reach the ears of the Castle or the town.

While Sapt was making his arrangements, Queen Flavia came to the room where Rudolf Rassendyll was. It was then nearing twelve, and young Bernenstein had been gone half an hour. Sapt attended her to the door, set a sentry at the end of the passage with orders that Her Majesty should on no pretence be disturbed, promised her very audibly to return as soon as he possibly could, and respectfully closed the door after she had entered. The Constable was well aware of the value in a secret business of doing openly all that can safely be done with openness.

All of what passed at that interview I do not know, but a part Queen Flavia herself told to me, or rather to Helga, my wife; for although it was meant to reach my ear, yet to me, a man, she would not disclose it directly. First she learnt from Mr Rassendyll the plans that had been made, and, although she trembled at the danger that he must run in meeting Rupert of Hentzau, she had such love of him and such a trust in his powers that she seemed to doubt little of his success. But she began to reproach herself for having brought him into this peril by writing her letter. At this he took from his pocket the copy that Rischenheim had carried. He had found time to read it, and now before her eyes he kissed it.

'Had I as many lives as there are words, my Queen,' he said softly, 'for each word I would gladly give a life.'

'Ah, Rudolf, but you've only one life, and that more mine than yours. Did you think we should ever meet again?'

'I didn't know,' said he; and now they were standing opposite one another.

'But I knew,' she said, her eyes shining brightly; 'I knew always that we should meet once more. Not how, nor where, but just that we should. So I lived, Rudolf.'

'God bless you,' he said.

'Yes, I lived through it all.'

He pressed her hand, knowing what that phrase meant and must mean for her.

'Will it last for ever?' she asked, suddenly gripping his hand tightly. But a moment later she went on: 'No, no, I mustn't make you unhappy, Rudolf. I'm half glad I wrote the letter, and half glad they stole it. It's so sweet to have you fighting for me, for me only this time, Rudolf—not for the King, for me!'

'Sweet indeed, my dearest lady. Don't be afraid; we shall win.'

'You will win, yes. And then you'll go?' And dropping his hands, she covered her face with hers.

'I mustn't kiss your face,' said he, 'but your hands I may kiss.' And he kissed her hands as they were pressed against her face.

'You wear my ring', she murmured through her fingers, 'always?'

'Why, yes,' he said, with a little laugh of wonder at her question.

'And there is—no one else?'

'My Queen!' said he, laughing again.

'No, I knew really, Rudolf, I knew really,' and now her hands flew out towards him, imploring his pardon. Then she began to speak quickly: 'Rudolf, last night I had a dream about you, a strange dream. I seemed to be in Strelsau, and all the people were talking about the King. It was you they meant; you were the King. At last you were the King, and I was your Queen. But I could see you only very dimly; you were somewhere, but I could not make out where; just sometimes your face came. Then I tried to tell you that you were King—yes, and Colonel Sapt and Fritz tried to tell you; the people too called out that you were King. What did it mean? But your face, when I saw it, was unmoved and very pale, and you seemed not to hear what we said, not even what I said. It almost seemed as if you were dead, and yet King. Ah, you mustn't die, even to be King,' and she laid a hand on his shoulder.

'Sweetheart,' said he gently, 'in dreams desires and fears blend in strange visions, so I seemed to you to be both a king and a dead man; but I'm not a king, and I am a very healthy fellow. Yet a thousand thanks to my dearest Queen for dreaming of me.'

'No, but what could it mean?' she asked again.

'What does it mean when I dream always of you, except that I always love you?'

'Was it only that?' she said, still unconvinced.

What more passed between them I do not know. I think that the Queen told my wife more, but women will sometimes keep women's secrets even from their husbands; though they love us, yet we are always in some sort the common enemy, against whom they join hands. Well, I would not look too far into such secrets, for to know must be, I suppose, to blame, and who is himself so blameless that in such a case he would be free with his censures?

Yet much cannot have passed, for almost close on their talk about the dream came Colonel Sapt, saying that the Guards were in line, and all the women streamed out to watch them, while the men followed, lest the gay uniforms should make them forgotten. Certainly a quiet fell over the old Castle, that only the Constable's curt tones broke, as he bade Rudolf come by the back way to the stables and mount his horse.

'There's no time to lose,' said Sapt, and his eye seemed to grudge the Queen even one word more with the man she loved.

But Rudolf was not to be hurried into leaving her in such a fashion. He clapped the Constable on the shoulder, laughing and bidding him think of what he would for a moment; then he went again to the Queen and would have knelt before her, but that she would not suffer, and they stood with hands locked. Then suddenly she drew him to her and kissed his forehead, saying:

'God go with you, Rudolf, my knight.'

Thus she turned away, letting him go. He walked towards the door. But a sound arrested his steps, and he waited in the middle of the room, his eyes on the door. Old Sapt flew to the threshold, his sword half way out of its sheath. There was a step coming down the passage, and the feet stopped outside the door.

'Is it the King?' whispered Rudolf.

'I don't know,' said Sapt.

'No, it's not the King,' came in unhesitating certainty from Queen Flavia.

They waited: a low knock sounded on the door. Still for a moment they waited. The knock was repeated urgently.

'We must open,' said Sapt. 'Behind the curtain with you, Rudolf!'

The Queen sat down and Sapt piled a heap of papers before her, that it might seem as though he and she transacted business. But his precautions were interrupted by a hoarse, eager, low cry from outside:

'Quick, in God's name, quick!'

They knew the voice for Bernenstein's. The Queen sprang up, Rudolf came out, Sapt turned the key. The lieutenant entered, hurried, breathless, pale.

'Well?' asked Sapt.

'He has got away?' cried Rudolf, guessing in a moment the misfortune that had brought Bernenstein back.

'Yes, he's got away. Just as we left the town and reached the open road towards Tarlenheim he said: "Are we going to walk all the way?" I was not loath to go quicker, and we broke into a trot. But I—ah, what a pestilent fool I am!'

'Never mind that—go on.'

'Why, I was thinking of him and my task, and having a bullet ready for him, and——'

'Of everything except your horse?' guessed Sapt, with a grim smile.

'Yes; and the horse pecked and stumbled, and I fell forward

'*I fired three times after him*'

on his neck. I put out my arm to recover myself, and—I jerked my revolver on to the ground.'

'And he saw?'

'He saw, curse him! For a second he waited; then he smiled, and turned, and dug his spurs in and was off, straight across country towards Strelsau. Well, I was off my horse in a moment, and I fired three times after him.'

'You hit?' asked Rudolf.

'I think so. He shifted the reins from one hand to the other and wrung his arm. I mounted and made after him, but his horse was better than mine and he gained ground. We began to meet people too, and I didn't dare to fire again. So I left him and rode here to tell you. Never employ me again, Constable, as long as you live.'

And the young man's face was twisted with misery and shame as, forgetting the Queen's presence, he sank despondently into a chair.

Sapt took no notice of his self-reproaches. But Rudolf went and laid a hand on his shoulder.

'It was an accident,' he said. 'No blame to you.'

The Queen rose and walked towards him; Bernenstein sprang to his feet.

'Sir,' said she, 'it is not success but effort that should gain thanks,' and she held out her hand.

Well, he was young; I do not laugh at the sob that escaped his lips as he turned his head.

'Let me try something else,' he implored.

'Mr Rassendyll,' said the Queen, 'you'll do my pleasure by employing this gentleman in my further service. I am already deep in his debt, and would be deeper.'

There was a moment's silence.

'Well, but what's to be done?' asked Colonel Sapt. 'He's gone to Strelsau.'

'He'll stop Rupert,' mused Mr Rassendyll.

'He may or he mayn't.'

'It's odds that he will.'

'We must provide for both.'

Sapt and Rudolf looked at one another.

'You must be here?' asked Rudolf of the Constable. 'Well, I'll go to Strelsau.' His smile broke out. 'That is, if Bernenstein will lend me a hat.'

The Queen made no sound; but she came and laid her hand on his arm. He looked at her, smiling still.

'Yes, I'll go to Strelsau,' said he, 'and I'll find Rupert, aye, and Rischenheim, too, if they're in the city.'

'Take me with you,' cried Bernenstein eagerly.

Rudolf glanced at Sapt. The Constable shook his head. Bernenstein's face fell.

'It's not that, boy,' said old Sapt, half in kindness, half in impatience. 'We want you here. Suppose Rupert comes here with Rischenheim!'

The idea was new, but the event by no means unlikely.

'But you'll be here, Constable,' urged Bernenstein, 'and Fritz von Tarlenheim will arrive in an hour.'

'Aye, young man,' said Sapt, nodding his head; 'but when I fight Rupert of Hentzau, I like to have a man to spare,' and he grinned broadly, being no whit afraid of what Bernenstein might think of his courage. 'Now go and get him a hat,' he added, and the lieutenant ran off on the errand.

But the Queen cried:

'Are you sending Rudolf alone, then—alone against two?'

'Yes, madame, if I may command the campaign,' said Sapt. 'I take it he should be equal to the task.'

He could not know the feelings of the Queen's heart. She dashed her hand across her eyes and turned in mute entreaty to Rudolf Rassendyll.

'I must go,' he said softly. 'We can't spare Bernenstein, and I mustn't stay here.'

She said no more. Rudolf walked across to Sapt.

'Take me to the stables. Is the horse good? I daren't take the train. Ah, here's the lieutenant and the hat.'

'The horse'll get you there tonight,' said Sapt. 'Come along. Bernenstein, stay with the Queen.'

At the threshold Rudolf paused, and, turning his head, glanced once at Queen Flavia, who stood still as a statue, watching him go. Then he followed the Constable, who brought him where the horse was. Sapt's devices for securing freedom from observation had served well, and Rudolf mounted unmolested.

'The hat doesn't fit very well,' said Rudolf.

'Like a crown better, eh?' suggested the colonel.

Rudolf laughed as he asked:

'Well, what are my orders?'

'Ride round by the moat to the road at the back; then through the forest to Hofbau; you know your way after that. You mustn't reach Strelsau till it's dark. Then, if you want a shelter——'

'To Fritz von Tarlenheim's, yes! From there I shall go straight to the address.'

'Aye. And——Rudolf!'

'Yes?'

'Make an end of him this time.'

'Please God. But if he goes to the lodge? He will unless Rischenheim stops him.'

'I'll be there in case, but I think Rischenheim will stop him.'

'If he comes here?'

'Young Bernenstein will die before he allows him to reach the King.'

'Sapt!'

'Aye?'

'Be kind to her.'

'Bless the man, yes!'

'Goodbye.'

'And good luck.'

At a swift canter Rudolf darted round the drive that led from the stables, by the moat, to the old forest road behind; five minutes brought him within the shelter of the trees, and he rode on confidently, meeting nobody save here and there a yokel, who, seeing a man ride hard with his head averted, took no more notice of him than to wish that he himself could ride abroad instead of being bound to work. Thus Rudolf Rassendyll set out again for the walls of Strelsau, through the forest of Zenda. And ahead of him, with an hour's start, galloped the Count of Luzau-Rischenheim, again a man, and a man with resolution, resentment and revenge in his heart.

The game was afoot now; who could tell the issue of it?

CHAPTER VII

The Message of Simon the Huntsman

I RECEIVED the telegram sent to me by the Constable of Zenda at my own house in Strelsau about one o'clock. It is needless to say that I made immediate preparations to obey the summons. My wife indeed protested—and I must admit with some show of reason—that I was unfit to endure fatigues, and that my bed was the only proper place for me. I could not listen, and James, Mr Rassendyll's servant, being informed of the message, was at my elbow with a card of the trains from Strelsau to Zenda, without waiting for any orders from me. I had talked to this man in the course of our journey, and discovered that he had been in the service of Lord Topham, formerly British ambassador to the court of Ruritania. How far he was acquainted with the secrets of his present master I did not know, but his familiarity with the city and the country made him of great use to me. We discovered, to our annoyance, that no train left till four o'clock, and then only a slow one; the result being that we could not arrive at the Castle till past six o'clock. This hour was not absolutely too late, but I was of course eager to be on the scene of action as early as possible.

'You'd better see if you can get a special, my lord,' James suggested; 'I'll run on to the station and arrange about it.'

I agreed. Since I was known to be often employed in the King's service, I could take a special train without exciting remark. James set out, and about a quarter of an hour later I got into my carriage to drive to the station. Just as the horses were about to start, the butler approached me.

'I beg your pardon, my lord,' said he, 'but Bauer didn't return with your lordship. Is he coming back?'

'No,' said I. 'Bauer was grossly impertinent on the journey, and I dismissed him.'

See page 71
Rudolf darted round the drive . . . to the old forest road behind

'Those foreign men are never to be trusted, my lord. And your lordship's bag?'

'What, hasn't it come?' I cried. 'I told him to send it.'

'It's not arrived, my lord.'

'Can the rogue have stolen it?' I exclaimed indignantly.

'If your lordship wishes it, I will mention the matter to the police.'

I appeared to consider this proposal.

'Wait till I come back,' I ended by saying. 'The bag may come, and I have no reason to doubt the fellow's honesty.'

This, I thought, would be the end of my connection with Master Bauer. He had served Rupert's turn, and would now disappear from the scene. Indeed it may be that Rupert would have liked to dispense with further aid from him; but he had few whom he could trust, and was compelled to employ those few more than once. At any rate, he had not done with Bauer, and I very soon received proof of the fact. My house is a couple of miles from the station, and we had to pass through a considerable part of the old town, where the streets are narrow and tortuous and progress necessarily slow. We had just entered the Königstrasse (and it must be remembered that I had at that time no reason for attaching any special significance to this locality) and were waiting impatiently for a heavy dray to move out of our path, when my coachman, who had overheard the butler's conversation with me, leant down from his box with an air of lively excitement.

'My lord,' he cried, 'there's Bauer—there, passing the butcher's shop!'

I sprang up in the carriage; the man's back was towards me, and he was threading his way through the people with a quick stealthy tread. I believe he must have seen me and was slinking off as fast as he could. I was not sure of him, but the coachman banished my doubt by saying: 'It's Bauer—it's certainly Bauer, my lord.'

I hardly stayed to form a resolution. If I could catch this fellow or even see where he went, a most important clue as to Rupert's doings and whereabouts might be put into my hand. I leapt out of the carriage, bidding the man wait, and at once started in pursuit

F

He was threading his way through the people with a quick stealthy tread

of my former servant. I heard the coachman laugh: he thought, no doubt, that anxiety for the missing bag inspired such eager haste.

The numbers of the houses in the Königstrasse begin, as anybody familiar with Strelsau will remember, at the end adjoining the station. The street being a long one, intersecting almost the entire length of the old town, I was, when I set out after Bauer, opposite number three hundred or thereabouts, and distant nearly three-quarters of a mile from that important number nineteen, towards which Bauer was hurrying like a rabbit to its burrow. I knew nothing and thought nothing of where he was going; to me nineteen was no more than eighteen or twenty; my only desire was to overtake him. I had no clear idea of what I meant to do when I caught him, but I had some hazy notion of intimidating him into giving up his secret by the threat of an accusation of theft. In fact, he had stolen my bag. After him I went; and he knew that I was after him. I saw him turn his face over his shoulder, and then bustle on faster. Neither of us, pursued or pursuer, dared quite to run; as it was, our eager strides and our carelessness of collisions created more than enough attention. But I had one advantage. Most folk in Strelsau knew me, and many got out of my way who were by no means inclined to pay a like civility to Bauer. Thus I began to gain on him, in spite of his haste; I had started fifty yards behind, but as we neared the end of the street and saw the station ahead of us, not more than twenty separated me from him. Then an annoying thing happened. I ran full into a stout old gentleman; Bauer had run into him before, and he was standing, as people will, staring in resentful astonishment at his first assailant's retreating figure. The second collision immensely increased his vexation: for me it had yet worse consequences; for when I disentangled myself, Bauer was gone! There was not a sign of him; I looked up: the number of the house above me was twenty-three; but the door was shut. I walked on a few paces, past twenty-two, past twenty-one—and up to nineteen. Nineteen was an old house, with a dirty dilapidated front and an air almost dissipated. It was a shop where provisions of the cheaper sort were on view in the window—things that one has never eaten but had heard of people eating.

The shop door stood open, but there was nothing to connect Bauer with the house. Muttering an oath in my exasperation, I was about to pass on, when an old woman put her head out of the door and looked round. I was full in front of her. I am sure that the old woman started slightly, and I think that I did. For I knew her, and she knew me. She was old Mother Holf, one of whose sons, Johann, had betrayed to us the secret of the dungeon at Zenda, while the other had died by Mr Rassendyll's hand by the side of the great pipe that masked the King's window. Her presence might mean nothing, yet it seemed to connect the house at once with the secret of the past and the crisis of the present.

She recovered herself in a moment, and curtsied to me.

'Ah, Mother Holf,' said I, 'how long is it since you set up shop in Strelsau?'

'About six months, my lord,' she answered, with a composed air and arms akimbo.

'I have not come across you before,' said I, looking keenly at her.

'Such a poor little shop as mine would not be likely to secure your lordship's patronage,' she answered, in a humility that seemed only half genuine.

I looked up at the windows. They were all closed and had their wooden lattices shut. The house was devoid of any signs of life.

'You've a good house here, mother, though it wants a splash of paint,' said I. 'Do you live all alone in it with your daughter?' For Max was dead and Johann abroad, and the old woman had, as far as I knew, no other children.

'Sometimes, sometimes not,' said she. 'I let lodgings to single men when I can.'

'Full now?'

'Not a soul, worse luck, my lord.'

Then I shot an arrow at a venture.

'That man who came in just now, then, was he only a customer?'

'I wish a customer had come in, but there has been nobody,' she replied in surprised tones.

I looked full in her eyes; she met mine with a blinking imperturbability. There is no face so inscrutable as a clever old woman's when she is on her guard. And her fat body barred the entrance; I could not so much as see inside, while the window, choked full with pig's trotters and such-like dainties, helped me very little. If the fox were there, he had got to earth and I could not dig him out.

At this moment I saw James approaching hurriedly. He was looking up the street, no doubt seeking my carriage and chafing at its delay. An instant later he saw me.

'My lord,' he said, 'your train will be ready in five minutes; if it doesn't start then, the line must be closed for another half-hour.'

I perceived a faint smile on the old woman's face. I was sure then that I was on the track of Bauer, and probably of more than Bauer. But my first duty was to obey orders and get to Zenda. Besides, I could not force my way in there in open daylight, without a scandal that would have set all the long ears in Strelsau aprick. I turned away reluctantly. I did not even know for certain that Bauer was within, and thus had no information of value to carry with me.

'If your lordship would kindly recommend me——' said the old hag.

'Yes, I'll recommend you,' said I. 'I'll recommend you to be careful whom you take for lodgers. There are queer fish about, mother.'

'I take the money beforehand,' she retorted with a grin; and I was as sure that she was in the plot as of my own existence.

There was nothing to be done; James's face urged me towards the station. I turned away. But at this instant a loud merry laugh sounded from inside the house. I started, and this time violently. The old woman's brow contracted in a frown, and her lips twitched for a moment; then her face regained its composure; but I knew the laugh, and she must have guessed that I knew it. Instantly I tried to appear as though I had noticed nothing. I nodded to her carelessly, and bidding James follow me set out for the station. But as we reached the platform I laid my hand on his shoulder, saying:

'The Count of Hentzau is in that house, James.'

He looked at me without surprise; he was as hard to stir to wonder as old Sapt himself.

'Indeed, sir. Shall I stay and watch?'

'No, come with me,' I answered. To tell the truth, I thought that to leave him alone in Strelsau to watch that house was in all likelihood to sign his death-warrant, and I shrank from imposing the duty on him. Rudolf might send him if he would; I dared not. So we got into our train, and I suppose that my coachman, when he had looked long enough for me, went home. I forgot to ask him afterwards. Very likely he thought it a fine joke to see his master hunting a truant servant and a truant bag through the streets in broad daylight. Had he known the truth, he would have been as interested, though, maybe, less amused.

I arrived at the town of Zenda at half past three, and was in the Castle before four. I may pass over the most kind and gracious words with which the Queen received me. Every sight of her face and every sound of her voice bound a man closer to her service, and now she made me feel that I was a poor fellow to have lost her letter and yet to be alive. But she would hear nothing of such talk, choosing rather to praise the little I had done than to blame the great thing in which I had failed. Dismissed from her presence, I flew open-mouthed to Sapt. I found him in his room with Bernenstein, and had the satisfaction of learning that my news of Rupert's whereabouts was confirmed by his information. I was also made acquainted with all that had been done, even as I have already related it, from the first successful trick played on Rischenheim to the moment of his unfortunate escape. But my face grew long and apprehensive when I heard that Rudolf Rassendyll had gone alone to Strelsau to put his head in that lion's mouth in the Königstrasse.

'There will be three of them there—Rupert, Rischenheim and my rascal Bauer,' said I.

'As to Rupert we don't know,' Sapt reminded me. 'He'll be there if Rischenheim arrives in time to tell him the truth. But we have also to be ready for him here, and at the hunting-lodge. Well, we're ready for him wherever he is: Rudolf will be in

Strelsau, you and I will ride to the lodge and Bernenstein will be here with the Queen.'

'Only one here?' I asked.

'Aye, but a good one,' said the Constable, clapping Bernenstein on the shoulder. 'We shan't be gone above four hours, and those while the King is safe in his bed. Bernenstein has only to refuse access to him, and stand to that with his life till we come back. You're equal to that, eh, lieutenant?'

I am by nature a cautious man, and prone to look at the dark side of every prospect and the risks of every enterprise; but I could not see what better dispositions were possible against the attack that threatened us. Yet I was sorely uneasy concerning Mr Rassendyll.

Now, after all our stir and runnings to and fro, came an hour or two of peace. We employed the time in having a good meal, and it was past five when, our repast finished, we sat back in our chairs enjoying cigars. James had waited on us, quietly usurping the office of the Constable's own servant, and thus we had been able to talk freely. The man's calm confidence in his master and his master's fortune also went far to comfort me.

'The King should be back soon,' said Sapt at last, with a glance at his big old-fashioned silver watch. 'Thank God, he'll be too tired to sit up long. We shall be free by nine o'clock, Fritz. I wish young Rupert would come to the lodge!'—and the colonel's face expressed a lively pleasure at the idea.

Six o'clock struck and the King did not appear. A few moments later a message came from the Queen, requesting our presence on the terrace in front of the *château*. The place commanded a view of the road by which the King would ride back, and we found the Queen walking restlessly up and down, considerably disquieted by the lateness of his return. In such a position as ours every unusual or unforeseen incident magnifies its possible meaning and invests itself with a sinister importance which would at ordinary times seem absurd. We three shared the Queen's feelings, and forgetting the many chances of the chase, any one of which would amply account for the King's delay, fell to speculating on remote possibilities of disaster. He might have met Rischenheim—though they had ridden in opposite directions;

Rupert might have intercepted him—though no known means could have brought Rupert to the forest so early. Our fears defeated common sense, and our conjectures outran possibility. Sapt was the first to recover from this foolish mood, and he rated us soundly, not sparing even the Queen herself. With a laugh we regained some of our equanimity, and felt rather ashamed of our weakness.

'Still it's strange that he doesn't come,' murmured the Queen, shading her eyes with her hand, and looking along the road to where the dark masses of the forest trees bounded our view. It was already dusk, but not so dark but that we could have seen the King's party as soon as it came into the open.

If the King's delay seemed strange at six, it was stranger at seven, and by eight most strange. We had long since ceased to talk lightly; by now we had lapsed into silence. Sapt's scoldings had died away. The Queen, wrapped in her furs (for it was very cold), sat sometimes on a seat, but oftener paced restlessly to and fro. Evening had fallen. We did not know what to do, nor even whether we ought to do anything. Sapt would not own to sharing our worse apprehensions, but his gloomy silence in face of our surmises witnessed that he was in his heart as disturbed as we were. For my part I had come to the end of my endurance, and I cried:

'For God's sake let's act! Shall I go and seek him?'

'A needle in a bundle of hay!' said Sapt with a shrug.

But at this moment my ear caught the sound of horses cantering on the road from the forest; at the same instant Bernenstein cried, 'Here they come!' The Queen paused, and we gathered round her. The horse-hoofs came nearer. Now we made out the figures of three men; they were the King's huntsmen, and they rode along merrily, singing a hunting chorus. The sound of it brought relief to us; so far at least there was no disaster. But why was not the King with them?

'The King is probably tired, and is following more slowly, madame,' suggested Bernenstein.

This explanation seemed very probable, and the lieutenant and I, as ready to be hopeful on slight grounds as fearful on small provocation, joyfully accepted it. Sapt, less easily turned to either mood, said, 'Aye, but let us hear,' and raising his voice called to the huntsmen, who had now arrived in the avenue. One of them, the King's chief huntsman, Simon, gorgeous in his uniform of green and gold, came swaggering along, and bowed low to the Queen.

'Well, Simon, where is the King?' she asked, trying to smile.

'The King, madame, has sent a message by me to Your Majesty.'

'Pray deliver it to me, Simon.'

'I will, madame. The King has enjoyed fine sport; and indeed, madame, if I may say so for myself, a better run——'

'You may say, friend Simon,' interrupted the Constable, tapping him on the shoulder, 'anything you like for yourself, but, as a matter of etiquette, the King's message should come first.'

'Oh, aye, Constable,' said Simon. 'You're always so down on a man, aren't you? Well then, madame, the King has enjoyed fine sport. For we started a boar at eleven, and——'

'Is this the King's message, Simon?' asked the Queen, smiling in genuine amusement, but impatiently.

'Why no, madame, not precisely His Majesty's message.'

'Then get to it, man, in Heaven's name!' growled Sapt testily. For here were we four (the Queen, too, one of us!) on tenterhooks, while the fool boasted about the sport that he had shown the King. For every boar in the forest Simon took as much credit as though he, and not Almighty God, had made the animal. It is always the way with such fellows.

Simon became a little confused under the combined influence of his own seductive memories and Sapt's brusque exhortations.

'As I was saying, madame,' he resumed, 'the boar led us a long way, but at last the hounds pulled him down, and His Majesty himself gave the *coup de grâce*. Well, then it was very late——'

'It's no earlier now,' grumbled the Constable.

'And the King, although indeed, madame, His Majesty was so gracious as to say that no huntsman whom His Majesty had ever had, had given His Majesty——'

'God help us!' groaned the Constable.

Simon shot an apprehensive apologetic glance at Colonel Sapt. The Constable was frowning ferociously.

In spite of the serious matters in hand I could not forbear a smile, while young Bernenstein broke into an audible laugh, which he tried to smother with his hand.

'Yes, the King was very tired, Simon?' said the Queen, at once encouraging him and bringing him back to the point with a woman's skill.

'Yes, madame, the King was very tired; and as we chanced to kill near the hunting-lodge——'

I do not know whether Simon noticed any change in the manner of his audience. But the Queen looked up with parted lips, and I believe that we three all drew a step nearer him. Sapt did not interrupt this time.

'Yes, madame, the King was very tired, and as we chanced to kill near the hunting-lodge, the King bade us carry our quarry there, and come back to dress it tomorrow; so we obeyed, and here we are—that is, except Herbert, my brother, who stayed with the King by His Majesty's orders. Because, madame, Herbert is a handy fellow, and my good mother taught him to cook a steak and——'

'Stayed where with the King?' roared Sapt.

'Why, at the hunting-lodge, Constable. The King stays there tonight, and will ride back tomorrow morning with Herbert. That, madame, is the King's message.'

We had come to it at last, and it was something to come to. Simon gazed from face to face. I saw him, and I understood at once that our feelings must be speaking too plainly. So I took on myself to dismiss him, saying:

'Thanks, Simon, thanks; we understand.'

He bowed to the Queen; she roused herself and added her thanks to mine. Simon withdrew, looking still a little puzzled.

After we were left alone there was a moment's silence. Then I said:

'Suppose Rupert——'

The Constable of Zenda broke in with a short laugh.

'On my life,' said he, 'how things fall out! We say he will go to the hunting-lodge, and—he goes!'

'If Rupert goes—if Rischenheim doesn't stop him!' I urged again.

The Queen rose from her seat and stretched out her hands towards us.

'Gentlemen, my letter!' said she.

Sapt wasted no time.

'Bernenstein,' said he, 'you stay here as we arranged. Nothing is altered. Horses for Fritz and myself in five minutes.'

Bernenstein turned and shot like an arrow along the terrace towards the stables.

'Nothing altered, madame,' said Sapt, 'except that we must be there before Count Rupert.'

I looked at my watch. It was twenty minutes past nine. Simon's cursed chatter had lost a quarter of an hour. I opened my lips to speak. A glance from Sapt's eyes told me that he discerned what I was about to say. I was silent.

'You'll be in time?' asked the Queen, with clasped hands and frightened eyes.

'Assuredly, madame,' returned Sapt with a bow.

'You won't let him reach the King?'

'Why, no, madame,' said Sapt with a smile.

'From my heart, gentlemen,' she said in a trembling voice, 'from my heart——'

'Here are the horses,' cried Sapt. He snatched her hand, brushed it with his grizzly moustache, and—well, I am not sure I heard, and I can hardly believe what I think I heard; but I will set it down for what it is worth. I think he said: 'Bless your sweet face, we'll do it.' At any rate she drew back with a little cry of surprise, and I saw the tears standing in her eyes. I kissed her hand also; then we mounted, and we started, and we rode, as if the devil were behind us, for the hunting-lodge.

But I turned once to watch her standing on the terrace, with young Bernenstein's tall figure beside her.

'Can we be in time?' said I. It was what I had meant to say before.

'I think not, but by God we'll try,' said Colonel Sapt.

And I knew why he had not let me speak.

Suddenly there was a sound behind us of a horse at the gallop.

'*Deuce take it, what horse is that?*'

Our heads flew round in the ready apprehension of men on a perilous errand. The hoofs drew near, for the unknown rode with reckless haste.

'We had best see what it is,' said the Constable, pulling up.

A second more, and the horseman was beside us. Sapt swore an oath half in amusement, half in vexation.

'Why, is it you, James?' I cried.

'Yes, sir,' answered Rudolf Rassendyll's servant.

'What the devil do you want?' asked Sapt.

'I came to attend on the Count von Tarlenheim, sir.'

'I did not give you any orders, James.'

'No, sir. But Mr Rassendyll told me not to leave you, unless you sent me away. So I made haste to follow you.'

Then Sapt cried:

'Deuce take it, what horse is that?'

'The best in the stables, so far as I could see, sir. I was afraid of not overtaking you.'

Sapt tugged at his moustache, scowled, but finally laughed.

'Much obliged for your compliment,' said he. 'The horse is mine.'

'Indeed, sir?' said James with respectful interest.

For a moment we were all silent. Then Sapt laughed again.

'Forward!' said he, and the three of us dashed into the forest.

CHAPTER VIII

The Temper of Boris the Hound

LOOKING back now, in the light of the information I have
gathered, I am able to trace very clearly, and almost hour by
hour, the events of this day, and to understand how chance,
laying hold of our cunning plan and mocking our wiliness,
twisted and turned our device to a predetermined but strange
issue, of which we were most guiltless in thought or intent.
Had the King not gone to the hunting-lodge our designs would
have found the fulfilment we looked for; had Rischenheim
succeeded in warning Rupert of Hentzau we should have stood
where we were. Fate or fortune would have it otherwise. The
King, being weary, went to the lodge, and Rischenheim failed
in warning his cousin. It was a narrow failure, for Rupert, as
his laugh told me, was in the house in the Königstrasse when I
set out from Strelsau, and Rischenheim arrived there at half past
four. He had taken the train at a roadside station, and thus easily
outstripped Mr Rassendyll, who, not daring to show his face, was
forced to ride all the way and enter the city under cover of night.
But Rischenheim had not ventured to send a warning, for he knew
that we were in possession of the address, and did not know what
steps we might have taken to intercept messages. Therefore he
was obliged to carry the news himself; when he came his man was
gone. Indeed Rupert must have left the house almost immediately
after I was safe away from the city. He was determined to be in
good time for his appointment; his only enemies were not in
Strelsau; there was no warrant on which he could be appre-
hended; and, although his connection with Black Michael was a
matter of popular gossip, he felt himself safe from arrest by
virtue of the secret that protected him. Accordingly he walked
out of the house, went to the station, took his ticket to Hofbau,
and, travelling by the four o'clock train, reached his destination

about half past five. He must have passed the train in which
Rischenheim travelled; the first news the latter had of his
departure was from a porter at the station, who, having recognized the Count of Hentzau, ventured to congratulate Rischenheim on his cousin's return. Rischenheim made no answer, but
hurried in great agitation to the house in the Königstrasse, where
the old woman Holf confirmed the tidings. Then he passed
through a period of great irresolution. Loyalty to Rupert urged
that he should follow him and share the perils into which his
cousin was hastening. But caution whispered that he was not
irrevocably committed, that nothing overt yet connected him
with Rupert's schemes, and that we who knew the truth should
be well content to purchase his silence as to the trick we had
played by granting him immunity. His fears won the day, and,
like the irresolute man he was, he determined to wait in Strelsau
till he heard the issue of the meeting at the lodge. If Rupert were
disposed of there, he had something to offer us in return for
peace; if his cousin escaped, he would be in the Königstrasse,
prepared to second the further plans of the desperate adventurer.
In any event his skin was safe, and I presume to think that this
weighed a little with him; for excuse he had the wound which
Bernenstein had given him, and which rendered one arm entirely
useless; had he gone then he would have been a most inefficient
ally.

Of all this we, as we rode through the forest, knew nothing.
We might guess, conjecture, hope or fear; but our certain knowledge stopped with Rischenheim's start for the capital and
Rupert's presence there at three o'clock. The pair might have
met or might have missed. We had to act as though they had
missed and Rupert were gone to meet the King. But we were
late. The consciousness of that pressed upon us, although we
evaded further mention of it; it made us spur and drive our
horses as quickly as, aye, and a little more quickly than, safety
allowed. Once James's horse stumbled in the darkness and its
rider was thrown; more than once a low bough hanging over the
path nearly swept me, dead or stunned, from my seat. Sapt paid
no attention to these mishaps or threatened mishaps. He had
taken the lead, and, sitting well down in the saddle, rode ahead,

turning neither to right nor left, never slackening his pace, sparing neither himself nor his beast. James and I were side by side behind him. We rode in silence, finding nothing to say to one another. My mind was full of a picture—the picture of Rupert with his easy smile handing to the King the Queen's letter. For the hour of the rendezvous was past. If that image had been translated into reality, what must we do? To kill Rupert would satisfy revenge, but of what other avail would it be when the King had read the letter? I am ashamed to say that I found myself girding at Mr Rassendyll for happening on a plan which the course of events had turned into a trap for ourselves and not for Rupert of Hentzau.

Suddenly Sapt, turning his head for the first time, pointed in front of him. The lodge was before us; we saw it looming dimly a quarter of a mile off. Sapt reined in his horse, and we followed his example. All dismounted, we tied our horses to trees and went forward at a quick silent walk. Our idea was that Sapt should enter on pretext of having been sent by the Queen to attend to her husband's comfort and arrange for his return without further fatigue next day. If Rupert had come and gone, the King's demeanour would probably betray the fact; if he had not yet come, I and James, patrolling outside, would bar his passage. There was a third possibility: he might be even now with the King. Our course in such a case we left unsettled; so far as I had any plan, it was to kill Rupert and try to convince the King that the letter was a forgery—a desperate hope, so desperate that we turned our eyes away from the possibility which would make it our only resource.

We were now very near the hunting-lodge, being about forty yards from the front of it. All at once Sapt threw himself on his stomach on the ground.

'Give me a match,' he whispered.

James struck a light, and the night being still the flame burnt brightly: it showed us the mark of a horse's hoof, apparently quite fresh, and leading away from the lodge. We rose and went on, following the tracks by the aid of more matches till we reached a tree twenty yards from the door. Here the hoof-marks ceased; but beyond there was a double track of human feet in

See page 81

Simon . . . bowed low to the Queen

the soft black earth; a man had gone thence to the house and returned from the house thither. On the right of the tree there were more hoof-marks, leading up to it and then ceasing. A man had ridden up from the right, dismounted, gone on foot to the house, returned to the tree, remounted, and ridden away along the track by which we had approached.

'It may be somebody else,' said I; but I do not think that we any of us doubted in our hearts that the tracks were made by the coming of Hentzau. Then the King had the letter; the mischief was done. We were too late.

Yet we did not hesitate. Since disaster had come, it must be faced. Mr Rassendyll's servant and I followed the Constable of Zenda up to the door, or within a few feet of it. Here Sapt, who was in uniform, loosened his sword in its sheath; James and I looked to our revolvers. There were no lights visible in the lodge; the door was shut; everything was still. Sapt knocked softly with his knuckles, but there was no answer from within. He laid hold of the handle and turned it; the door opened, and the passage lay dark and apparently empty before us.

'You stay here, as we arranged,' whispered the colonel. 'Give me the matches, and I'll go in.'

James handed him the box of matches, and he crossed the threshold. For a yard or two we saw him plainly, then his figure grew dim and indistinct. I heard nothing except my own hard breathing. But in a moment there was another sound—a muffled exclamation, and the noise of a man stumbling; a sword, too, clattered on the stones of the passage. We looked at one another: the noise did not produce any answering stir in the house; then came the sharp little explosion of a match struck on its box, next we heard Sapt raising himself, his scabbard scraping along the stones; his footsteps came towards us, and in a second he appeared at the door.

'What was it?' I whispered.

'I fell,' said Sapt.

'Over what?'

'Come and see. James, stay here.'

I followed the Constable for the distance of eight or ten feet along the passage.

G

'Isn't there a lamp anywhere?' I asked.

'We can see enough with a match,' he answered. 'Here, this is what I fell over.'

Even before the match was struck I saw a dark body lying across the passage.

'A dead man!' I guessed instantly.

'Why, no,' said Sapt, striking a light; 'a dead dog, Fritz.'

An exclamation of wonder escaped me as I fell on my knees. At the same instant Sapt muttered, 'Ay, there's a lamp,' and stretching up his hand to a little oil lamp that stood on a bracket, he lit it, took it down, and held it over the body. It served to give a fair though unsteady light, and enabled us to see what lay in the passage.

'It's Boris, the boar-hound,' said I, still in a whisper, although there was no sign of any listeners.

I knew the dog well; he was the King's favourite, and always accompanied him when he went hunting. He was obedient to every word of the King's, but of a rather uncertain temper towards the rest of the world. However, *De mortuis nil nisi bonum*; there he lay dead in the passage. Sapt put his hand on the beast's head. There was a bullet-hole right through his forehead. I nodded, and in my turn pointed to the dog's right shoulder, which was shattered by another ball.

'And see here,' said the Constable. 'Have a pull at this.'

I looked where his hand now was. In the dog's mouth was a piece of grey cloth, and on the piece of grey cloth was a horn coat-button. I took hold of the cloth and pulled. Boris held on even in death. Sapt drew his sword, and, inserting the point of it between the dog's teeth, parted them enough for me to draw out the piece of cloth.

'You'd better put it in your pocket,' said the Constable. 'Now come along'; and, holding the lamp in one hand and his sword (which he did not resheathe) in the other, he stepped over the body of the boar-hound, and I followed him.

We were now in front of the door of the room where Rudolf Rassendyll had supped with us on the day of his first coming to Ruritania, and whence he had set out to be crowned in Strelsau. On the right of it was the room where the King slept, and farther along in the same direction the kitchen and the cellars. The officer or officers in attendance on the King used to sleep on the other side of the dining-room.

'We must explore, I suppose,' said Sapt; in spite of his outward calmness I caught in his voice the ring of excitement rising and ill-repressed. But at this moment we heard from the passage on our left (as we faced the door) a low moan, and then a dragging sound, as if a man were crawling along the floor, painfully trailing his limbs after him. Sapt held the lamp in that direction, and we saw Herbert the forester, pale-faced and wide-eyed, raised from the ground on his two hands, while his legs stretched behind him and his stomach rested on the boards.

'Who is it?' he said in a faint voice.

'Why, man, you know us,' said the Constable, stepping up to him. 'What's happened here?'

The poor fellow was very faint, and, I think, wandered a little in his brain.

'I've got it, sir,' he murmured. 'I've got it, fair and straight. No more hunting for me, sir. I've got it here in the stomach. Oh, my God!' He let his head fall with a thud on the floor.

I ran and raised him. Kneeling on one knee, I propped his head against my leg.

'Tell us about it,' commanded Sapt in a curt crisp voice, while I got the man into the easiest position that I could contrive.

In slow struggling tones he began his story, repeating here, omitting there, often confusing the order of his narrative, oftener still arresting it while he waited for strength. Yet we were not impatient, but heard without a thought of time. I looked round once at a sound, and found that James, anxious about us, had stolen along the passage and joined us. Sapt took no notice of him, nor of anything save the words that dropped in irregular utterance from the stricken man's lips. Here is the story, a strange instance of the turning of a great event on a small cause.

The King had eaten a little supper, and, having gone to his bedroom, had stretched himself on the bed and fallen asleep without undressing. Herbert was clearing the dining-table and performing similar duties, when suddenly (thus he told it) he found a man standing beside him. He did not know (he was new to the King's service) who the unexpected visitor was, but he was of middle height, dark, handsome, and 'looked like a gentleman all over'. He was dressed in a shooting-tunic, and a revolver was thrust through the belt of it. One hand rested on the belt, while the other held a small square box.

'Tell the King I am here. He expects me,' said the stranger.

Herbert, alarmed at the suddenness and silence of the intruder's approach, and guiltily conscious of having left the door unbolted, drew back. He was unarmed, but, being a stout fellow, was prepared to defend his master as best he could. Rupert—beyond doubt it was Rupert—laughed lightly, saying again: 'Man, he expects me. Go and tell him,' and sat himself on the table, swinging his leg. Herbert, influenced by the visitor's air of command, began to retreat towards the bedroom, keeping his face towards Rupert. 'If the King asks more, tell him I have the packet and the letter,' said Rupert. The man bowed and passed into the bedroom. The King was asleep; when roused he seemed to know nothing of letter or packet, and to expect no visitor. Herbert's ready fears revived; he whispered that the stranger carried a revolver. Whatever the King's faults might be—and God forbid that I should speak hardly of him whom fate used so hardly!—he was no coward. He sprang from his bed; at the same moment the great boar-hound uncoiled himself and came from beneath, yawning and fawning. But in an instant the beast caught the scent of a stranger: his ears pricked and he gave a low growl, as he looked up in his master's face. Then Rupert of Hentzau, weary perhaps of waiting, perhaps only doubtful whether his message would be properly delivered, appeared in the doorway.

The King was unarmed, and Herbert in no better plight; their hunting weapons were in the adjoining room, and Rupert seemed to bar the way. I have said that the King was no coward, yet I think that the sight of Rupert, bringing back the memory of his torments in the dungeon, half cowed him; for he shrank back crying, 'You!' The hound, in subtle understanding of his master's movement, growled angrily.

'You expected me, sire?' said Rupert with a bow; but he smiled. I know that the sight of the King's alarm pleased him. To inspire terror was his delight, and it does not come to every man to strike fear into the heart of a king and an Elphberg. It had come more than once to Rupert of Hentzau.

'No,' muttered the King. Then, recovering his composure a little, he said angrily, 'How dare you come here?'

'You didn't expect me?' cried Rupert, and in an instant the thought of a trap seemed to flash across his alert mind. He drew the revolver half way from his belt, probably in a scarcely conscious movement born of the desire to assure himself of its presence. With a cry of alarm Herbert flung himself before the King, who sank back on the bed. Rupert, puzzled, vexed, yet half amused (for he smiled still, the man said), took a step forward, crying out something about Rischenheim—what, Herbert could not tell us. 'Keep back!' exclaimed the King. 'Keep back!' Rupert paused; then as though with a sudden thought he held up the box that was in his left hand, saying:

'Well, look at this, sire, and we'll talk afterwards,' and he stretched out his hand with the box in it.

Now the thing stood on a razor's edge, for the King whispered to Herbert:

'What is it? Go and take it.'

But Herbert hesitated, fearing to leave the King, whom his body now protected as though with a shield. Rupert's impatience overcame him: if there were a trap, every moment's delay doubled his danger. With a scornful laugh, he exclaimed:

'Catch it, then, if you're afraid to come for it,' and he flung the packet to Herbert or the King, or which of them might chance to catch it.

This insolence had a strange result. In an instant, with a fierce growl and a mighty bound, Boris was at the stranger's throat. Rupert had not seen or had not heeded the dog. A startled oath rang out from him. He snatched the revolver from his belt and fired at his assailant. This shot must have broken the beast's shoulder, but it only half arrested his spring. His great weight was still hurled on Rupert's chest, and bore him back on his knee. The packet that he had flung lay unheeded. The King, wild with alarm and furious with anger at his favourite's fate, jumped up and ran past Rupert into the next room. Herbert followed; even as they went Rupert flung the wounded weakened beast from

He raised his left hand

him and darted to the doorway. He found himself facing Herbert, who held a boar-spear, and the King, who had a double-barrelled hunting gun. He raised his left hand, Herbert said—no doubt he still asked a hearing—but the King levelled his weapon. With a spring Rupert gained the shelter of the door; the bullet sped by him and buried itself in the wall of the room. Then Herbert was at him with the boar-spear. Explanations must wait now: it was life or death; without hesitation Rupert fired at Herbert, bringing him to the ground with a mortal wound. The King's gun was at his shoulder again.

'You damned fool!' roared Rupert. 'If you must have it, take it!' And gun and revolver rang out at the same moment. But Rupert—never did his nerve fail him—hit, the King missed; Herbert saw the count stand for an instant with his smoking barrel in his hand, looking at the King who lay on the ground.

Then Rupert walked towards the door. I wish I had seen his face then! Did he frown or smile? Was triumph or chagrin uppermost? Remorse? Not he!

He reached the door and passed through. That was the last Herbert saw of him; but the fourth actor in the drama, the wordless player whose part had been so momentous, took the stage. Limping along, now whining in sharp agony, now growling in fierce anger, with blood flowing but hair bristling, the hound Boris dragged himself across the room, through the door, after Rupert of Hentzau. Herbert listened, raising his head from the ground. There was a growl, an oath, the sound of a scuffle. Rupert must have turned in time to receive the dog's spring. The beast, maimed and crippled by his shattered shoulder, did not reach his enemy's face, but his teeth tore away the bit of cloth that we had found held in the vice of his jaws. Then came another shot, a laugh, retreating steps, and a door slammed. With that last sound Herbert awoke to the fact of the count's escape; with weary efforts he dragged himself into the passage. The idea that he could go on if he got a drink of brandy turned him in the direction of the cellar. But his strength failed, and he sank down where we found him, not knowing whether the King were dead or still alive, and unable even to make his way back to the room where his master lay stretched on the ground.

I had listened to the story, bound as though by a spell. Half way through, James's hand had crept to my arm and rested there; when Herbert finished I heard the little man licking his lips, again and again slapping his tongue against them. Then I looked at Sapt. He was pale as a ghost, and the lines on his face seemed to have grown deeper. He glanced up and met my regard. Neither of us spoke; we exchanged thoughts with our eyes. 'This is our work,' we said to one another. 'It was our trap— these are our victims.' I cannot even now think of that hour, for by our act the King lay dead.

But was he dead? I seized Sapt by the arm. His glance questioned me.

'The King?' I whispered hoarsely.

'Yes, the King,' he returned.

Facing round, we walked to the door of the dining-room.

Here I turned suddenly faint, and clutched at the Constable. He held me up and pushed the door wide open. The smell of powder was in the room; it seemed as if the smoke hung about, curling in dim coils round the chandelier, which gave a subdued light. James had the lamp now, and followed us with it. But the King was not there. A sudden hope filled me. He had not been killed then! I regained strength, and darted across towards the inside room. Here, too, the light was dim, and I turned to beckon for the lamp. Sapt and James came together, and stood peering over my shoulder in the doorway.

The King lay prone on the floor, face downwards, near the bed. He had crawled there, seeking for some place to rest, as we supposed. He did not move. We watched him for a moment; the silence seemed deeper than silence could be. At last, moved by a common impulse, we stepped forward, but timidly, as though we approached the throne of Death itself. I was the first to kneel by the King and raise his head. Blood had flowed from his lips, but it ceased to flow now. He was dead.

I felt Sapt's hand on my shoulder. Looking up, I saw his other hand stretched out towards the ground. I turned my eyes where he pointed. There, in the King's hand, stained with the King's blood, was the box that I had carried to Wintenberg and Rupert of Hentzau had brought to the lodge that night. It was not rest, but the box, that the dying King had sought in his last moment. I bent, and lifting his hand unclasped the fingers, still limp and warm.

Sapt bent down with sudden eagerness.

'Is it open?' he whispered.

The string was round it; the sealing wax was unbroken. The secret had outlived the King, and he had gone to his death unknowing. All at once—I cannot tell why—I put my hand over my eyes; I found my eyelashes were wet.

'Is it open?' asked Sapt again, for in the dim light he could not see.

'No,' I answered.

'Thank God!' said he. And, for Sapt's, the voice was soft.

CHAPTER IX

The King in the Hunting-Lodge

THE moment with its shock and tumult of feeling brings one judgment, later reflection another. Among the sins of Rupert of Hentzau I do not assign the first and greatest place to his killing of the King. It was indeed the act of a reckless man who stood at nothing and held nothing sacred; but when I consider Herbert's story, and trace how the deed came to be done and the impulsion of circumstances that led to it, it seems to have been in some sort thrust upon him by the same perverse fate that dogged our steps. He had meant the King no harm—indeed it may be argued that, from whatever motive, he had sought to serve him—and save under the sudden stress of self-defence he had done him none. The King's unlooked-for ignorance of his errand, Herbert's honest hasty zeal, the temper of Boris the hound, had forced on him an act unmeditated and utterly against his interest. His whole guilt lay in preferring the King's death to his own—a crime perhaps in most men, but hardly deserving a place in Rupert's catalogue. All this I can admit now, but on that night, with the dead body lying there before us, with the story piteously told by Herbert's faltering voice fresh in our ears, it was hard to allow any such extenuation. Our hearts cried out for vengeance, although we ourselves served the King no more. Nay, it may well be that we hoped to stifle some reproach of our own consciences by a louder clamour against another's sin, or longed to offer some fancied empty atonement to our dead master by executing swift justice on the man who had killed him. I cannot tell fully what the others felt, but in me at least the dominant impulse was to waste not a moment in proclaiming the crime, and raising the whole country in pursuit of Rupert, so that every man in Ruritania should quit his work, his pleasure or his bed, and make it his concern to take the Count of Hentzau, alive or dead. I remember

97

that I walked over to where Sapt was sitting, and caught him by
the arm, saying:

'We must raise the alarm. If you'll go to Zenda, I'll start for
Strelsau.'

'The alarm?' said he, looking up at me and tugging his
moustache.

'Yes: when the news is known, every man in the kingdom will
be on the look-out for him, and he can't escape.'

'So that he'd be taken?' asked the Constable.

'Yes, to a certainty!' I cried, hot in excitement and emotion.

Sapt glanced across at Mr Rassendyll's servant. James had,
with my help, raised the King's body on to the bed, and had
aided the wounded forester to reach a couch. He stood now near
the Constable, in his usual unobtrusive readiness. He did not
speak, but I saw a look of understanding in his eyes as he nodded
his head to Colonel Sapt. They were well-matched, that pair,
hard to move, hard to shake, not to be turned from the purpose
in their minds and the matter that lay to their hands.

'Yes, he'd probably be taken or killed,' said Sapt.

'Then let's do it!' I cried.

'With the Queen's letter on him,' said Colonel Sapt.

I had forgotten.

'We have the box, he has the letter still,' said Sapt.

I could have laughed even at that moment. He had left the
box (whether from haste or heedlessness or malice we could not
tell), but the letter was on him. Taken alive, he would use that
powerful weapon to save his life or satisfy his anger; if it were
found on his body, its evidence would speak loud and clear to all
the world. Again he was protected by his crime: while he had
the letter, he must be kept inviolate from all attack except at our
own hands. We desired his death, but we must be his bodyguard
and die in his defence rather than let any other but ourselves
come at him. No open means must be used, and no allies sought.
All this rushed to my mind at Sapt's words, and I saw what the
Constable and James had never forgotten. But what to do I could
not see. For the King of Ruritania lay dead.

An hour or more had passed since our discovery, and it was
now close on midnight. Had all gone well we ought by this time

to have been far on our road back to the Castle; by this time
Rupert must be miles away from where he had killed the King;
already Mr Rassendyll would be seeking his enemy in Strelsau.

'But what are we to do about—about that, then?' I asked,
pointing with my finger through the doorway towards the bed.

Sapt gave a last tug at his moustache, then crossed his hands on the
hilt of the sword between his knees and leant forward in his chair.

'Nothing,' he said, looking in my face. 'Until we have the
letter, nothing.'

'But it's impossible!' I cried.

'Why, no, Fritz,' he answered thoughtfully. 'It's not impossible yet; it may become so. But if we can catch Rupert in the
next day, or even in the next two days, it's not impossible. Only
let me have that letter, and I'll account for the concealment.
What? Is the fact that crimes are known never concealed, for
fear of putting the criminal on his guard?'

'You'll be able to make a story, sir,' James put in, with a grave
but reassuring air.

'Yes, James, I shall be able to make a story, or your master
will make one for me. But, by God, story or no story, the letter
mustn't be found. Let them say we killed him ourselves if they
like, but——'

I seized his hand and gripped it.

'You don't doubt I'm with you?' I asked.

'Not for a moment, Fritz,' he answered.

'Then how can we do it?'

We drew nearer together; Sapt and I sat, while James leant
over Sapt's chair.

The oil in the lamp was almost exhausted, and the light burnt
very dim. Now and again poor Herbert, for whom our skill could
do nothing, gave a low moan. I am ashamed to remember how
little we thought of him, but great schemes make the actors in
them careless of humanity; the life of a man goes for nothing
against a point in the game. Except for his groans—and they grew
fainter and less frequent—our voices alone broke the silence of
the little lodge.

'The Queen must know,' said Sapt. 'Let her stay at Zenda and
give out that the King is at the lodge for a day or two longer.

Then you, Fritz—for you must ride to the Castle at once—and Bernenstein must get to Strelsau as quick as you can, and find Rudolf Rassendyll. You three ought to be able to track young Rupert down and get the letter from him. If he is not in the city you must catch Rischenheim and force him to say where he is; we know Rischenheim can be persuaded. If Rupert's there, I need give no advice either to you or to Rudolf.'

'And you?'

'James and I stay here. If anyone comes whom we can keep out, the King is ill. If rumours get about, and great folk come, why, they must enter.'

'But the body?'

'This morning, when you're gone, we shall make a temporary grave. I dare say two,' and he jerked his thumb towards poor Herbert. 'Or even,' he added with his grim smile, 'three—for our friend Boris, too, must be out of sight.'

'You'll bury the King?'

'Not so deep but that we can take him out again, poor fellow. Well, Fritz, have you a better plan?'

I had no plan, and I was not in love with Sapt's plan. Yet it offered us four-and-twenty hours. For that time, at least, it seemed as if the secret could be kept. Beyond that we could hardly hope for success: after that we must produce the King; dead or alive, the King must be seen. Yet it might be that before the respite ran out Rupert would be ours. In fine, what else could be chosen? For now a greater peril threatened than that against which we had at the first sought to guard. Then the worst we feared was that the letter should come to the King's hands. That could never be. But it would be a worse thing if it were found on Rupert, and all the kingdom, nay, all Europe, knew that it was written in the hand of her who was now in her own right Queen of Ruritania. To save her from that no chance was too desperate, no scheme too perilous; yes, if, as Sapt said, we ourselves were held to answer for the King's death, still we must go on. I, through whose negligence the whole train of disaster had been laid, was the last man to hesitate. In all honesty I held my life due and forfeit, should it be demanded of me—my life, and, before the world, my honour.

So the plan was made. A grave was to be dug ready for the King; if need arose, his body should be laid in it, and the place chosen was under the floor of the wine-cellar. When death came to poor Herbert, he could lie in the yard behind the house; for Boris they meditated a resting-place under the tree where our horses were tethered. There was nothing to keep me, and I rose; but as I rose, I heard the forester's voice call plaintively for me. The unlucky fellow knew me well, and now cried to me to sit by him. I think Sapt wanted me to leave him; but I could not refuse his last request, even though it consumed some precious minutes. He was very near his end, and, sitting by him, I did my best to soothe his passing. His fortitude was good to see, and I believe that we all at last found new courage for our enterprise from seeing how this humble man met death. At last even the Constable ceased to show impatience, and let me stay till I could close the sufferer's eyes.

But thus time went, and it was nearly five in the morning before I bade them farewell and mounted my horse. They took theirs and led them away to the stables behind the lodge; I waved my hand and galloped off on my return to the Castle. Day was dawning, and the air was fresh and pure. The new light brought new hope; fears seemed to vanish before it; my nerves were strung to effort and to confidence. My horse moved freely under me and carried me easily along the grassy avenues. It was hard then to be utterly despondent, hard to doubt skill of brain, strength of hand, or fortune's favour.

The Castle came in sight, and I hailed it with a glad cry that echoed among the trees. But a moment later I gave an exclamation of surprise, and raised myself a little from the saddle while I gazed earnestly at the summit of the keep. The flagstaff was naked; the royal standard that had flapped in the wind last night was gone. But by immemorial custom the flag flew on the keep when the King or the Queen was at the Castle. It would fly for Rudolf V no more; but why did it not proclaim and honour the presence of Queen Flavia? I sat down in my saddle and spurred my horse to the top of his speed. We had been buffeted by fate sorely; but now I feared yet another blow.

In a quarter of an hour more I was at the door. A servant ran

The Castle came in sight

out and I dismounted leisurely and easily. Pulling off my gloves,
I dusted my boots with them, turned to the stableman and bade
him look to the horse, and then said to the footman:

'As soon as the Queen is dressed, find out if she can see me. I
have a message from His Majesty.'

The fellow looked a little puzzled; but at this moment Hermann, the King's majordomo, came to the door.

'Isn't the Constable with you, my lord?' he asked.

'No, the Constable remains at the lodge with the King,' said
I, carelessly, though I was very far from careless. 'I have a message
for Her Majesty, Hermann. Find out from some of the women
when she will receive me.'

'The Queen's not here,' said he. 'Indeed we've had a lively
time, my lord. At five o'clock she came out, ready dressed, from
her room, sent for Lieutenant von Bernenstein, and announced
that she was about to set out from the Castle. As you know, the
mail train passes here at six.' Hermann took out his watch. 'Yes,
the Queen must just have left the station.'

'Where for?' I asked, with a shrug for the woman's whim.

'Why, for Strelsau. She gave no reasons for going, and took with her only one lady, Lieutenant von Bernenstein being in attendance. It was a bustle, if you like, with everybody to be roused and got out of bed, and a carriage to be made ready, and messages to go to the station, and——'

'She gave no reasons?'

'None, my lord. She left with me a letter to the Constable, which she ordered me to give into his own hands as soon as he arrived at the Castle. She said it contained a message of importance, which the Constable was to convey to the King, and that it must be entrusted to nobody except Colonel Sapt himself. I wonder, my lord, that you didn't notice that the flag was hauled down.'

'Tut, man, I wasn't staring at the keep. Give me the letter.' For I saw that the clue to this fresh puzzle must lie under the cover of Sapt's letter. That letter I must myself carry to Sapt, and without loss of time.

'Give you the letter, my lord? But, pardon me, you're not the Constable.' He laughed a little.

'Why, no,' said I, mustering a smile. 'It's true that I'm not the Constable, but I'm going to the Constable. I had the King's orders to rejoin him as soon as I had seen the Queen; and since Her Majesty isn't here, I shall return to the lodge directly a fresh horse can be saddled for me. And the Constable's at the lodge. Come, the letter!'

'I can't give it you, my lord. Her Majesty's orders were positive.'

'Nonsense. If she had known I should come and not the Constable, she would have told me to carry it to him.'

'I don't know about that, my lord: her orders were plain, and she doesn't like being disobeyed.'

The stableman had led the horse away, the footman had disappeared. Hermann and I were alone.

'Give me the letter,' I said; and I know that my self-control failed, and eagerness was plain in my voice. Plain it was, and Hermann took alarm. He started back, clapping his hand to the breast of his laced coat. The gesture betrayed where the letter was: I was past prudence; I sprang on him and wrenched his hand away, catching him by the throat with my other hand. Diving into his pocket, I got the letter. Then I suddenly loosed hold of him, for his eyes were starting out of his head. I took out a couple of gold pieces and gave them to him.

'It's urgent, you fool,' said I. 'Hold your tongue about it.' And without waiting to study his amazed red face I turned and ran towards the stables. In five minutes I was on a fresh horse; in six I was clear of the Castle, heading back as fast as I could for the hunting-lodge. Even now Hermann remembers the grip I gave him—though doubtless he has long spent the pieces of gold.

When I reached the end of this second journey I came in for the obsequies of Boris. James was just patting the ground under the tree with a mattock when I rode up; Sapt was standing by, smoking his pipe. The boots of both were stained and sticky with mud. I flung myself from my saddle and blurted out my news. The Constable snatched at his letter with an oath; James levelled the ground with careful accuracy; I do not remember doing anything except wiping my forehead and feeling very hungry.

'Good Lord, she's gone after him!' said Sapt, as he read. Then he handed me the letter.

I will not set out what the Queen wrote. The purport seemed to us, who did not share her feelings, pathetic indeed and moving, but in the end (to speak plainly) folly. She had tried to endure her sojourn at Zenda, she said; but it drove her mad. She could not rest; she did not know how we fared, nor those in Strelsau: for hours she had lain awake; then, at last falling asleep, she had dreamed. 'I had had the same dream before. Now it came again. I saw him so plain. He seemed to me to be the King, and to be called King. But he did not answer nor move. He seemed dead; and I could not rest.' So she wrote, ever excusing herself, ever repeating how something drew her to Strelsau, telling her that she must go if she would see 'him whom you know' alive again. 'And I must see him—ah, I must see him! If the King has had the letter, I am ruined already. If he has not, tell him what you will or what you can contrive. I must go. It came a second time, and all so plain. I saw him, I tell you I saw him. Ah, I must see him again. I swear that I will only see him once. He is in danger—I know he's in danger; or what does the dream mean? Bernenstein will go with me, and I shall see him. Do, do forgive me: I can't stay, the dream was so plain.' Thus she ended, seeming, poor lady, half frantic with the visions that her own troubled brain and desolate heart had conjured up to torment her. I did not know that she had before told Mr Rassendyll himself of this strange dream; though I lay small store by such matters, believing that we ourselves make our dreams, fashioning out of the fears and hopes of today what seems to come by night in the guise of a mysterious revelation. Yet there are some things that a man cannot understand, and I do not profess to measure with my mind the ways of God.

However, not why the Queen went, but that she had gone, concerned us. We had returned to the house now, and James, remembering that men must eat though kings die, was getting us some breakfast. In fact I had great need of food, being utterly worn out; and they, after their labours, were hardly less weary. As we ate, we talked; and it was plain to us that I also must go to Strelsau. There, in the city, the drama must be played out. There was Rudolf, there Rischenheim, there in all likelihood Rupert of Hentzau, there now the Queen. And of these Rupert alone, or perhaps Rischenheim also, knew that the King was dead, and how the issue of last night had shaped itself under the compelling hand of wayward fortune. The King lay in peace on his bed, his grave was dug; Sapt and James held the secret with solemn faith and ready lives. To Strelsau I must go, to tell the Queen that she was widowed, and to aim the stroke at young Rupert's heart.

At nine in the morning I started from the lodge. I was bound to ride to Hofbau, and there wait for a train which would carry me to the capital. From Hofbau I could send a message; but the message must announce only my own coming, not the news I carried. To Sapt, thanks to the cypher, I could send word at any time, and he bade me ask Mr Rassendyll whether he should come to our aid or stay where he was.

'A day must decide the whole thing,' he said. 'We can't conceal the King's death long. For God's sake, Fritz, make an end of that young villain, and get the letter.'

So, wasting no time in farewells, I set out. By ten o'clock I was

H

at Hofbau, for I rode furiously. From there I sent to Bernenstein, at the Palace, word of my coming. But there I was delayed. There was no train for an hour.

'I'll ride!' I cried to myself, only to remember the next moment that, if I rode, I should come to my journey's end much later. There was nothing for it but to wait, and it may be imagined in what mood I waited. Every minute seemed an hour, and I know not to this day how the hour wore itself away. I ate, I drank, I smoked, I walked, sat and stood. The station-master knew me, and thought I had gone mad, till I told him that I carried most important dispatches, and that the delay imperilled great interests. Then he became sympathetic; but what could he do? No special train was to be had at a roadside station: I must wait; and wait somehow, and without blowing my brains out, I did.

At last I was in the train; now indeed we moved, and I came nearer. An hour's run brought me in sight of the city. Then, to my unutterable wrath, we were stopped, and waited twenty minutes or half an hour. At last we started again; had we not, I should have jumped out and run, for to sit longer motionless would have driven me mad. Now we entered the station. With a great effort I calmed myself. I lolled back in my seat; when we stopped I sat there till a porter opened the door. In lazy leisureliness I bade him get me a cab, and followed him across the station. He held the door for me, and, giving him his *douceur*, I set my foot on the step.

'Tell him to drive to the Palace,' said I, 'and to be quick. I'm late already, thanks to this cursed train.'

'The old mare will soon take you there, sir,' said the driver.

I jumped in. But at this moment I saw a man on the platform beckoning with his hand and hastening towards me. The cabman also saw him and waited. I dared not tell him to drive on, for I feared to betray any undue haste, and it would have looked strange not to spare a moment to my wife's cousin, Anton von Strofzin. He came up, holding out his hand delicately gloved in pearl-grey kid, for young Anton was a leader of the Strelsau dandies.

'Ah, my dear Fritz!' said he. 'I am glad I hold no appointment at court. How dreadfully active you all are! I thought you were settled at Zenda for a month?'

'The Queen changed her mind suddenly,' said I, smiling. 'Ladies do, as you know well—you who know all about them.'

My compliment, or insinuation, produced a pleased smile and a gallant twirling of his moustache.

'Well, I thought you'd be here soon,' he said; 'but I didn't know that the Queen had come.'

'*Precisely*,' said he

'You didn't? Then why did you look out for me?'

He opened his eyes a little in languid elegant surprise.

'Oh, I supposed you'd be on duty, or something, and have to come. Aren't you in attendance?'

'On the Queen? No, not just now.'

'But on the King?'

'Why, yes,' said I, and I leant forward. 'At least I'm engaged now on the King's business.'

'Precisely,' said he. 'So I thought you'd come, as soon as I heard that the King was here.'

It may be that I ought to have preserved my composure. But I am not Sapt nor Rudolf Rassendyll.

'The King here?' I gasped, clutching him by the arm.

'Of course. You didn't know? Yes, he's in town.'

But I heeded him no more. For a moment I could not speak, then I cried to the cabman:

'To the Palace. And drive like the devil!'

We shot away, leaving Anton open-mouthed in wonder. I sank back on the cushions, fairly aghast. The King lay dead in the hunting-lodge, but the King was in his capital!

Of course the truth soon flashed through my mind, but it brought no comfort. Rudolf Rassendyll was in Strelsau. He had been seen by somebody and taken for the King. But comfort? What comfort was there, now that the King was dead and could never come to the rescue of his counterfeit?

In fact the truth was worse than I conceived. Had I known it all, I might well have yielded to despair. For not by the chance uncertain sight of a passer-by, not by mere rumour which might had been sturdily denied, not by the evidence of one only or of two, was the King's presence in the city known. That day, by the witness of a crowd of people, by his own claim and his own voice, aye, and by the assent of the Queen herself, Mr Rassendyll was taken to be the King in Strelsau, while neither he nor Queen Flavia knew that the King was dead. I must now relate the strange and perverse succession of events which forced them to employ a resource so dangerous and face a peril so immense. Yet great and perilous as they knew the risk to be, even when they dared it, in the light of what they did not know it was more fearful and more fatal still.

CHAPTER X

The King in Strelsau

MR RASSENDYLL reached Strelsau from Zenda without accident
about nine o'clock in the evening of the same day as that which
witnessed the tragedy of the hunting-lodge. He could have
arrived sooner, but prudence did not allow him to enter the
populous suburbs of the town till the darkness guarded him from
notice. The gates of the city were no longer shut at sunset, as
they used to be in the days when Duke Michael was governor,
and Rudolf passed them without difficulty. Fortunately the night,
fine where we were, was wet and stormy at Strelsau; thus there
were few people in the streets, and he was able to gain the door
of my house still unremarked. Here, of course, a danger presented itself. None of my servants were in the secret; only my
wife, in whom the Queen herself had confided, knew Rudolf,
and she did not expect to see him, since she was ignorant of the
recent course of events. Rudolf was quite alive to the peril, and
regretted the absence of his faithful attendant, who could have
cleared the way for him. The pouring rain gave him an excuse
for twisting a scarf about his face and pulling his coat-collar up
to his ears, while the gusts of wind made the cramming of his
hat low over his eyes no more than a natural precaution against
its loss. Thus masked from curious eyes, he drew rein before my
door, and, having dismounted, rang the bell. When the butler
came, a strange, hoarse voice, half-stifled by folds of scarf, asked
for the countess, alleging for pretext a message from myself. The
man hesitated, as well he might, to leave the stranger alone with
the door open and the contents of the hall at his mercy. Murmuring an apology in case his visitor should prove to be a gentleman,
he shut the door and went in search of his mistress. His description of the untimely caller at once roused my wife's quick wit;
she had heard from me how Rudolf had ridden once from Strelsau

to the hunting-lodge with muffled face: a very tall man with his face wrapped in a scarf and his hat over his eyes, who came with a private message, suggested to her at least a possibility of Mr Rassendyll's arrival. Helga never will admit that she is clever, yet I find she discovers from me what she wants to know, and I suspect hides successfully the small matters of which she in her wifely discretion deems I had best remain ignorant. Being able thus to manage me, she was equal to coping with the butler. She laid aside her embroidery most composedly.

'Ah, yes,' she said, 'I know the gentleman. Surely you haven't left him out in the rain?' She was anxious lest Rudolf's features should have been exposed too long to the light of the hall lamps.

The butler stammered an apology, explaining his fear for our goods and the impossibility of distinguishing social rank on a dark night. Helga cut him short with an impatient gesture, crying: 'How stupid of you!' and herself ran quickly down and opened the door—a little way only, though. The first sight of Mr Rassendyll confirmed her suspicions; in a moment, she said, she knew his eyes.

'It is you, then?' she cried. 'And my foolish servant has left you in the rain! Pray come in. Oh, but your horse!' She turned to the penitent butler, who had followed her downstairs. 'Take the baron's horse round to the stables,' she said.

'I will send someone at once, my lady.'

'No, no, take it yourself—take it at once. I'll look after the baron.'

Reluctantly and ruefully the fat fellow stepped out into the storm. Rudolf drew back and let him pass, then he entered quickly, to find himself alone with Helga in the hall. With a finger on her lips, she led him swiftly into a small sitting-room on the ground floor, which I used as a sort of office or place of business. It looked out on the street, and the rain could be heard driving against the broad panes of the window. Rudolf turned to her with a smile, and, bowing, kissed her hand.

'The baron what, my dear countess?' he inquired.

'He won't ask,' said she, with a shrug. 'Do tell me what brings you here, and what has happened.'

He told her very briefly all he knew. She hid bravely her alarm
at hearing that I might perhaps meet Rupert at the lodge, and at
once listened to what Rudolf wanted of her.

'Can I get out of the house and, if need be, back again unnoticed?' he asked.

'The door is locked at night, and only Fritz and the butler have
keys.'

Mr Rassendyll's eye travelled to the window of the room.

'I haven't grown so fat that I can't get through there,' said he.
'So we'd better not trouble the butler. He'd talk, you know.'

'I will sit here all night and keep everybody from the room.'

'I may come back pursued if I bungle my work and an alarm is
raised.'

'Your work?' she asked, shrinking back a little.

'Yes,' said he. 'Don't ask what it is, countess. It is in the
Queen's service.'

'For the Queen I will do anything and everything, as Fritz
would.'

He took her hand and pressed it in a friendly encouraging way.

'Then I may issue my orders?' he asked, smiling.

'They shall be obeyed.'

'Then a dry cloak, a little supper and this room to myself,
except for you.'

As he spoke the butler turned the handle of the door. My
wife flew across the room, opened the door, and, while Rudolf
turned his back, directed the man to bring some cold meat, or
whatever could be ready with as little delay as possible.

'Now, come with me,' she said to Rudolf, directly the servant
was gone.

She took him to my dressing-room, where he got dry clothes;
then she saw the supper laid, ordered a bedroom to be prepared,
told the butler that she had business with the baron and that he
need not sit up if she were later than eleven, dismissed him
and went to tell Rudolf that the coast was clear for his return to
the sitting-room. He came, expressing admiration for her
courage and address: I take leave to think that she deserved his
compliments. He made a hasty supper; then they talked together,
Rudolf smoking his cigar. Eleven came and went. It was not yet

time. My wife opened the door and looked out. The hall was dark, the door locked and its key in the hands of the butler. She closed the door again and softly locked it. As the clock struck twelve Rudolf rose and turned the lamp very low. Then he unfastened the shutters noiselessly, raised the window and looked out.

'Shut them again when I'm gone,' he whispered. 'If I come back I'll knock like this, and you'll open for me.'

'For heaven's sake be careful!' she murmured, catching at his hand.

He nodded reassuringly, and crossing his leg over the window-sill sat there for a moment listening. The storm was as fierce as ever, and the street was deserted. He let himself down on to the pavement, his face again wrapped up. She watched his tall figure stride quickly along till a turn of the road hid it. Then, having closed the window and the shutters again, she sat down to keep her watch, praying for him, for me and for her dear mistress the Queen. For she knew that perilous work was afoot that night, and did not know whom it might threaten or whom destroy.

From the moment that Mr Rassendyll thus left my house at midnight on his search for Rupert of Hentzau, every hour and almost every moment brought its incident in the swiftly moving drama which decided the issues of our fortune. What we were doing has been told; by now Rupert himself was on his way back to the city, and the Queen was meditating, in her restless vigil, on the resolve that in a few hours was to bring her also to Strelsau. Even in the dead of night both sides were active. For, plan cautiously and skilfully as he might, Rudolf fought with an antagonist who lost no chances, and who had found an apt and useful tool in that same Bauer, a rascal, and a cunning rascal, if ever one were bred in the world. From the beginning even to the end our error lay in taking too little count of this fellow, and dear was the price we paid.

Both to my wife and to Rudolf himself the street had seemed empty of any living being when she watched and he set out. Yet everything had been seen, from his first arrival to the moment when she closed the window after him. At either end of my house there runs out a projection, formed by the bay windows of the principal drawing-room and of the dining-room respectively.

These projecting walls form shadows, and in the shade of one of them—of which I do not know, nor is it of moment—a man watched all that passed; had he been anywhere else Rudolf must have seen him. If we had not been too engrossed in playing our own hands it would doubtless have struck us as probable that Rupert would direct Rischenheim and Bauer to keep an eye on my house during his absence; for it was there that any of us who found our way to the city would naturally resort in the first instance. As a fact, he had not omitted this precaution. The night was so dark that the spy, who had seen the King but once and never Mr Rassendyll, did not recognize who the visitor was; but he rightly conceived that he would serve his employer by tracking the steps of the tall man who made so mysterious an arrival and so surreptitious a departure from the suspected house. Accordingly, as Rudolf turned the corner and Helga left the window, a short thickset figure started cautiously out of the projecting shadow, and followed in Rudolf's wake through the storm. The pair, tracker and tracked, met nobody, save here and there a police-constable keeping a most unwilling beat. Even such were few, and for the most part more intent on sheltering in the lee of a friendly wall and thereby keeping a dry stitch or two on them than on taking note of passers-by. On the pair went. Now Rudolf turned into the Königstrasse. As he did so, Bauer, who must have been nearly a hundred yards behind (for he could not start till the shutters were closed), quickened his pace and reduced the interval between them to about seventy yards. This he might well have thought a safe distance on a night so wild, when the rush of the wind and the pelt of the rain joined to hide the sound of footsteps.

But Bauer reasoned as a townsman, and Rudolf Rassendyll had the quick ear of a man bred in the country and trained to the woodland. All at once there was a jerk of his head; I know so well the motion which marked awakened attention in him. He did not pause nor break his stride: to do either would have been to betray his suspicions to his follower; but he crossed the road to the opposite side to that where No. 19 was situated, and slackened his pace a little, so that there might be a longer interval between his footfalls. The steps behind him grew slower, even as his did; their sound came no nearer: the follower would not overtake. Now a man who loiters on such a night, just because another ahead of him is fool enough to loiter, has a reason for his action other than what can be detected at first sight. So thought Rudolf Rassendyll, and his brain was busy with finding it out.

Then an idea seized him, and, forgetting the precautions that had hitherto served so well, he came to a sudden stop on the pavement, engrossed in deep thought. Was the man who dogged his steps Rupert himself? It would be like Rupert to track him, like Rupert to conceive such an attack, like Rupert to be ready either for a fearless assault from the front or a shameless shot from behind, and indifferent utterly which chance offered, so it threw him one of them. Mr Rassendyll asked no better than to meet his enemy thus in the open. They could fight a fair fight, and if he fell the lamp would be caught up and carried on by Sapt's hand or mine; if he got the better of Rupert, the letter would be his; a moment would destroy it and give safety to the Queen. I do not suppose that he spent time in thinking how he should escape arrest at the hands of the police whom the fracas would probably rouse; if he did, he may well have reckoned on declaring plainly who he was, of laughing at their surprise over a chance likeness to the King, and of trusting to us to smuggle him beyond the arm of the law. What mattered all that, so that there was a moment in which to destroy the letter? At any rate he turned full round and began to walk straight towards Bauer, his hand resting on the revolver in the pocket of his coat.

Bauer saw him coming, and must have known that he was suspected or detected. At once the cunning fellow slouched his head between his shoulders, and set out along the street at a quick shuffle, whistling as he went. Rudolf stood still now in the middle of the road, wondering who the man was: whether Rupert, purposely disguising his gait, or a confederate, or, after all, some person innocent of our secret and indifferent to our schemes. On came Bauer, softly whistling and slushing his feet carelessly through the liquid mud. Now he was nearly opposite where Mr Rassendyll stood. Rudolf was wellnigh convinced that the man had been on his track: he would make certainty surer. The bold game was always his choice and his delight: this trait he shared with Rupert of Hentzau, and hence arose, I think, the strange secret inclination he had for his unscrupulous opponent. Now he walked suddenly across to Bauer, and spoke to him in his natural voice, at the same time removing the scarf partly, but not altogether, from his face:

'You're out late, my friend, for a night like this.'

Bauer, startled though he was by the unexpected challenge, had his wits about him. Whether he identified Rudolf at once I do not know; I think that he must at least have suspected the truth.

'A lad that has no home to go to must needs be out both late and early, sir,' said he, arresting his shuffling steps, and looking up with that honest stolid air which had made a fool of me.

I had described him very minutely to Mr Rassendyll; if Bauer knew or guessed who his challenger was, Mr Rassendyll was as well equipped for the encounter.

'No home to go to!' cried Rudolf in a pitying tone. 'How's that? But anyhow heaven forbid that you or any man should walk the streets a night like this! Come, I'll give you a bed. Come with me, and I'll find you good shelter, my boy.'

Bauer shrank away. He did not see the meaning of this stroke, and his eye, travelling up the street, showed that his thoughts had turned towards flight. Rudolf gave no time for putting any such notion into effect. Maintaining his air of genial compassion, he passed his left arm through Bauer's right, saying as he led him across the road:

'I'm a Christian man, and a bed you shall have this night, my lad, as sure as I'm alive. Come along with me. The devil, it's not weather for standing still!'

The carrying of arms in Strelsau was forbidden. Bauer had no wish to get into trouble with the police, and, moreover, he had intended nothing but a reconnaissance; he was therefore without any weapon, and he was a child in Rudolf's grasp. He had no alternative but to obey the suasion of Mr Rassendyll's arm, and they two began to walk down the Königstrasse. Bauer's whistle had died away, not to return; but from time to time Rudolf hummed softly a cheerful tune, his fingers beating time on Bauer's captive arm. Presently they crossed the road again.

Bauer's lagging steps indicated that he took no pleasure in the change of side, but he could not resist.

'Aye, you shall go where I'm going, my lad,' said Rudolf encouragingly; and he laughed a little as he looked down at the fellow's face.

Along they went; soon they came to the small numbers at the station end of the Königstrasse. Rudolf began to peer at the shop fronts.

'It's cursed dark,' said he. 'Pray, lad, can you make out which is nineteen?'

The moment he had spoken the smile broadened on his face. The shot had gone home. Bauer was a clever scoundrel, but his nerves were not under perfect control, and his arm had quivered under Rudolf's.

'Nineteen, sir?' he stammered.

'Aye, nineteen. That's where we're bound for, you and I. There I hope we shall find—what we want.'

Bauer seemed bewildered; no doubt he was at a loss how either to understand or to parry the bold attack.

'Ah, this looks like it,' said Rudolf in a tone of great satisfaction, as they came to old Mother Holf's little shop. 'Isn't that a one and a nine over the door, my lad? Ah, and Holf! Yes, that's the name. Pray ring the bell. My hands are occupied.'

Rudolf's hands were indeed occupied: one held Bauer's arm, now no longer with a friendly pressure, but with a grip of iron; in the other the captive saw the revolver, which had till now lain hidden.

'You see?' asked Rudolf pleasantly. 'You must ring for me, mustn't you? It would startle them if I aroused them with a shot.' A motion of the barrel told Bauer the direction which the shot would take.

'There's no bell,' said Bauer sullenly.

'Ah, then you knock?'

'I suppose so.'

'In any particular way, my friend?'

'I don't know,' growled Bauer.

'Nor I. Can't you guess?'

'No, I know nothing of it.'

'Well, we must try. You knock, and——— Listen, my lad. You must guess right. You understand?'

'How can I guess?' asked Bauer, in an attempt at bluster.

'Indeed I don't know,' smiled Rudolf. 'But I hate waiting, and if the door is not open in two minutes I shall arouse the good folk with a shot. You see? You quite see, don't you?' Again the barrel's motion pointed and explained Mr Rassendyll's meaning.

Under this powerful persuasion Bauer yielded. He lifted his hand and knocked on the door with his knuckles, first loudly, then very softly, the gentler stroke being repeated five times in rapid succession. Clearly he was expected, for without any sound of approaching feet the chain was unfastened with a subdued rattle. Then came the noise of the bolt being cautiously worked back into its socket. As it shot home a chink of the door opened. At the same moment Rudolf's hand slipped from Bauer's arm. With a swift movement he caught the fellow by the nape of the neck and flung him violently into the roadway, where, losing his footing, he fell sprawling face downwards in the mud. Rudolf threw himself against the door: it yielded, he was inside, and in an instant he had shut the door and driven the bolt home again, leaving Bauer in the gutter outside. Then he turned with his hand on the butt of his revolver. I know that he hoped to find Rupert of Hentzau's face within a foot of his.

Neither Rupert nor Rischenheim, nor even the old woman, fronted him: a tall, handsome dark girl faced him, holding an oil lamp in her hand. He did not know her, but I could have told him that she was old Mother Holf's youngest child, Rosa, for I had often seen her as I rode through the town of Zenda with the King, before the old lady moved her dwelling to Strelsau. Indeed the girl had seemed to dog the King's footsteps, and he had himself joked on her obvious efforts to attract his attention, and the languishing glances of her great black eyes. But it is the lot of prominent personages to inspire these strange passions, and the King had spent as little thought on her as on any of the romantic girls who found a naughty delight in half-fanciful devotion to him —devotion starting, in many cases, by an irony of which the King was happily unconscious, from the brave figure that he made at his coronation and his picturesque daring in the affair of Black

Michael. The worshippers never came near enough to perceive the alteration in their idol.

The half, then, at least of Rosa's attachment was justly due to the man who now stood opposite to her, looking at her with surprise by the murky light of the strong-smelling oil lamp. The lamp shook and almost fell from her hand when she saw him; for the scarf had slid away, and his features were exposed to full view. Fright, delight and excitement vied with one another in her eyes.

'The King!' she whispered in amazement. 'No, but——' And she searched his face wonderingly.

'Is it the beard you miss?' asked Rudolf, fingering his chin. 'Mayn't kings shave when they please as well as other men?' Her face still expressed bewilderment, and still a lingering doubt. He bent towards her, whispering: 'Perhaps I wasn't over-anxious to be known at once.'

She flushed with pleasure at the confidence he seemed to put in her.

'I should know you anywhere,' she whispered with a glance of the great black eyes. 'Anywhere, Your Majesty.'

'Then you'll help me perhaps?'

'With my life!'

'No, no, my dear young lady, merely with a little information. Whose house is this?'

'My mother's.'

'Ah! She takes lodgers?'

The girl appeared vexed at his cautious approaches.

'Tell me what you want to know,' she said simply.

'Then who's here?'

'My lord the Count of Luzau-Rischenheim.'

'And what's he doing?'

'He's lying on the bed moaning and swearing because his wounded arm gives him pain.'

'And is nobody else here?'

She looked round warily, and sank her voice to a whisper as she answered:

'No, not now—nobody else.'

'I was seeking a friend of mine,' said Rudolf. 'I want to see him alone. It's not easy for a King to see people alone.'

'You mean——?'

'Well, you know who I mean.'

'Yes. No, he's gone; but he's gone to find you.'

'To find me? Plague take it! How do you know that, my pretty lady?'

'Bauer told me.'

'Ah, Bauer! And who's Bauer?'

'The man who knocked. Why did you shut him out?'

'To be alone with you, to be sure. So Bauer tells you his master's secrets?'

She acknowledged his raillery with a coquettish laugh. It was not amiss for the King to see that she had her admirers.

'Well, and where has this foolish count gone to meet me?' asked Rudolf lightly.

'You haven't seen him?'

'No; I come straight from the Castle of Zenda.'

'But,' she cried, 'he expected to find you at the hunting-lodge. Ah, but now I recollect! The Count of Rischenheim was greatly vexed to find, on his return, that his cousin was gone.'

'Ah, he was gone! Now I see! Rischenheim brought a message from me to Count Rupert.'

'And they missed one another, Your Majesty?'

'Exactly, my dear young lady. Very vexatious it is, upon my word!' In this remark, at least, Rudolf spoke no more and no other than he felt. 'But when do you expect the Count of Hentzau?' he pursued.

'Early in the morning, Your Majesty—at seven or eight.'

Rudolf came nearer to her, and took a couple of gold coins from his pocket.

'I don't want money, Your Majesty,' she murmured.

'Oh, make a hole in them and hang them round your neck.'

'Ah, yes: yes, give them to me!' she cried, holding out her hand eagerly.

'You'll earn them?' he asked, playfully holding them out of her reach.

'How?'

'By being ready to open to me when I come at eleven and knock as Bauer knocked.'

'Yes, I'll be there.'

'And by telling nobody that I've been here tonight. Will you promise me that?'

'Not my mother?'

'No.'

'Nor the Count of Luzau-Rischenheim?'

'Him least of all. You must tell nobody. My business is very private, and Rischenheim doesn't know it.'

'I'll do all you tell me. But—but Bauer knows.'

'True,' said Rudolf, 'Bauer knows. Well, we'll see about Bauer.'

As he spoke he turned towards the door. Suddenly the girl bent, snatched at his hand, and kissed it.

'I would die for you,' she murmured.

'Poor child!' said he gently. I believe he was loath to make profit, even in the Queen's service, of her poor foolish love. He laid his hand on the door, but paused a moment to say:

'If Bauer comes, you have told me nothing. Mind, nothing! I threatened you, but you told me nothing.'

'He'll tell them you have been here.'

'That can't be helped; at least they won't know when I shall arrive again. Good night.'

Rudolf opened the door and slipped through, closing it hastily behind him. If Bauer got back to the house, his visit must be known; but if he could intercept Bauer, the girl's silence was assured. He stood just outside, listening intently and searching the darkness with eager eyes.

CHAPTER XI

What the Chancellor's Wife Saw

THE night, so precious in its silence, solitude and darkness, was waning fast; soon the first dim approaches of day would be visible, soon the streets would become alive and people be about. Before then Rudolf Rassendyll, the man who bore a face that he dared not show in open day, must be under cover; else men would say that the King was in Strelsau, and the news would flash in a few hours throughout the kingdom and (so Rudolf feared) reach even those ears which we knew to be shut to all earthly sounds. But there was still some time at Mr Rassendyll's disposal, and he could not spend it better than in pursuing his fight with Bauer. Taking a leaf out of the rascal's own book, he drew himself back into the shadow of the house walls and prepared to wait. At the worst he could keep the fellow from communicating with Rischenheim for a little longer, and his hope was that Bauer would steal back after a while and reconnoitre with a view to discovering how matters stood, whether the unwelcome visitor had taken his departure and the way to Rischenheim were open. Wrapping his scarf closely round his face, Rudolf waited, patiently enduring the tedium as best he might, drenched by the rain which fell steadily, and very imperfectly sheltered from the buffeting of the wind. Minutes went by; there were no signs of Bauer nor of anybody else in the silent street. Yet Rudolf did not venture to leave his post; Bauer would seize the opportunity to slip in; perhaps Bauer had seen him come out, and was in his turn waiting till the coast should be clear; or, again, perhaps the useful spy had gone off to intercept Rupert of Hentzau, and warn him of the danger in the Königstrasse. Ignorant of the truth and compelled to accept all these chances, Rudolf waited, still watching the distant beginnings of dawning day, which must soon drive him to his hiding-place again. Meanwhile, my poor wife waited also, a prey to every fear that a woman's sensitive mind can imagine and feed upon.

Rudolf turned his head this way and that, seeking always the darker blot of shadow that would mean a human being. For a while his search was in vain, but presently he found what he looked for—aye, and even more. On the same side of the street, to his left hand, from the direction of the station, not one but three blurred shapes moved up the street. They came stealthily, yet quickly; with caution, but without pause or hesitation. Rudolf, scenting danger, flattened himself close against the wall and felt for his revolver. Very likely they were only early workers or late revellers, but he was ready for something else; he had not yet sighted Bauer, and action was to be looked for from the man. By infinitely gradual sidelong slitherings he moved a few paces from the door of Mother Holf's house, and stood six feet perhaps, or eight, on the right-hand side of it. The three came on. He strained his eyes in the effort to discern their features. In that dim light certainty was impossible, but the one in the middle might well be Bauer; the height, the walk and the make were much what Bauer's were. If it were Bauer, then Bauer had friends, and Bauer and his friends seemed to be stalking some game. Always most carefully and gradually, Rudolf edged yet farther from the shop. At a distance of some five yards he halted finally, drew out his revolver, covered the man whom he took to be Bauer, and thus waited his fortune and his chance.

Now it was plain that Bauer—for Bauer it was—would look for one of two things: what he hoped was to find Rudolf still in the house, what he feared was to be told that Rudolf, having fulfilled the unknown purpose of his visit, was gone whole and sound. If the latter tidings met him, these two good friends of his whom he had enlisted for his reinforcement were to have five crowns each and go home in peace; if the former, they were to do their work and make ten crowns. Years after, one of them told me the whole story without shame or reserve. What their work was, the heavy bludgeons they carried and the long knife that one of them had lent to Bauer showed pretty clearly. But neither to Bauer nor to them did it occur that their quarry might be crouching near, hunting as well as hunted. Not that the pair of ruffians who had been thus hired would have hesitated for that thought, as I imagine. For it is strange, yet certain, that the zenith of courage and the acme of villainy can both be bought for the price of a lady's glove; among such outcasts as those from whom Bauer drew his recruits the murder of a man is held serious only when the police are by, and death at the hands of him they seek to kill is no more than an everyday risk of their employment.

'Here's the house,' whispered Bauer, stopping at the door. 'Now I'll knock, and you stand by to knock him on the head if he runs out. He's got a six-shooter, so lose no time.'

'He'll only fire it in heaven,' growled a hoarse guttural voice that ended in a chuckle.

'But if he's gone?' objected the other auxiliary.

'Then I know where he's gone,' answered Bauer. 'Are you ready?'

A ruffian stood on either side of the door with uplifted bludgeon. Bauer raised his hand to knock.

Rudolf knew that Rischenheim was within, and he feared that Bauer, hearing that the stranger had gone, would take the opportunity of telling the count of his visit. The count would in his turn warn Rupert of Hentzau, and the work of catching the ringleader would all fall to be done again. At no time did Mr Rassendyll take count of odds against him, but in this instance he may well have thought himself, with his revolver, a match for the three ruffians. At any rate, before Bauer had time to give the signal, he sprang out suddenly from the wall and darted at the fellow. His onset was so sudden that the other two fell back a pace; Rudolf caught Bauer fairly by the throat. I do not suppose that he meant to strangle him, but the anger, long stored in his heart, found vent in the fierce grip of his fingers. It is certain that Bauer thought his time was come, unless he struck a blow for himself. Instantly he raised his hand and thrust fiercely at Rudolf with his long knife. Mr Rassendyll would have been a dead man, had he not loosed his hold and sprung lightly away. But Bauer sprang at him again, thrusting with the knife, and crying to his associates: 'Club him, you fools, club him!'

Thus exhorted, one jumped forward. The moment for hesitation was gone. In spite of the noise of wind and pelting rain, the

sound of a shot risked much; but not to fire was death. Rudolf
fired full at Bauer: the fellow saw his intention and tried to leap
behind one of his companions; he was just too late, and fell with
a groan to the ground.

Again the other ruffians shrank back, appalled by the sudden
ruthless decision of the act. Mr Rassendyll laughed. A half-
smothered yet uncontrolled oath broke from one of them. 'By
God!' he whispered hoarsely, gazing at Rudolf's face and letting
his arm fall to his side. 'My God!' he said, and his mouth hung
open. Again Rudolf laughed at his terrified stare.

'A bigger job than you fancied, is it?' he asked, pushing his
scarf well away from his chin.

The man gaped at him; the other's eyes asked wondering
questions, but neither did he attempt to resume the attack. The
first at last found voice, and he said:

'Well, it'd be damned cheap at ten crowns, and that's the
living truth.'

His friend—or confederate rather, for such men have no
friends—looked on, still amazed.

'Take up that fellow by his head and his heels,' ordered Rudolf.
'Quickly! I suppose you don't want the police to find us here
with him, do you? Well, no more do I. Lift him up.'

As he spoke Rudolf turned to knock on the door of No. 19.

But even as he did so Bauer groaned. Dead perhaps he ought to
have been, but it seems to me that fate is always ready to take the
cream and leave the scum. His leap aside had served him well
after all; he had nearly escaped scot free. As it was, the bullet,
without missing his head altogether, had just glanced on his
temple as it passed; its impact had stunned but not killed. Friend
Bauer was in unusual luck that night; I wouldn't have taken a
hundred to one about his chance of life. Rudolf arrested his hand.
It would not do to leave Bauer at the house, if Bauer were likely
to regain speech. He stood for a moment considering what to do,
but in an instant the thoughts that he tried to gather were
scattered again.

'The patrol, the patrol!' hoarsely whispered the fellow who
had not yet spoken. There was a sound of the hoofs of horses.
Down the street from the station end there appeared two

'The patrol, the patrol!'

mounted men. Without a second's hesitation the two rascals dropped their friend Bauer with a thud on the ground; one ran at his full speed across the street, the other bolted no less quickly up the Königstrasse. Neither could afford to meet the constables; and who could say what story this red-haired gentleman might tell, ay, or what powers he might command?

But in truth Rudolf gave no thought to either his story or his powers. If he were caught, the best he could hope would be to lie in the lock-up while Rupert played his game unmolested. The device that he had employed against the amazed ruffians could be used against lawful authority only as a last and desperate resort. While he could run, run he would. In an instant he also took to his heels, following the fellow who had darted up the Königstrasse. But before he had gone very far, coming to a narrow turning, he shot down it; then he paused for a moment to listen.

The patrol had seen the sudden dispersal of the group, and, struck with natural suspicion, quickened pace. A few minutes brought them where Bauer was. They jumped from their horses and ran to him. He was unconscious, and could, of course, give them no account of how he came to be in his present state. The fronts of all the houses were dark, the doors shut; there was nothing to connect the man stretched on the ground with either No. 19 or any other dwelling. Moreover the constables were not sure that the sufferer was himself a meritorious object, for his hand still held a long ugly knife. They were perplexed; they were but two; there was a wounded man to look after; there were three men to pursue, and the three had fled in three different directions. They looked up at No. 19; No. 19 remained dark, quiet, absolutely indifferent. The fugitives were out of sight. Rudolf Rassendyll, hearing nothing, had started again on his way. But a minute later he heard a shrill whistle. The patrol were summoning assistance; the man must be carried to the station, and a report made; but other constables might be warned of what had happened, and dispatched in pursuit of the culprits. Rudolf heard more than one answering whistle; he broke into a run, looking for a turning on the left that would take him back into the direction of my house, but he found none. The narrow street twisted and curved in the bewildering way that charac- terizes the old parts of the town. Rudolf had spent some time once in Strelsau; but a king learns little of back streets, and he was soon fairly puzzled as to his whereabouts. Day was dawning, and he began to meet people here and there. He dared run no more, even had his breath lasted him; winding the scarf about his face, and cramming his hat over his forehead again, he fell into an easy walk, wondering whether he could venture to ask his way, relieved to find no signs that he was being pursued, trying to persuade himself that Bauer, though not dead, was at least incapable of embarrassing disclosures; above all conscious of the danger of his tell-tale face, and of the necessity of finding some shelter before the city was all stirring and awake.

At this moment he heard horses' hoofs behind him. He was now at the end of the street, where it opened on the square in which the barracks stand. He knew his bearings now and, had he not been interrupted, could have been back to safe shelter in my house in twenty minutes. But looking back, he saw the figure of a mounted constable just coming into sight behind him. The man seemed to see Rudolf, for he broke into a quick trot. Mr Rassendyll's position was critical; this fact alone accounts for the dangerous step into which he allowed himself to be forced. Here he was, a man unable to give account of himself, of remarkable appearance, and carrying a revolver, of which one barrel was discharged. And there was Bauer, a wounded man, shot by somebody with a revolver a quarter of an hour before. Even to be questioned was dangerous; to be detained meant ruin to the great business that engaged his energies. For all he knew, the patrol had actually sighted him as he ran. His fears were not vain; for the constable raised his voice, crying:

'Hi, sir—you there—stop a minute!'

Resistance was the one thing worse than to yield. Wit, and not force, must find escape this time. Rudolf stopped, looking round again with a surprised air. Then he drew himself up with an assumption of dignity, and waited for the constable. If that last card must be played, he would win the hand with it.

'Well, what do you want?' he asked coldly, when the man was a few yards from him; and, as he spoke, he withdrew the scarf almost entirely from his features, keeping it only over his chin.

'You call very peremptorily,' he continued, staring contemptuously. 'What's your business with me?'

With a violent start, the sergeant—for such the star on his collar and the lace on his cuff proclaimed him—leant forward in the saddle to look at the man whom he had hailed. Rudolf said nothing and did not move. The man's eyes studied his face intently. Then he sat bold upright and saluted, his face dyed to a deep red in his sudden confusion.

'And why do you salute me now?' asked Rudolf in a mocking tone. 'First you hunt me, then you salute me. By heaven, I don't know why you put yourself out at all about me!'

'I—I——' the fellow stuttered. Then trying a fresh start, he stammered, 'Your Majesty, I didn't know—I didn't suppose——'

Rudolf stepped towards him with a quick decisive tread.

'And why do you call me "Your Majesty"?'

'It—it—— Isn't it Your Majesty?'

Rudolf was close by him now, his hand on the horse's neck. He looked up in the sergeant's face with steady eyes, saying:

'You make a mistake, my friend. I am not the King.'

'You are not——' stuttered the bewildered fellow.

'By no means. And, sergeant?'

'Your Majesty?'

'Sir, you mean.'

'Yes, sir.'

'A zealous officer, sergeant, can make no greater mistake than to take for the King a gentleman who is not the King. It might injure his prospects, since the King, not being here, mightn't wish to have it supposed that he was here. Do you follow me, sergeant?'

The man said nothing, but stared hard. After a moment Rudolf continued:

'In such a case,' said he, 'a discreet officer would not trouble the gentleman any more, and would be very careful not to mention that he had made such a silly mistake. Indeed, if questioned, he would answer without hesitation that he hadn't seen anybody even like the King, much less the King himself.'

A doubtful puzzled little smile spread under the sergeant's moustache.

'You see, the King is not even in Strelsau,' said Rudolf.

'Not in Strelsau, sir?'

'Why, no; he's at Zenda.'

'Ah! At Zenda, sir?'

'Certainly. It is therefore impossible—physically impossible —that he should be here.'

The fellow was convinced that he understood now.

'It's certainly impossible, sir,' said he, smiling more broadly.

'Absolutely, and therefore impossible also that you should have seen him.' With this Rudolf took a gold piece from his pocket and handed it to the sergeant. The fellow took it with something like a wink. 'As for you, you've searched here and found nobody,' concluded Mr Rassendyll. 'So hadn't you better at once search somewhere else?'

'Without doubt, sir,' said the sergeant; and with the most deferential salute, and another confidential smile, he turned and rode back by the way he had come. No doubt he wished that he could meet a gentleman who was—not the King—every morning of his life. It need hardly be said that all idea of connecting the gentleman with the crime committed in the Königstrasse had vanished from his mind. Thus Rudolf won freedom from the man's interference, but at a dangerous cost—how dangerous he did not know. It was indeed most impossible that the King could be in Strelsau.

He lost no time now in turning his steps towards his refuge. It was past five o'clock, day came quickly, and the streets began to be peopled by men and women on their way to open stalls or to buy in the market. Rudolf crossed the square at a rapid walk, for he was afraid of the soldiers who were gathering for early duty opposite to the barracks. Fortunately he passed by them unobserved, and gained the comparative seclusion of the street in which my house stands without encountering any further difficulties. In truth he was almost in safety; but bad luck was now to have its turn. When Mr Rassendyll was no more than fifty yards from my door, a carriage suddenly drove up and stopped a few paces in front of him. The footman sprang down and opened the door. Two ladies got out; they were dressed in evening costume, and were returning from a ball. One was middle-aged, the other young and rather pretty. They stood for a moment on the pavement, the younger saying: 'Isn't it pleasant, mother? I wish I could always be up at five o'clock.'

'My dear, you wouldn't like it for long,' answered the elder. 'It's very nice for a change, but——'

She stopped abruptly. Her eye had fallen on Rudolf Rassendyll. He knew her: she was no less a person than the wife of Helsing the Chancellor; his was the house at which the carriage had stopped. The trick that had served with the sergeant of police would not do now. She knew the King too well to believe that she could be mistaken about him; she was too much of a busybody to be content to pretend that she was mistaken.

'Good gracious!' she whispered loudly, and, catching her

daughter's arm, she murmured: 'Heavens, my dear, it's the King!'

Rudolf was caught. Not only the ladies but their servants were looking at him.

Flight was impossible. He walked by them. The ladies curtsied, the servants bowed bareheaded. Rudolf touched his hat and bowed slightly in return. He walked straight on towards my house; they were watching him, and he knew it. Most heartily did he curse the untimely hours to which folks keep up their dancing, but he thought that a visit to my house would afford as plausible an excuse for his presence as any other. So he went on, surveyed by the wondering ladies, and by the servants, who, smothering smiles, asked one another what brought His Majesty abroad in such a plight (for Rudolf's clothes were soaked and his boots muddy) at such an hour—and that in Strelsau, when all the world thought he was at Zenda.

Rudolf reached my house; knowing that he was watched, he had abandoned all intention of giving the signal agreed on between my wife and himself and of making his way in through the window. Such a sight would indeed have given the excellent Baroness von Helsing matter for gossip! It was better to let every servant in my house see his open entrance. But alas! virtue itself sometimes leads to ruin. My dearest Helga, sleepless and watchful in the interest of her mistress, was even now behind the shutter, listening with all her ears and peering through the chinks. No sooner did Rudolf's footsteps become audible than she cautiously unfastened the shutter, opened the window, put her pretty head out, and called softly:

'All's safe! Come in!'

The mischief was done then, for the faces of Helsing's wife and daughter, aye, and the faces of Helsing's servants, were intent on this most strange spectacle. Rudolf, turning his head over his shoulder, saw them; a moment later poor Helga saw them also. Innocent and untrained in controlling her feelings, she gave a shrill little cry of dismay, and hastily drew back. Rudolf looked round again. The ladies had retreated to the cover of the porch, but he still saw their eager faces peering from between the pillars that supported it.

'All's safe! Come in!'

'I may as well go in now,' said Rudolf, and in he sprang. There was a merry smile on his face as he ran forward to meet Helga, who leant against the table, pale and agitated.

'They saw you?' she gasped.

'Undoubtedly,' said he. Then his sense of amusement conquered everything else, and he sat down in a chair, laughing.

'I'd give my life,' said he, 'to hear the story that the chancellor will be wakened up to hear in a minute or two from now!'

But a moment's thought made him grave again. For whether he were the King or Rudolf Rassendyll, he knew that my wife's name was in equal peril. Knowing this, he stood at nothing to serve her. He turned to her and spoke quickly:

'You must rouse one of the servants at once. Send him round to the chancellor's and tell the chancellor to come here directly. No, write a note. Say the King has come by appointment to see Fritz on some private business, but that Fritz has not kept the appointment, and that the King must now see the chancellor at once. Say there's not a moment to lose.'

She was looking at him with wondering eyes.

'Don't you see,' he said, 'if I can impose on Helsing, I may stop those women's tongues? If nothing's done, how long do you suppose it'll be before all Strelsau knows that Fritz von Tarlenheim's wife let the King in at the window at five o'clock in the morning?'

'I don't understand,' murmured poor Helga in bewilderment.

'No, my dear lady, but for heaven's sake do what I ask of you. It's the only chance now.'

'I'll do it,' she said, and sat down to write.

Thus it was that, hard on the marvellous tidings which, as I conjecture, the Baroness von Helsing poured into her husband's drowsy ears, came an imperative summons that the chancellor should wait on the King at the house of Fritz von Tarlenheim.

Truly we had tempted fate too far by bringing Rudolf Rassendyll again to Strelsau.

CHAPTER XII

Before them All!

GREAT as was the risk and immense as were the difficulties created by the course which Mr Rassendyll adopted, I cannot doubt that he acted for the best in the light of the information which he possessed. His plan was to disclose himself to Helsing in the character of the King, to bind him to secrecy, and make him impose the same obligation on his wife, daughter and servants. The chancellor was to be quieted with the excuse of urgent business, and conciliated by a promise that he should know its nature in the course of a few hours; meanwhile, an appeal to his loyalty must suffice to ensure obedience. If all went well in the day that had now dawned, by the evening of it the letter would be destroyed, the Queen's peril past and Rudolf once more far away from Strelsau. Then enough of the truth— no more—must be disclosed. Helsing would be told the story of Rudolf Rassendyll and persuaded to hold his tongue about the harum-scarum Englishman (we are ready to believe much of an Englishman) having been audacious enough again to play the King in Strelsau. The old chancellor was a very good fellow, and I do not think that Rudolf did wrong in relying upon him. Where he miscalculated was, of course, just where he was ignorant. The whole of what the Queen's friends, ay, and the Queen herself, did in Strelsau became useless and mischievous by reason of the King's death; their action must have been utterly different had they been aware of that catastrophe; but their wisdom should be judged only according to their knowledge.

In the first place, the chancellor himself showed much good sense. Even before he obeyed the King's summons he sent for the two servants and charged them, on pain of instant dismissal and worse things to follow, to say nothing of what they had seen. His commands to his wife and daughter were more polite, doubtless, but no less peremptory. He may well have supposed that the King's business was private as well as important when it led His Majesty to be roaming the streets of Strelsau at a moment when he was supposed to be at the Castle of Zenda, and to enter a friend's house by the window at such untimely hours. The mere facts were eloquent of secrecy. Moreover the King had shaved his beard—the ladies were sure of it—and this again, though it might be merely an accidental coincidence, was also capable of signifying a very urgent desire to be unknown. So the chancellor, having given his orders, and being himself aflame with the liveliest curiosity, lost no time in obeying the King's commands, and arrived at my house before six o'clock.

When the visitor was announced Rudolf was upstairs, having a bath and some breakfast. Helga had learnt her lesson well enough to entertain the visitor until Rudolf appeared. She was full of apologies for my absence, protesting that she could in no way explain it: neither could she so much as conjecture what was the King's business with her husband. She played the dutiful wife whose virtue was obedience, whose greatest sin would be an indiscreet prying into what it was not her part to know.

'I know no more,' she said, 'than that Fritz wrote to me to expect the King and him at about five o'clock, and to be ready to let them in by the window, as the King did not wish the servants to be aware of his presence.'

The King came and greeted Helsing most graciously. The tragedy and comedy of these busy days were strangely mingled; even now I can hardly help smiling when I picture Rudolf, with grave lips but that distant twinkle in his eye (I swear he enjoyed the sport), sitting down by the old chancellor in the darkest corner of the room, covering him with flattery, hinting at most strange things, deploring a secret obstacle to immediate confidence, promising that tomorrow, at the latest, he would seek the advice of the wisest and most tried of his counsellors, appealing to the chancellor's loyalty to trust him till then. Helsing, blinking through his spectacles, followed with devout attention the long narrative that told nothing, and the urgent exhortation that masked a trick. His accents were almost broken with emotion as he put himself absolutely at the King's disposal, and declared that he could answer for the discretion of his family and household as completely as for his own.

'Then you're a very lucky man, my dear chancellor,' said Rudolf, with a sigh which seemed to hint that the King in his palace was not so fortunate. Helsing was immensely pleased. He was all agog to go and tell his wife how entirely the King trusted to her honour and silence.

There was nothing that Rudolf more desired than to be relieved of the excellent old fellow's presence; but, well aware of the supreme importance of keeping him in a good temper, he would not hear of his departure for a few minutes.

'At any rate the ladies won't talk till after breakfast, and since they got home only at five o'clock they won't breakfast yet awhile,' said he.

So he made Helsing sit down, and talked to him. Rudolf had not failed to notice that the Count of Luzau-Rischenheim had been a little surprised at the sound of his voice; in this conversation he studiously kept his tones low, affecting a certain weakness and huskiness such as he had detected in the King's utterances, as he listened behind the curtain in Sapt's room at the Castle. The part was played as completely and triumphantly as in the old days when he ran the gauntlet of every eye in Strelsau. Yet if he had not taken such pains to conciliate old Helsing, but had let him depart, he might not have found himself driven to a greater and even more hazardous deception.

They were conversing together alone. My wife had been prevailed on by Rudolf to lie down in her room for an hour. Sorely needing rest, she had obeyed him, having first given strict orders that no member of the household should enter the room where the two were except on an express summons. Fearing suspicion, she and Rudolf had agreed that it was better to rely on these injunctions than to lock the door again, as they had the night before.

But while these things passed at my house, the Queen and Bernenstein were on their way to Strelsau. Perhaps had Sapt been at Zenda, his powerful influence might have availed to check the impulsive expedition; Bernenstein had no such authority, and could only obey the Queen's peremptory orders and pathetic prayers. Ever since Rudolf Rassendyll left her, three years before, she had lived in stern self-repression, never her true self, never for a moment able to be or to do what every hour her heart urged on her. How are these things done? I doubt if a man lives who could do them; but women live who do them. Now his sudden coming and the train of stirring events that accompanied it, his danger and hers, his words and her enjoyment of his presence, had all worked together to shatter her self-control; and the strange dream, heightening the emotion which was its own cause, left her with no conscious desire save to be near Mr Rassendyll, and scarcely with a fear except for his safety. As they journeyed her talk was all of his peril, never of the disaster which threatened herself, and which we were all striving with might and main to avert from her head. She travelled alone with Bernenstein, getting rid of the lady who attended her by some careless pretext, and she urged on him continually to bring her as speedily as might be to Mr Rassendyll. I cannot find much blame for her. Rudolf stood for all the joy in her life, and Rudolf had gone to fight with the Count of Hentzau. What wonder that she saw him as it were dead? Yet still she would have it that, in his seeming death, all men hailed him for their King. Well, it was her love that crowned him. As they reached the city she grew more composed, being persuaded by Bernenstein that nothing in her bearing must rouse suspicion. Yet she was none the less resolved to seek Mr Rassendyll at once. In truth she feared even then to find him dead, so strong was the hold of her dream on her: until she knew that he was alive she could not rest. Bernenstein, fearful that the strain would kill her or rob her of reason, promised everything; and declared, with a confidence which he did not feel, that beyond doubt Mr Rassendyll was alive and well.

'But where—where?' she cried eagerly, with clasped hands.

'We're most likely, madame, to find him at Fritz von Tarlenheim's,' answered the lieutenant. 'He would wait there till the time came to attack Rupert, or, if the thing is over, he will have returned there.'

'Then let us drive there at once,' she urged.

Bernenstein, however, persuaded her to go to the palace first and let it be known that she was going to pay a visit to my wife.

See page 145

'I'll tell you about that directly,' he said, glancing at the girl

She arrived at the palace at eight o'clock, took a cup of chocolate, and then ordered her carriage. Bernenstein alone accompanied her when she set out for my house about nine. He was, by now, hardly less excited than the Queen herself.

In her entire preoccupation with Mr Rassendyll she gave little thought to what might have happened at the hunting-lodge; but Bernenstein drew gloomy auguries from the failure of Sapt and myself to return at the proper time. Either evil had befallen us, or the letter had reached the King before we arrived at the lodge; the probabilities seemed to him to be confined to these alternatives. Yet when he spoke in this strain to the Queen, he could get from her nothing except: 'If we can find Mr Rassendyll, he will tell us what to do.'

Thus, then, a little after nine in the morning, the Queen's carriage drove up to my door. The ladies of the chancellor's family had enjoyed a very short night's rest, for their heads came bobbing out of window the moment the wheels were heard; many people were about now, and the crown on the panels attracted the usual small crowd of loiterers. Bernenstein sprang out and gave his hand to the Queen. With a hasty slight bow to the onlookers she hastened up the two or three steps of the porch, and with her own hand rang the bell. Inside, the carriage had just been observed. My wife's waiting-maid ran hastily to her mistress: Helga was lying on her bed; she rose at once, and after a few minutes of necessary preparations (or such preparations as seem to ladies necessary, however great the need of haste may be) hurried downstairs, to receive Her Majesty—and to warn Her Majesty. She was too late. The door was already open. The butler and the footman both had run to it, and thrown it open for the Queen. As Helga reached the foot of the stairs, Her Majesty was just entering the room where Rudolf was, the servants attending her, and Bernenstein standing behind, his helmet in his hand.

Rudolf and the chancellor had been continuing their conversation. To avoid the observation of passers-by (for the interior of the room is easy to see from the street), the blind had been drawn down, and the room was in deep shadow. They had heard the wheels, but neither of them dreamt that the visitor

K

could be the Queen. It was an utter surprise to them when, without their orders, the door was suddenly flung open. The chancellor, slow of movement and not, if I may say it, over-quick of brain, sat in his corner for half a minute or more before he rose to his feet. On the other hand Rudolf Rassendyll was the best part of the way across the room in an instant. Helga was at the door now, and she thrust her head round young Bernenstein's broad shoulder. Thus she saw what happened. The Queen, forgetting the servants, and not observing Helsing —seeming indeed to stay for nothing and to think of nothing, but to have her thoughts and heart filled with the sight of the man she loved and the knowledge of his safety—met him as he ran towards her, and, before Helga or Bernenstein or Rudolf himself could stay her or conceive what she was about to do, caught both his hands in hers with an intense grasp, crying:

'Rudolf, you're safe! Thank God, oh, thank God!' and she carried his hands to her lips and kissed them passionately.

A moment of absolute silence followed, dictated in the servants by decorum, in the chancellor by consideration, in Helga and Bernenstein by utter consternation. Rudolf himself also was silent, but whether from bewilderment or an emotion answering to hers I know not. Either it might well be. The stillness struck her. She looked up in his eyes; she looked round the room and saw Helsing, now bowing profoundly from the corner; she turned her head with a sudden frightened jerk and glanced at my motionless deferential servants. Then it came upon her what she had done. She gave a quick gasp for breath, and her face, always pale, went white as marble. Her features set in a strange stiffness, and suddenly she reeled where she stood, and fell forward. Only Rudolf's hand bore her up. Thus for a moment too short to reckon they stood. Then he, a smile of great love and pity coming on his lips, drew her to him and passing his arm about her waist thus supported her. Then, smiling still, he looked down on her, and said in a low tone, yet distinct enough for all to hear:

'All is well, dearest.'

My wife gripped Bernenstein's arm, and he turned to find her pale-faced too, with quivering lips and shining eyes. But the eyes had a message and an urgent one for him. He read it; he knew that it bade him second what Rudolf Rassendyll had done. He came forward and approached Rudolf; then he fell on one knee, and kissed Rudolf's left hand that was extended to him.

'I'm very glad to see you, Lieutenant von Bernenstein,' said Rudolf Rassendyll.

For the moment the thing was done, ruin averted and safety secured. Everything had been at stake: that there was such a man as Rudolf Rassendyll might have been disclosed; that he had once filled the King's throne was a high secret which they were prepared to trust to Helsing under stress of necessity; but there remained something which must be hidden at all costs, and which the Queen's passionate exclamation had threatened to expose. There was a Rudolf Rassendyll, and he had been King, but, more than all this, the Queen loved him and he the Queen. That could be told to none, not even to Helsing; for Helsing, though he would not gossip to the town, would yet hold himself bound to carry the matter to the King. So Rudolf chose to take any future difficulties rather than that present and certain disaster. Sooner than entail it on her he loved, he claimed for himself the place of her husband and the name of King. And she, clutching at the only chance that her act left, was content to have it so. It may be that for an instant her weary tortured brain found sweet rest in the dim dream that so it was, for she let her head lie there on his breast and her eyes closed, her face looking very peaceful, and a soft little sigh escaping in pleasure from her lips.

But every moment bore its peril and extracted its effort. Rudolf led the Queen to a couch, and then briefly charged the servants not to speak of his presence for a few hours. As they had no doubt perceived, said he, from the Queen's agitation, important business was on foot; it demanded his presence in Strelsau, but required also that his presence should not be known. A short time would free them from the obligation which he now asked of their loyalty. When they had withdrawn, bowing obedience, he turned to Helsing, pressed his hand warmly, reiterated his request for silence, and said that he would summon the chancellor to his presence again later in the day, either where he was or at the palace. Then he bade all withdraw and leave him alone for a little with the Queen. He was obeyed, but Helsing had hardly left the house when Rudolf called Bernenstein back, and with him my wife. Helga hastened to the Queen, who was still sorely agitated; Rudolf drew Bernenstein aside, and exchanged with him all their news. Mr Rassendyll was much disturbed at finding that no tidings had come from Colonel Sapt and myself, but his apprehension was greatly increased on learning the untoward accident by which the King himself had been at the lodge the night before. Indeed he was utterly in the dark; where the King was, where Rupert, where we were, he did not know. And he was here in Strelsau, known as the King to half a dozen people or more, protected only by their promises, liable at any moment to be exposed by the coming of the King himself, or even by a message from him.

Yet in face of all perplexities, perhaps even the more because of the darkness in which he was enveloped, Rudolf held firm to his purpose. There were two things that seemed plain. If Rupert had escaped the trap, and was still alive with the letter on him, Rupert must be found; here was the first task. That accomplished, there remained for Rudolf himself nothing save to disappear as quietly and secretly as he had come, trusting that his presence could be concealed from the man whose name he had usurped. Nay, if need were, the King must be told that Rudolf Rassendyll had played a trick on the chancellor, and, having enjoyed his pleasure, was gone again. Everything could, in the last resort, be told, save that which touched the Queen's honour.

At this moment the message which I dispatched from the station at Hofbau reached my house. There was a knock at the door. Bernenstein opened it and took the telegram, which was addressed to my wife. I had written all that I dared to trust to such a means of communication, and here it is:

'I am coming to Strelsau. The King will not leave the lodge today. The count came, but left before we arrived. I do not know whether he has gone to Strelsau. He gave no news to the King.'

'Then they didn't get him!' cried Bernenstein in deep disappointment.

'No, but "He gave no news to the King",' said Rudolf triumphantly.

They were all standing now round the Queen, who sat on the couch. She seemed very faint and weary, but at peace. It was enough for her that Rudolf fought and planned for her.

'And see this,' Rudolf went on: '"The King will not leave the lodge today." Thank God, then, we have today!'

'Yes, but where's Rupert?'

'We shall know in an hour, if he's in Strelsau.' And Mr Rassendyll looked as though it would please him well to find Rupert in Strelsau. 'Yes, I must seek him. I shall stand at nothing to find him. If I can only get to him as the King, then I'll be the King. We have today!'

My message put them in heart again, although it left so much still unexplained. Rudolf turned to the Queen.

'Courage, my Queen,' said he. 'A few hours now will see an end of all our dangers.'

'And then?' she asked.

'Then you'll be safe and at rest,' said he, bending over her and speaking softly. 'And I shall be proud in the knowledge of having saved you.'

'And you?'

'I must go,' Helga heard him whisper, as he bent lower still, and she and Bernenstein moved away.

Chapter XIII

A King up his Sleeve

THE tall, handsome girl was taking down the shutters from the shop-front at No. 19 in the Königstrasse. She went about her work languidly enough, but there was a tinge of dusky red on her cheeks, and her eyes were brightened by some suppressed excitement. Old Mother Holf, leaning against the counter, was grumbling angrily because Bauer did not come. Now it was not likely that Bauer would come just yet, for he was still in the infirmary attached to the police-cells, where a couple of doctors were very busy setting him on his legs again. The old woman knew nothing of this, but only that he had gone the night before to reconnoitre; where he was to play the spy she did not know, on whom perhaps she guessed.

'You're sure he never came back?' she asked her daughter.

'He never came back that I saw,' answered the girl. 'And I was on the watch with my lamp here in the shop till it grew light.'

'He's twelve hours gone now, and never a message! Aye, and Count Rupert should be here soon, and he'll be in a fine taking if Bauer's not back.'

The girl made no answer; she had finished her task and stood in the doorway, looking out on the street. It was past eight, and many people were about, still for the most part humble folk; the more comfortably placed would not be moving for an hour or two yet. In the road the traffic consisted chiefly of country carts and wagons, bringing in produce for the day's victualling of the great city. The girl watched the stream, but her thoughts were occupied with the stately gentleman who had come to her by night and asked a service of her. She had heard the revolver shot outside; as it sounded she had blown out her lamp, and there, behind the door in the dark, had heard the swiftly retreating feet of the

142

fugitives and, a little later, the arrival of the patrol. Well, the
patrol would not dare to touch the King; as for Bauer, let him be
alive or dead: what cared she, who was the King's servant, able to
help the King against his enemies? If Bauer were the King's
enemy, right glad would she be to hear that the rogue was dead.
How finely the King had caught him by the neck and thrown him
out! She laughed to think how little her mother knew the
company she had kept that night.

The row of country carts moved slowly by. One or two stopped
before the shop, and the carters offered vegetables for sale. The
old woman would have nothing to say to them, but waved them
on irritably. Three had thus stopped and again proceeded, and an
impatient grumble broke from the old lady as a fourth, a covered
wagon, drew up before the door.

'We don't want anything: go on, go on with you!' she cried
shrilly.

The carter got down from his seat without heeding her, and
walked round to the back.

'Here you are, sir,' he cried. 'Nineteen, Königstrasse.'

A yawn was heard, and the long sigh a man gives as he stretches
himself in the mingled luxury and pain of an awakening after
sound, refreshing sleep.

'All right; I'll get down,' came in answer from inside.

'Ah, it's the count!' said the old lady to her daughter in
satisfied tones. 'What will he say, though, about that rogue
Bauer?'

Rupert of Hentzau put his head out from under the wagon-tilt,
looked up and down the street, gave the carter a couple of
crowns, leapt down and ran lightly across the pavement into the
little shop. The wagon moved on.

'A lucky thing I met him,' said Rupert cheerily. 'The wagon
hid me very well, and handsome as my face is, I can't let Strelsau
enjoy too much of it just now. Well, mother, what cheer? And
you, my pretty, how goes it with you?' He carelessly brushed the
girl's cheek with the glove that he had drawn off. 'Faith, though,
I beg your pardon,' he added a moment later; 'the glove's not
clean enough for that,' and he looked at his buff glove, which was
stained with patches of dull rusty brown.

Rupert leapt down and ran lightly across the pavement

'It's all as when you left, Count Rupert,' said Mother Holf, 'except that that rascal Bauer went out last night——'

'That's right enough. But hasn't he come back?'

'No, not yet.'

'Hum. No signs of—anybody else?' His look defined the vague question.

The old woman shook her head. The girl turned away to hide a smile. 'Anybody else' meant the King, so she suspected. Well, they should hear nothing from her. The King himself had charged her to be silent.

'But Rischenheim has come, I suppose?' pursued Rupert.

'Oh, yes; he came, my lord, soon after you went. He wears his arm in a sling.'

'Ah!' cried Rupert in sudden excitement. 'As I guessed! The
devil! If only I could do everything myself, and not have to trust
to fools and bunglers! Where's the count?'

'Why, in the attic. You know the way.'

'True. But I want some breakfast, mother.'

'Rosa shall serve you at once, my lord.'

The girl followed Rupert up the narrow crazy staircase of the
tall old house. They passed three floors, all uninhabited; a last
steep flight brought them right under the deep arched roof.
Rupert opened a door that stood at the top of the stairs, and,
followed still by Rosa with her mysterious happy smile, entered
a long narrow room. The ceiling, high in the centre, sloped
rapidly down on either side, so that at door and window it was
little more than six feet above the floor. There was an oak table,
and a few chairs; a couple of iron bedsteads stood by the wall
near the window. One was empty; the Count of Luzau-Rischenheim lay on the other, fully dressed, his right arm supported in
a sling of black silk. Rupert paused on the threshold, smiling at
his cousin; the girl passed on to a high press or cupboard,
and, opening it, took out plates, glasses, and the other furni-
ture of the table. Rischenheim sprang up and ran across the
room.

' What news?' he cried eagerly. ' You escaped them,
Rupert?'

'It appears so,' said Rupert airily; and, advancing into the
room, he threw himself into a chair, tossing his hat on to the
table. 'It appears that I escaped, although some fool's stupidity
nearly made an end of me.'

Rischenheim flushed.

'I'll tell you about that directly,' he said, glancing at the girl,
who had put some cold meat and a bottle of wine on the table,
and was now completing the preparations for Rupert's meal in a
very leisurely fashion.

'Had I nothing to do but look at pretty faces—which, by
heaven, I wish heartily were the case—I would beg you to stay,'
said Rupert, rising and making a profound bow.

'I've no wish to hear what doesn't concern me,' she retorted
scornfully.

'What a rare and blessed disposition!' said he, holding the door for her and bowing again.

'I know what I know!' she cried to him triumphantly from the landing. 'Maybe you'd give something to know it too, Count Rupert!'

'It's very likely, for, by Jove, girls know wonderful things!' smiled Rupert; but he shut the door, and came quickly back to the table, now frowning again. 'Come, tell me, how did they make a fool of you, or why did you make a fool of me, cousin?'

While Rischenheim related how he had been trapped and tricked at the Castle of Zenda, Rupert of Hentzau made a very good breakfast. He offered no interruption and no comments, but when Rudolf Rassendyll came into the story he looked up for an instant with a quick jerk of his head and a sudden light in his eyes. The end of Rischenheim's narrative found him tolerant and smiling again.

'Ah, well, the snare was cleverly set,' he said. 'I don't wonder you fell into it.'

'And now you? What happened to you?' asked Rischenheim eagerly.

'I? Why, having your message which was not your message, I obeyed your directions which were not your directions.'

'You went to the lodge?'

'Certainly.'

'And found Sapt there?—Anybody else?'

'Why, not Sapt at all.'

'Not Sapt? But surely they laid a trap for you?'

'Very possibly, but the jaws didn't bite.' Rupert crossed his legs and lit a cigarette.

'But what did you find?'

'I? I found the King's forester and the King's boar-hound, and —well, I found the King himself too.'

'The King at the lodge?'

'You weren't so wrong as you thought, were you?'

'But surely Sapt, or Bernenstein, or someone was with him?'

'As I tell you, his forester and his boar-hound. No other man or beast, on my honour.'

'Then you gave him the letter?' cried Rischenheim, trembling with excitement.

'Alas, no, my dear cousin. I threw the box at him, but I don't think he had time to open it. We didn't get to that stage of the conversation at which I had intended to produce the letter.'

'But why not—why not?'

Rupert rose to his feet, and, coming just opposite to where Rischenheim sat, balanced himself on his heels and looked down at his cousin, blowing the ash from his cigarette and smiling pleasantly.

'Have you noticed,' he asked, 'that my coat's torn?'

'I see it is.'

'Yes. The boar-hound tried to bite me, cousin. And the forester would have stabbed me. And—well, the King wanted to shoot me.'

'Yes, yes! For God's sake what happened?'

'Well, they none of them did what they wanted. That's what happened, dear cousin.'

Rischenheim was staring at him now with wide-opened eyes. Rupert smiled down on him composedly.

'Because, you see,' he added, 'Heaven helped me. So that, my dear cousin, the dog will bite no more, and the forester will stab no more. Surely the country is well rid of them?'

A silence followed. Then Rischenheim, leaning forward, said in a low whisper, as though afraid to hear his own question:

'And the King?'

'The King? Well, the King will shoot no more.'

For a moment Rischenheim, still leaning forward, gazed at his cousin. Then he sank slowly back into his chair.

'My God!' he murmured, 'my God!'

'The King was a fool,' said Rupert. 'Come, I'll tell you a little more about it.' He drew a chair up and seated himself in it.

While he talked Rischenheim seemed hardly to listen. The story gained in effect from the contrast of Rupert's airy telling; his companion's pale face and twitching hands tickled his fancy to more shameless jesting. But when he had finished he gave a

pull to his small smartly curled moustache, and said with a
sudden gravity:

'After all, though, it's a serious matter.'

Rischenheim was appalled at the issue. His cousin's influence
had been strong enough to lead him into the affair of the letter;
he was aghast to think how Rupert's reckless daredevilry had led
on from stage to stage till the death of a King seemed but an
incident in his schemes. He sprang suddenly to his feet, crying:

'But we must fly—we must fly!'

'No, we needn't fly. Perhaps we'd better go, but we needn't
fly.'

'But when it becomes known——?' He broke off, and then
cried: 'Why did you tell me? Why did you come back here?'

'Well, I told you because it was interesting, and I came back
here because I had no money to go elsewhere.'

'I would have sent money.'

'I find that I can get more when I ask in person. Besides, is
everything finished?'

'I'll have no more to do with it.'

'Ah, my good cousin, you despond too soon. The good King is
unhappily gone from us, but we still have our dear Queen. We
have also, by the kindness of Heaven, our dear Queen's letter.'

'I'll have no more to do with it.'

'Your neck feeling . . . ?' Rupert delicately imitated the
putting of a noose about a man's throat.

Rischenheim rose suddenly and flung the window open wide.

'I'm suffocated,' he muttered with a sullen frown, avoiding
Rupert's eyes.

'Where's Rudolf Rassendyll?' asked Rupert. 'Have you heard
of him?'

'No, I don't know where he is.'

'We must find that out, I think.'

Rischenheim turned abruptly on him.

'I had no hand in this thing,' he said, 'and I'll have no more
to do with it. I was not there. What did I know of the King being
there? I'm not guilty of it: on my soul, I know nothing of it.'

'That's all very true,' nodded Rupert.

'Rupert,' cried he, 'let me go, let me alone! If you want

money, I'll give it you. For God's sake take it and get out of Strelsau!'

'I'm ashamed to beg, my dear cousin, but in fact I want a little money until I can contrive to realize my valuable property. Is it safe, I wonder? Ah, yes, here it is.'

He drew from his inner pocket the Queen's letter.

'Now if the King hadn't been a fool!' he murmured regretfully, as he regarded it.

Then he walked across to the window and looked out; he could not himself be seen from the street, and nobody was visible at the windows opposite. Men and women passed to and fro on their daily labours or pleasures; there was no unusual stir in the city. Looking across the roofs, Rupert could see the royal standard floating in the wind over the palace and barracks. He took out his watch; Rischenheim imitated his action: it was ten minutes to ten.

'Rischenheim,' he called, 'come here a moment. Here—look out.'

Rischenheim obeyed, and Rupert let him look for a minute or two before speaking again.

'Do you see anything remarkable?' he asked then.

'No, nothing,' answered Rischenheim, still curt and sullen in his fright.

'Well, no more do I. And that's very odd. For don't you think that Sapt or some other of Her Majesty's friends must have gone to the lodge last night?'

'They meant to, I swear,' said Rischenheim with sudden attention.

'Then they would have found the King. There's a telegraph wire at Hofbau, only a few miles away. And it's ten o'clock. My cousin, why isn't Strelsau mourning for our lamented King? Why aren't the flags at half-mast? I don't understand it.'

'No,' murmured Rischenheim, his eyes now fixed on his cousin's face.

Rupert broke into a smile and tapped his teeth with his fingers.

'I wonder,' said he meditatively, 'if that old player Sapt has got a king up his sleeve again! If that were so——' He stopped and seemed to fall into deep thought. Rischenheim did not interrupt him, but stood looking now at him, now out of the window. Still there was no stir in the streets, and still the standards floated at the summit of the flagstaffs. The King's death was not yet known in Strelsau.

'Where's Bauer?' asked Rupert suddenly. 'Where the plague can Bauer be? He was my eyes. Here we are cooped up, and I don't know what's going on.'

'I don't know where he is. Something must have happened to him.'

'Of course, my wise cousin. But what?'

Rupert began to walk up and down the room, smoking another cigarette at a great pace. Rischenheim sat down by the table, resting his head on his hand. He was wearied out by the strain and excitement, his wounded arm pained him greatly, and he was full of horror and remorse at the event which had happened unknown to him the night before.

'I wish I was quit of it,' he moaned at last.

Rupert stopped before him.

'You repent of your misdeeds?' he asked. 'Well, then, you shall be allowed to repent. Nay, you shall go and tell the King that you repent. Rischenheim, I must know what they are doing. You must go and ask an audience of the King.'

'But the King is——'

'We shall know that better when you've asked for your audience. See here.'

Rupert sat down by his cousin and instructed him in his task. This was no other than to discover whether there were a King in Strelsau, or whether the only King lay dead in the hunting-lodge. If there were no attempt being made to conceal the King's death, Rupert's plan was to seek safety in flight. He did not abandon his designs: from the secure vantage of foreign soil he would hold the Queen's letter over her head, and by the threat of publishing it ensure at once immunity for himself and almost any further terms which he chose to exact from her. If, on the other hand, the Count of Luzau-Rischenheim found a King in Strelsau, if the royal standards continued to wave at the summit of their flagstaffs, and Strelsau knew nothing of the dead man in the lodge, then Rupert had laid his hand on another secret; for he knew who the King in Strelsau must be. Starting from this point, his audacious mind darted forward to new and bolder schemes. He could offer again to Rudolf Rassendyll what he had offered once before, three years ago—a partnership in crime and the profits of crime—or, if this advance were refused, then he declared that he would himself descend openly into the streets of Strelsau and proclaim the death of the King from the steps of the cathedral.

'Who can tell,' he cried, springing up, enraptured and merry with the inspiration of his plan, 'who can tell whether Sapt or I came to the lodge first? Who found the King alive, Sapt or I? Who left him dead, Sapt or I? Who had most interest in killing him—I, who only sought to make him aware of what touched his honour, or Sapt, who was and is hand and glove with the man that now robs him of his name and usurps his place while his body is still warm? Ah, they haven't done with Rupert of Hentzau yet!'

He stopped, looking down on his companion. Rischenheim's fingers still twitched nervously and his cheeks were pale. But now his face was alight with interest and eagerness. Again the fascination of Rupert's audacity and the infection of his courage caught on his kinsman's weaker nature, and inspired him to a temporary emulation of the will that dominated him.

'You see,' pursued Rupert, 'it's not likely that they'll do you any harm.'

'I'll risk anything.'

'Most gallant gentleman! At the worse they'll only keep you a prisoner. Well, if you're not back in a couple of hours, I shall draw my conclusions. I shall know that there's a King in Strelsau.'

'But where shall I look for the King?'

'Why, first in the palace, and secondly at Fritz von Tarlenheim's. I expect you will find him at Fritz's, though.'

'Shall I go there first, then?'

'No. That would be seeming to know too much.'

'You'll wait here?'

'Certainly, cousin—unless I see cause to move, you know.'

'And I shall find you on my return?'

'Me, or directions from me. By the way, bring money too. There's never any harm in having a full pocket. I wonder what the devil does without a breeches pocket!'

Rischenheim let that curious speculation alone, although he remembered the whimsical air with which Rupert delivered it. He was now on fire to be gone, his ill-balanced brain leaping from the depths of despondency to the certainty of brilliant success, and not heeding the gulf of danger that it surpassed in buoyant fancy.

'We shall have them in a corner, Rupert!' he cried.

'Aye, perhaps. But wild beasts in a corner bite hard.'

'I wish my arm were well!'

'You'll be safer with it wounded,' said Rupert with a smile.

'By God! Rupert, I can defend myself.'

'True, true; but it's your brain I want now, cousin.'

'You shall see that I have something in me.'

'If it please God, dear cousin.'

With every mocking encouragement and every careless taunt Rischenheim's resolve to prove himself a man grew stronger. He snatched up a revolver that lay on the mantelpiece and put it in his pocket.

'Don't fire, if you can help it,' advised Rupert.

Rischenheim's answer was to make for the door at a great speed. Rupert watched him go, and then returned to the window. The last his cousin saw was his figure standing straight and lithe against the light, while he looked out on the city. Still there was no stir in the streets, still the royal standard floated at the top of the flagstaffs.

Rischenheim plunged down the stairs: his feet were too slow for his eagerness. At the bottom he found the girl Rosa sweeping the passage with great apparent diligence.

'You're going out, my lord?' she asked.

'Why, yes; I have business. Pray stand on one side—this passage is so cursedly narrow.'

Rosa showed no haste in moving.

'And Count Rupert, is he going out also?' she asked.

'You see he's not with me. He'll wait——' Rischenheim

broke off, and asked angrily, 'What business is it of yours, girl? Get out of the way!'

She moved aside now, making him no answer. He rushed past; she looked after him with a smile of triumph. Then she fell again to her sweeping. The King had bidden her to be ready at eleven. It was half-past ten. Soon the King would have need of her.

Chapter XIV

The News Comes to Strelsau

On leaving No. 19, Rischenheim walked swiftly some little way up the Königstrasse, and then hailed a cab. He had hardly raised his hand when he heard his name called, and, looking round, saw Anton von Strofzin's smart phaeton pulling up beside him. Anton was driving, and on the other seat was a large nosegay of choice flowers.

'Where are you off to?' cried Anton, leaning forward with a gay smile.

'Well, where are you? To a lady's I presume from your bouquet there,' answered Rischenheim, as lightly as he could.

'The little bunch of flowers,' simpered young Anton, 'is a cousinly offering to Helga von Tarlenheim, and I'm going to present it. Can I give you a lift anywhere?'

Although Rischenheim had intended to go first to the palace, Anton's offer seemed to give him a good excuse for drawing the more likely covert first.

'I was going to the palace, to find out where the King is. I want to see him, if he'll give me a minute or two,' he remarked.

'I'll drive you there afterwards. Jump up. That your cab? Here you are, cabman,' and, flinging the cabman a crown, he displaced the bouquet and made room for Rischenheim beside him.

Anton's horses, of which he was not a little proud, made short work of the distance to my home. The phaeton rattled up to the door, and both the young men got out. The moment of their arrival found the chancellor just leaving to return to his own house. Helsing knew them both, and stopped to rally Anton on the matter of his bouquet. Anton was famous for his bouquets, which he distributed widely among the ladies of Strelsau.

'I hoped it was for my daughter,' said the chancellor slyly. 'For I love flowers, and my wife has ceased to provide me with them; moreover I've ceased to provide her with them—so but for my daughter we should have none.'

Anton answered his chaff, promising a bouquet for the young lady the next day, but declaring that he could not disappoint his cousin. He was interrupted by Rischenheim, who, looking round on the group of bystanders, now grown numerous, exclaimed:

'What's going on here, my dear chancellor? What are all these people hanging about here for? Ah, that's a royal carriage!'

'The Queen's with the countess,' answered Helsing. 'The people are waiting to see her come out.'

'She's always worth seeing,' Anton pronounced, sticking his glass in his eye.

'And you've been to visit her?' pursued Rischenheim.

'Why, yes. I—I went to pay my respects, my dear Rischen-heim.'

'An early visit!'

'It was more or less on business.'

'Ah, I have business also, and very important business. But it's with the King.'

'I won't keep you a moment, Rischenheim,' called Anton, as, bouquet in hand, he knocked at the door.

'With the King?' said Helsing. 'Ah, yes, but the King——'

'I'm on my way to the palace to find out where he is. If I can't see him, I must write at once. My business is very urgent.'

'Indeed, my dear count, indeed! Dear me! Urgent, you say?'

'But perhaps you can help me. Is he at Zenda?'

The chancellor was becoming very embarrassed; Anton had disappeared into the house; Rischenheim buttonholed him resolutely.

'At Zenda? Well, now, I don't—— Excuse me, but what's your business?'

'Excuse me, my dear chancellor: it's a secret.'

'I have the King's confidence.'

'Then you'll be indifferent to not enjoying mine,' smiled Rischenheim.

'I perceive that your arm is hurt,' observed the chancellor, seeking a diversion.

'Between ourselves, that has something to do with my business. Well, I must go to the palace. Or—stay—would Her Majesty condescend to help me? I think I'll risk a request. She can but refuse,' and so saying Rischenheim approached the door.

'Oh, my friend, I wouldn't do that,' cried Helsing, darting after him. 'The Queen is—well, very much engaged. She won't like to be troubled.'

Rischenheim took no notice of him, but knocked loudly. The door was opened, and he told the butler to carry his name to the Queen and beg a moment's speech with her. Helsing stood in perplexity on the steps. The crowd was delighted with the coming of these great folk and showed no sign of dispersing. Anton von Strofzin did not reappear. Rischenheim edged himself inside the doorway and stood on the threshold of the hall. There he heard voices proceeding from the sitting-room on the left. He recognized the Queen's, my wife's and Anton's. Then came the butler's, saying:

'I will inform the count of Your Majesty's wishes.'

The door of the room opened; the butler appeared, and immediately behind him Anton von Strofzin and Bernenstein. Bernenstein had the young fellow by the arm, and hurried him through the hall. They passed the butler, who made way for them, and came to where Rischenheim stood.

'We meet again,' said Rischenheim with a bow.

The chancellor rubbed his hands in nervous perturbation. The butler stepped up and delivered his message: the Queen regretted her inability to receive the count. Rischenheim nodded, and, standing so that the door could not be shut, asked Bernenstein whether he knew where the King was.

Now Bernenstein was most anxious to get the pair of them away and the door shut, but he dared show no eagerness.

'Do you want another interview with the King already?' he asked with a smile. 'The last was so pleasant, then?'

Rischenheim took no notice of the taunt, but observed sarcastically:

'There's a strange difficulty in finding our good King. The chancellor here doesn't know where he is, or at least he won't answer my questions.'

'Possibly the King has his reasons for not wishing to be disturbed,' suggested Bernenstein.

'It's very possible,' retorted Rischenheim significantly.

'Meanwhile, my dear count, I shall take it as a personal favour if you'll move out of the doorway.'

'Do I incommode you by standing here?' asked the count.

'Infinitely, my lord,' answered Bernenstein stiffly.

'Hallo, Bernenstein, what's the matter?' cried Anton, seeing that their tones and glances had grown angry. The crowd also had noticed the raised voices and hostile manner of the disputants, and began to gather round in a more compact group.

Suddenly a voice came from inside the hall; it was distinct and loud, yet not without a touch of huskiness. The sound of it hushed the rising quarrel and silenced the crowd into expectant stillness. Bernenstein looked aghast, Rischenheim nervous yet triumphant, Anton amused and gratified.

'The King!' he cried, and burst into a laugh. 'You've drawn him, Rischenheim!'

The crowd heard his boyish exclamation and raised a cheer. Helsing turned as though to rebuke them. Had not the King himself desired secrecy? Yes, but he who spoke as the King chose any risk sooner than let Rischenheim go back and warn Rupert of his presence.

'Is that the Count of Luzau-Rischenheim?' called Rudolf from within. 'If so, let him enter and then shut the door.'

There was something in his tone that alarmed Rischenheim. He started back on the step. But Bernenstein caught him by the arm.

'Since you wished to come in, come in,' he said with a grim smile.

Rischenheim looked round, as though he meditated flight. The next moment Bernenstein was thrust aside. For one short instant a tall figure appeared in the doorway; the crowd had but a glimpse, yet they cheered again. Rischenheim's hand was clasped in a firm grip; he passed unwillingly but helplessly through the door. Bernenstein followed; the door was shut. Anton faced round on Helsing, a scornful twist on his lips.

'There was a deuced lot of mystery about nothing,' said he.

'Why couldn't you say he was there?' And without waiting for
an answer from the outraged and bewildered chancellor he swung
down the steps and climbed into his phaeton.

The people round were chatting noisily, delighted to have
caught a glimpse of the King, speculating what brought him and
the Queen to my house, and hoping that they would soon come
out and get into the royal carriage that still stood waiting.

Had they been able to see inside the door, their emotion would
have been stirred to a keener pitch. Rudolf himself caught
Rischenheim by the arm, and without a moment's delay led him
towards the back of the house. They went along a passage and
reached a small room that looked out on the garden. Rudolf had
known my house in old days, and did not forget its resources.

'Shut the door, Bernenstein,' said Rudolf. Then he turned to
Rischenheim. 'My lord,' he said, 'I suppose you came to find out
something. Do you know it now?'

Rischenheim plucked up courage to answer him.

'Yes, I know now that I have to deal with an impostor,' said he
defiantly.

'Precisely. And impostors cannot afford to be exposed.'

Rischenheim's cheek turned rather pale. Rudolf faced him,
and Bernenstein guarded the door. He was absolutely at their
mercy; and he knew their secret. Did they know his—the news
that Rupert of Hentzau had brought?

'Listen,' said Rudolf. 'For a few hours today I am King in
Strelsau. In those few hours I have an account to settle with
your cousin; something that he has I must have. I'm going now to
seek him, and while I seek him you will stay here with Bernenstein. Perhaps I shall fail, perhaps I shall succeed. Whether I
succeed or fail, by tonight I shall be far from Strelsau and the
King's place will be free for him again.'

Rischenheim gave a slight start, and a look of triumph spread
over his face. They did not know that the King was dead.

Rudolf came nearer to him, fixing his eyes steadily on his
prisoner's face.

'I don't know', he continued, 'why you are in this business,
my lord. Your cousin's motives I know well. But I wonder that
they seemed to you great enough to justify the ruin of an unhappy

lady who is your Queen. Be assured that I will die sooner than let that letter reach the King's hand.'

Rischenheim made him no answer.

'Are you armed?' asked Rudolf.

Rischenheim sullenly flung his revolver on the table. Bernenstein came forward and took it.

'Keep him here, Bernenstein. When I return I'll tell you what more to do. If I don't return, Fritz will be here soon, and you and he must make your own plans.'

'He shan't give me the slip a second time,' said Bernenstein.

'We hold ourselves free', said Rudolf to Rischenheim, 'to do what we please with you, my lord. But I have no wish to cause your death unless it be necessary. You will be wise to wait till your cousin's fate is decided before you attempt any further steps against us.' And with a slight bow he left the prisoner in Bernenstein's charge, and went back to the room where the Queen awaited him. Helga was with her. The Queen sprang up to meet him.

'I mustn't lose a moment,' he said. 'All that crowd of people know now that the King is here. The news will filter through the town in no time. We must send word to Sapt to keep it from the King's ears at all costs: I must go and do my work, and then disappear.'

The Queen stood facing him. Her eyes seemed to devour his face; but she said only:

'Yes, it must be so.'

'You must return to the palace as soon as I am gone. I shall send out and ask the people to disperse, and then I must be off.'

'To seek Rupert of Hentzau?'

'Yes.'

She struggled for a moment with the contending feelings that filled her heart. Then she came to him and seized hold of his hand.

'Don't go,' she said, in low trembling tones. 'Don't go, Rudolf. He'll kill you. Never mind the letter. Don't go: I had rather a thousand times that the King had it than that you should . . . Oh, my dear, don't go!'

'I must go,' he said softly.

Again she began to implore him, but he would not yield. Helga moved towards the door, but Rudolf stopped her.

'No,' he said, 'you must stay with her, you must go to the palace with her.'

Even as he spoke they heard the wheels of a carriage driven

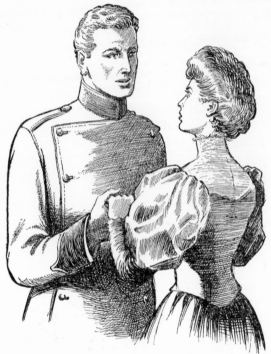

'I must go,' he said softly

quickly to the door. By now I had met Anton von Strofzin, and heard from him that the King was at my house. As I dashed up, the news was confirmed by the comments and jokes of the crowd.

'Ah, he's in a hurry,' they said. 'He's kept the King waiting. He'll get a wigging.'

As may be supposed, I paid little heed to them. I sprang out and ran up the steps to the door. I saw my wife's face at the window: she herself ran to the door and opened it for me.

'Good God!' I whispered, 'do all these people know he's here, and take him for the King?'

'Yes,' she said. 'We couldn't help it: he showed himself at the door.'

It was worse than I dreamt: not two or three people but all that crowd were victims of the mistake; all of them had heard that the King was in Strelsau—aye, and had seen him.

'Where is he? Where is he?' I asked, and followed her hastily to the room.

The Queen and Rudolf were standing side by side. What I have told from Helga's description had just passed between them. Rudolf ran to meet me.

'Is all well?' he asked eagerly.

I forgot the Queen's presence and paid no sign of respect to her. I caught Rudolf by the arm and cried to him:

'Do they take you for the King?'

'Yes,' he said. 'Heavens, man, don't look so white! We shall manage it. I can be gone by tonight.'

'Gone? How will that help, since they believe you to be the King?'

'You can keep it from the King,' he urged. 'I couldn't help it. I can settle with Rupert and disappear.'

The three were standing round me, surprised at my great and terrible agitation. Looking back now, I wonder that I could speak to them at all.

Rudolf tried again to reassure me. He little knew the cause of what he saw.

'It won't take long to settle affairs with Rupert,' said he. 'And we must have the letter, or it will get to the King after all.'

'The King will never see the letter,' I blurted out, as I sank back in a chair.

They said nothing. I looked round on their faces. I had a strange feeling of helplessness, and seemed to be able to do nothing but throw the truth at them in blunt plainness. Let them make what they could of it, I could make nothing.

'The King will never see the letter,' I repeated. 'Rupert himself has ensured that.'

'What do you mean? You've not met Rupert? You've not got the letter?'

'No, no; but the King can never read it.'

Then Rudolf seized me by the shoulder and fairly shook me; indeed, I must have seemed like a man in a dream or a torpor.

'Why not, man, why not?' he asked in urgent low tones.

Again I looked at them, but somehow this time my eyes were attracted and held by the Queen's face. I believe that she was the first to catch a hint of the tidings I brought. Her lips were parted, and her gaze eagerly strained upon me. I rubbed my hands across my forehead, and, looking up stupidly at her, I said:

'He can never see the letter. He's dead.'

There was a little scream from Helga; Rudolf neither spoke nor moved; the Queen continued to gaze at me in motionless wonder and horror.

'Rupert killed him,' said I. 'The boar-hound attacked Rupert; then Herbert and the King attacked him; and he killed them all. Yes, the King is dead. He's dead.'

Now none spoke. The Queen's eyes never left my face.

'Yes, he's dead!' said I; and I watched her eyes still. For a long while (or long it seemed) they were on my face; at last, as though drawn by some irresistible force, they turned away. I followed the new line they took. She looked at Rudolf Rassendyll, and he at her. Helga had taken out her handkerchief and, utterly upset by the horror and shock, was lying back in a low chair, sobbing half hysterically; I saw the swift look that passed from the Queen to her lover, carrying in it grief, remorse and most unwilling joy. He did not speak to her, but put out his hand and took hers. She drew it away almost sharply, and covered her face with both hands. Rudolf turned to me.

'When was it?'

'Last night.'

'And the . . . He's at the lodge?'

'Yes, with Sapt and James.'

I was recovering my senses and my coolness.

'Nobody knows yet,' I said. 'We were afraid you might be taken for him by somebody. But, my God, Rudolf, what's to be done now?'

Mr Rassendyll's lips were set firm and tight. He frowned slightly, and his blue eyes wore a curious entranced expression. He seemed to me to be forgetful of everything, even of us who were with him, in some one idea that possessed him. The Queen herself came nearer to him and lightly touched his arm with her hand. He started as though surprised, then fell again into his reverie.

'What's to be done, Rudolf?' I asked again.

'I'm going to kill Rupert of Hentzau,' he said. 'The rest we'll talk of afterwards.'

He walked rapidly across the room and rang the bell.

'Clear those people away,' he ordered. 'Tell them that I want to be quiet. Then send a closed carriage round for me. Don't be more than ten minutes.'

The servant received his peremptory orders with a low bow, and left us. The Queen, who had been all this time outwardly calm and composed, now fell into great agitation, which even the consciousness of our presence could not enable her to hide.

'Rudolf, must you go? Since—since this has happened——'

'Hush, my dearest lady,' he whispered. Then he went on more loudly: 'I won't quit Ruritania a second time leaving Rupert of Hentzau alive. Fritz, send word to Sapt that the King is in Strelsau—he will understand—and that instructions from the King will follow by midday. When I have killed Rupert, I shall visit the lodge on my way to the frontier.'

He turned to go, but the Queen, following, detained him for a minute.

'You'll come and see me before you go?' she pleaded.

'But I ought not,' said he, his resolute eyes suddenly softening in a marvellous fashion.

'You will?'

'Yes, my Queen.'

Then I sprang up, for a sudden dread laid hold on me.

'Heavens, man!' I cried. 'What if he kills you—there in the Königstrasse?'

Rudolf turned to me; there was a look of surprise on his face.

'He won't kill me,' he answered.

The Queen, looking still in Rudolf's face, and forgetful now, it seemed, of the dream that had so terrified her, took no notice of what I said, but urged again:

'You'll come, Rudolf?'

'Yes, once, my Queen,' and with a last kiss of her hand he was gone.

The Queen stood for yet another moment where she was, still and almost rigid. Then suddenly she walked or stumbled to where my wife sat, and, flinging herself on her knees, hid her face in Helga's lap; I heard her sobs break out fast and tumultuously. Helga looked up at me, the tears streaming down her cheeks. I turned and went out. Perhaps Helga could comfort her; I prayed that God in His pity might send her comfort, although she for her sin's sake dared not ask it of Him. Poor soul! I hope there may be nothing worse scored to my account.

CHAPTER XV

A Pastime for Colonel Sapt

THE Constable of Zenda and James, Mr Rassendyll's servant, sat at breakfast in the hunting-lodge. They were in the small room which was ordinarily used as the bedroom of the gentleman in attendance on the King: they chose it now because it commanded a view of the approach. The door of the house was securely fastened: they were prepared to refuse admission; in case refusal were impossible, the preparations for concealing the King's body and that of his huntsman Herbert were complete. Inquirers would be told that the King had ridden out with his huntsman at daybreak, promising to return in the evening, but not stating where he was going; Sapt was under orders to await his return, and James was expecting instructions from his master the Count of Tarlenheim. Thus armed against discovery, they looked for news from me which should determine their future action.

Meanwhile there was an interval of enforced idleness. Sapt, his meal finished, puffed away at his great pipe; James, after much pressure, had consented to light a small black clay, and sat at his ease with his legs stretched before him. His brows were knit, and a curious half-smile played about his mouth.

'What may you be thinking about, friend James?' asked the Constable between two puffs. He had taken a fancy to the alert, ready little fellow.

James smoked for a moment, then took his pipe from his mouth.

'I was thinking, sir, that since the King is dead——' He paused.

'The King is no doubt dead, poor fellow,' said Sapt, nodding.

'That since he's certainly dead, and since my master, Mr Rassendyll, is alive——'

'So far as we know, James,' Sapt reminded him.

'I venture to differ from you'

'Why, yes, sir, so far as we know. Since, then, Mr Rassendyll is alive and the King is dead, I was thinking that it was a great pity, sir, that my master can't take his place and be King.'

James looked across at the Constable with an air of a man who offers a respectful suggestion.

'A remarkable thought, James,' observed the Constable with a grin.

'You don't agree with me, sir?' asked James deprecatingly.

'I don't say that it isn't a pity, for Rudolf makes a good king. But you see it's impossible, isn't it?'

James nursed his knee between his hands, and his pipe, which he had replaced, stuck out of one corner of his mouth.

'When you say impossible, sir,' he remarked deferentially, 'I venture to differ from you.'

'You do? Come, we're at leisure. Let's hear how it would be possible.'

'My master is in Strelsau, sir,' began James.

'Well, most likely.'

'I'm sure of it, sir. If he's seen there, he will be taken for the King.'

'That has happened before, and no doubt may happen again, unless——'

'Why, of course, sir, unless the King's body should be dis-covered.'

'That's what I was about to say, James.'

James kept silence for a few minutes. Then he observed:

'It will be very awkward to explain how the King was killed.'

'The story will need good telling,' admitted Sapt.

'And it will be difficult to make it appear that the King was killed in Strelsau; yet if my master should chance to be killed in Strelsau——'

'Heaven forbid, James! On all grounds, Heaven forbid!'

'Even if my master is not killed, it will be difficult for us to get the King killed at the right time, and by means that will seem plausible.'

Sapt seemed to fall into the humour of the speculation.

'That's all very true. But if Mr Rassendyll is to be King, it will be both awkward and difficult to dispose of the King's body and of this poor fellow Herbert,' said he, sucking at his pipe.

Again James paused for a little while before he remarked:

'I am, of course, sir, only discussing the matter by way of passing the time. It would probably be wrong to carry any such plan into effect.'

'It might be, but let us discuss it—to pass the time,' said Sapt; and he leant forward, looking into the servant's quiet shrewd face.

'Well, then, sir, since it amuses you, let us say that the King came to the lodge last night, and was joined there by his friend Mr Rassendyll.'

'And did I come too?'

'You, sir, came also in attendance on the King.'

'Well, and you, James? You came. How came you?'

'Why, sir, by the Count of Tarlenheim's orders, to wait on Mr Rassendyll, the King's friend. Now the King, sir . . . This is my story, you know, sir, only my story.'

'Your story interests me. Go on with it.'

'The King went out very early this morning, sir.'

'That would be on private business?'

'So we should have understood. But Mr Rassendyll, Herbert and ourselves remained here.'

'Had the Count of Hentzau been?'

'Not to our knowledge, sir. But we were all tired and slept very soundly.'

'Now did we?' said the Constable with a grim smile.

'In fact, sir, we were all overcome with fatigue—Mr Rassendyll like the rest—and full morning found us still in our beds. There we should be to this moment, sir, had we not been suddenly aroused in a startling and fearful manner.'

'You should write story-books, James. Now what was this fearful manner in which we were aroused?'

James laid down his pipe, and resting his hands on his knees, continued his story.

'This lodge, sir, this wooden lodge—for the lodge is all of wood, sir, without and within.'

'This lodge is undoubtedly of wood, James, and, as you say, both inside and out.'

'And since it is, sir, it would be mighty careless to leave a candle burning where the oil and firewood are stored.'

'Most criminal!'

'But hard words don't hurt dead men; and you see, sir, poor Herbert is dead.'

'It is true. He wouldn't feel aggrieved.'

'But we, sir, you and I, awaking——'

'Aren't the others to awake, James?'

'Indeed, sir, I should pray that they had never awaked. For you and I, waking first, would find the lodge a mass of flames. We should have to run for our lives.'

'What? Should we make no effort to rouse the others?'

'Indeed, sir, we should do all that men could do; we should even risk death by suffocation.'

'But we should fail, in spite of our heroism, should we?'

'Alas, sir, in spite of all our efforts we should fail. The flames would envelop the lodge in one blaze; before help could come,

the lodge would be in ruins and my unhappy master and poor
Herbert would be consumed to ashes.'

'Hum!'

'They would, at least, sir, be entirely unrecognizable.'

'You think so?'

'Beyond doubt, if the oil and the firewood and the candle were
placed to the best advantage.'

'Ah, yes. And there would be an end of Rudolf Rassendyll?'

'Sir, I should myself carry the tidings to his family.'

'Whereas the King of Ruritania——'

'Would enjoy a long and prosperous reign, God willing, sir.'

'And the Queen of Ruritania, James?'

'Do not misunderstand me, sir. They could be secretly married
—I should say remarried.'

'Yes, certainly remarried.'

'By a trustworthy priest.'

'You mean an untrustworthy priest?'

'It's the same thing, sir, from a different point of view.'

For the first time James smiled a thoughtful smile.

Sapt in his turn laid down his pipe now, and was tugging at
his moustache. There was a smile on his lips, too, and his eyes
looked hard into James's. The little man met his glance composedly.

'It's an ingenious fancy, this of yours, James,' the Constable
remarked. 'What, though, if your master's killed, too? That's
quite possible. Count Rupert's a man to be reckoned with.'

'If my master is killed, sir, he must be buried,' answered James.

'In Strelsau?' came in quick question from Sapt.

'He won't mind where, sir.'

'True, he won't mind, and we needn't mind for him.'

'Why, no, sir. But to carry a body secretly from here to
Strelsau——'

'Yes, that is, as we agreed at the first, difficult. Well, it's a pretty
story, but—your master wouldn't approve of it. Supposing he
were not killed, I mean.'

'It's waste of time, sir, disapproving of what's done: he might
think the story better than the truth, although it's not a good
story.'

M

The two men's eyes met again in a long glance.

'Where do you come from?' asked Sapt suddenly.

'London, sir, originally.'

'They make good stories there?'

'Yes, sir, and act them sometimes.'

The instant he had spoken, James sprang to his feet and pointed out of the window.

A man on horseback was cantering towards the lodge. Exchanging one quick look, both hastened to the door, and, advancing some twenty yards, waited under the tree, on the spot where Boris lay buried.

'By the way,' said Sapt, 'you forgot the dog,' and he pointed to the ground.

'The affectionate beast will be in his master's room, and die there, sir.'

'Eh, but he must rise again first!'

'Certainly, sir. That won't be a long matter.'

Sapt was still smiling in grim amusement when the messenger came up and, leaning from his horse, handed him a telegram.

'Special and urgent, sir,' said he.

Sapt tore it open and read. It was the message that I sent in obedience to Mr Rassendyll's orders. He would not trust my cipher, but, indeed, none was necessary. Sapt would understand the message, although it said simply:

'The King is in Strelsau. Wait orders at the lodge. Business here in progress, but not finished. Will wire again.'

Sapt handed it to James, who took it with a respectful bow. James read it with attention, and returned it with another bow.

'I'll attend to what it says, sir,' he remarked.

'Yes,' said Sapt. 'Thanks, my man,' he added to the messenger. 'Here's a crown for you. If any other message comes for me and you bring it in good time, you shall have another.'

'You shall have it as quick as a horse can bring it from the station, sir.'

'The King's business won't bear delay, you know,' nodded Sapt.

'You shan't have to wait, sir,' and, with a parting salute, the fellow turned his horse and trotted away.

'You see,' remarked Sapt, 'that your story is quite imaginary. For that fellow can see for himself that the lodge was not burnt down last night.'

'That's true; but excuse me, sir——'

'Pray go on, James. I've told you that I'm interested.'

'He can't see that it won't be burnt down tonight. A fire, sir, is a thing that may happen any night.'

Then old Sapt suddenly burst into a roar, half-speech, half-laughter.

'By God, what a thing!' he roared; and James smiled complacently.

'There's a fate about it,' said the Constable. 'There's a strange fate about it. The man was born to it. We'd have done it before if Michael had throttled the King in that cellar, as I thought he would. Yes, by Heaven, we'd have done it! Why, we wanted it! God forgive us, in our hearts both Fritz and I wanted it. But Rudolf would have the King out. He would have him out, though he lost a throne—and what he wanted more— by it. But he would have him out. So he thwarted the fate. But it's not to be thwarted. Young Rupert may think this new affair is his doing. No, it's the fate using him. The fate brought Rudolf here again, the fate will have him King. Well, you stare at me. Do you think I'm mad, Mr Valet?'

'I think, sir, that you talk very good sense, if I may say so,' answered James.

'Sense?' echoed Sapt, with a chuckle. 'I don't know about that. But the fate's there, depend on it!'

The two were back in their little room now, past the door that hid the bodies of the King and his huntsman. James stood by the table, old Sapt roamed up and down, tugging his moustache and now and again sawing the air with his sturdy hairy hand.

'I daren't do it,' he muttered. 'I daren't do it. It's a thing a man can't set his hand to of his own will. But the fate'll do it— the fate'll do it. The fate'll force it on us.'

'Then we'd best be ready, sir,' suggested James quietly.

Sapt turned on him quickly, almost fiercely.

'They used to call me a cool hand,' said he. 'By Jove! what are you?'

'There's no harm in being ready, sir,' said James the servant.
Sapt came to him and caught hold of his shoulders.

'Ready?' he asked in a gruff whisper.

'The oil, the firewood, the light,' said James.

'Where, man, where? Do you mean by the bodies?'

'Not where the bodies are now. Each must be in the proper place.'

'We must move them, then?'

'Why, yes. And the dog too.'

Sapt almost glared at him; then he burst into a laugh.

'So be it,' he said. 'You take command. Yes, we'll be ready.
The fate drives.'

Then and there they set about what they had to do. It seemed
indeed as though some strange influence were dominating Sapt:
he went about the work like a man who is hardly awake. They
placed the bodies each where the living man would be by night—
the King in the guest-room, the huntsman in the sort of cupboard where the honest fellow had been wont to lie. They dug
up the buried dog, Sapt chuckling convulsively, James grave as
the mute whose grim doings he seemed to travesty; they carried
the shot-pierced earth-grimed thing in, and laid it in the King's
room. Then they made their piles of wood, pouring the store of
oil over them, and setting bottles of spirits near, that the flames,
having cracked the bottles, might gain fresh fuel. To Sapt it
seemed now as if they played some foolish game that was to end
with the playing, now as if they obeyed some mysterious power
which kept its great purpose hidden from the instruments. Mr
Rassendyll's servant moved and arranged and ordered all as deftly
as he folded his master's clothes or stropped his master's razor.
Old Sapt stopped him once as he went by.

'Don't think me a mad fool, because I talk of the fate,' he said,
almost anxiously.

'Not I, sir,' answered James; 'I know nothing of that. But I
like to be ready.'

'It would be a thing!' muttered Sapt.

The mockery, real or assumed, in which they had begun their
work had vanished now. If they were not serious, they played at
seriousness. If they entertained no intention such as their acts
seemed to indicate, they could no longer deny that they cherished

a hope. They shrank, or at least Sapt shrank, from setting such a ball rolling; but they longed for the fate that would give it a kick, and they made smooth the incline down which it, when thus impelled, was to run. When they had finished their task and sat down again opposite to one another in the little front room, the whole scheme was ready, the preparations were made, all was in train; they waited only for that impulse from chance or fate which was to turn the servant's story into reality and action. And when the thing was done, Sapt's coolness, so rarely upset, yet so completely beaten by the force of that wild idea, came back to him. He lit his pipe again and lay back in his chair, puffing freely, with a meditative look on his face.

'It's two o'clock, sir,' said James. 'Something should have happened before now in Strelsau.'

'Ah, but what?' asked the Constable.

Suddenly breaking on their ears came a loud knock at the door. Absorbed in their own thoughts, they had not noticed two men riding up to the lodge. The visitors wore the green and gold of the King's huntsmen; the one who had knocked was Simon, the chief huntsman, and brother of Herbert who lay dead in the little room inside.

'Rather dangerous!' muttered the Constable of Zenda as he hurried to the door, James following him.

Simon was astonished when Sapt opened the door.

'Beg pardon, Constable, but I want to see Herbert. Can I go in?' And he jumped down from his horse, throwing the reins to his companion.

'What's the good of your going in?' asked Sapt. 'Herbert's not here.'

'Not here? Then where is he?'

'Why, he went with the King this morning.'

'Oh, he went with the King, sir? Then he's in Strelsau, I suppose?'

'If you know that, Simon, you're wiser than I am.'

'But the King is in Strelsau, sir.'

'The deuce he is! He said nothing of going to Strelsau. He rose early and rode off with Herbert, merely saying they would be back tonight.'

'He went to Strelsau, sir. I am just from Zenda, and His Majesty is known to have been in town with the Queen. They were both at Count Fritz's.'

'I'm much interested to hear it. But didn't the telegram say where Herbert was?'

Simon laughed.

'Herbert's not a king, you see,' he said. 'Well, I'll come again tomorrow morning, for I must see him soon. He'll be back by then, sir?'

'Yes, Simon, your brother will be here tomorrow morning.'

'Or what's left of him after such a two days of work,' suggested Simon jocularly.

'Why, yes, precisely,' said Sapt, biting his moustache and darting one swift glance at James. 'Or what's left of him, as you say.'

'And I'll bring a cart and carry the boar down to the Castle at the same time, sir. At least I suppose you haven't eaten it all?'

Sapt laughed; Simon was gratified at the tribute, and laughed even more heartily himself.

'We haven't even cooked it yet,' said Sapt, 'but I won't answer for it that we shan't have by tomorrow.'

'All right, sir; I'll be here. By the way, there's another bit of news come on the wires. They say Count Rupert of Hentzau has been seen in the city.'

'Rupert of Hentzau? Oh, pooh! Nonsense, my good Simon. He daren't show his face there for his life.'

'Ah, but it may be no nonsense. Perhaps that's what took the King to Strelsau.'

'It's enough to take him if it's true,' admitted Sapt.

'Well, good day, sir.'

'Good day, Simon.'

The two huntsmen rode off. James watched them for a little while.

'The King,' he said then, 'is known to be in Strelsau; and now Count Rupert is known to be in Strelsau. How is Count Rupert to have killed the King here in the forest of Zenda, sir?'

Sapt looked at him almost apprehensively.

'How is the King's body to come to the forest of Zenda?'

asked James. 'Or how is the King's body to go to the city of
Strelsau?'

'Stop your damned riddles!' roared Sapt. 'Man, are you bent
on driving me into it?'

The servant came near to him, and laid a hand on his shoulder.

'You went into as great a thing once before, sir,' said he.

'It was to save the King.'

'And this is to save the Queen and yourself. For if we don't do
it, the truth about my master must be known.'

Sapt made him no answer. They sat down again in silence.
There they sat, sometimes smoking, never speaking, while the
tedious afternoon wore away and the shadows from the trees of
the forest lengthened. They did not think of eating or drinking;
they did not move, save when James rose and lit a little fire of
brushwood in the grate. It grew dusk, and again James moved to
light the lamp. It was hard on six o'clock, and still no news from
Strelsau.

Then there was the sound of a horse's hoofs. The two rushed
to the door, beyond it, and far along the grassy road that gave
approach to the hunting-lodge. They forgot to guard the secret,
and the door gaped open behind them. Sapt ran as he had not run
for many a day, and outstripped his companion. There was a
message from Strelsau!

The Constable, without a word of greeting, snatched the
envelope from the hand of the messenger and tore it open. He
read it hastily, muttering under his breath, 'Good God!' Then
he turned suddenly round and began to walk quickly back to
James, who, seeing himself beaten in the race, had dropped to a
walk. But the messenger had his cares as well as the Constable.
If the Constable's thoughts were on a crown, so were his. He
called out in indignant protest:

'I've never drawn rein since Hofbau, sir. Am I not to have
my crown?'

Sapt stopped, turned, and retraced his steps. He took a crown
from his pocket. As he looked up in giving it, there was a queer
smile on his broad, weather-beaten face.

'Aye,' he said, 'every man that deserves a crown shall have one,
if I can give it him.'

Then he turned again to James, who had now come up, and laid his hand on his shoulder.

'Come along, my king-maker,' said he.

James looked in his face for a moment. The Constable's eyes met his, and the Constable nodded.

So they turned to the lodge where the dead King and his hunstman lay. Verily the fate drove.

CHAPTER XVI

A Crowd in the Königstrasse

THE project that had taken shape in the thoughts of Mr Rassendyll's servant, and had inflamed Sapt's daring mind as the
dropping of a spark kindles dry shavings, had suggested itself
vaguely to more than one of us in Strelsau. We did not indeed
coolly face and plan it, as the little servant had, nor seize on it at
once with an eagerness to be convinced of its necessity like the
Constable of Zenda; but it was there in my mind, sometimes
figuring as a dread, sometimes as a hope, now seeming the one
thing to be avoided, again the only resource against a more
disastrous issue. I knew that it was in Bernenstein's thoughts no
less than in my own; for neither of us had been able to form any
reasonable scheme by which the living King, whom half Strelsau
now knew to be in the city, could be spirited away, and the dead
King set in his place. The change could take place, as it seemed,
only in one way and at one cost; the truth, or the better part of it,
must be told, and every tongue set wagging with gossip and
guesses concerning Rudolf Rassendyll and his relations with the
Queen. Who that knows what men and women are would not
have shrunk from that alternative? To adopt it was to expose the
Queen to all, or nearly all, the peril she had run by the loss of
the letter. We indeed assumed, influenced by Rudolf's unhesitating self-confidence, that the letter would be won back,
and the mouth of Rupert of Hentzau shut; but enough would
remain to furnish material for eager talk and conjectures un-
restrained by respect or charity. Therefore, alive as we were
to its difficulties and its unending risks, we yet conceived of the
thing as possible, had it in our hearts, and hinted it to one
another—my wife to me, I to Bernenstein, and he to me—in
quick glances and half-uttered sentences that declared its presence
while shunning the open confession of it. For the Queen herself

I cannot speak. Her thoughts, as I judged them, were bounded by
the longing to see Mr Rassendyll again, and dwelt on the visit that
he promised as the horizon of hope. To Rudolf we had dared to
disclose nothing of the part our imaginations set him to play: if
he were to accept it, the acceptance would be of his own act,
because the fate that old Sapt talked of drove him and on no
persuasion of ours. As he had said, he left the rest, and had
centred all his efforts on the immediate task which fell to his hand
to perform, the task that was to be accomplished at the dingy old
house in the Königstrasse. We were fully awake to the fact that
even Rupert's death would not make the secret safe. Rischenheim, although for a moment a prisoner and helpless, was alive
and could not be mewed up for ever; Bauer was we knew not
where, free to act and free to talk. Yet in our hearts we feared
none but Rupert, and the doubt was not whether we could do the
thing so much as whether we should. For in moments of excitement and intense feeling a man makes light of obstacles which
look large enough as he turns reflective eyes on them in the quiet
of after days.

A message in the King's name had persuaded the best part of
the idle crowd to disperse reluctantly. Rudolf himself had entered
one of my carriages and driven off. He started, not towards the
Königstrasse, but in the opposite direction; I supposed that he
meant to approach his destination by a circuitous way, hoping to
gain it without attracting notice. The Queen's carriage was still
before my door, for it had been arranged that she was to proceed
to the palace and await tidings there. My wife and I were to
accompany her; and I went to her now, where she sat alone, and
asked if it were her pleasure to start at once. I found her thoughtful but calm. She listened to me; then, rising, she said: 'Yes, I
will go.' But then she asked suddenly, 'Where is the Count of
Luzau-Rischenheim?'

I told her how Bernenstein kept guard over the count in the
room at the back of the house. She seemed to consider for a
moment, then she said: 'I will see him. Go and bring him to me.
You must be here while I talk to him, but nobody else.'

I did not know what she intended, but I saw no reason to
oppose her wishes, and I was glad to find for her any means of

employing this time of suspense. I obeyed her commands and brought Rischenheim to her. He followed me slowly and reluctantly; his unstable mind had again jumped from rashness to despondency: he was pale and uneasy, and, when he found himself in her presence, the bravado of his bearing, maintained before Bernenstein, gave place to a shamefaced sullenness. He could not meet the grave eyes that she fixed on him.

I withdrew to the farther end of the room; but it was small, and I heard all that passed. I had my revolver ready to cover Rischenheim in case he should be moved to make a dash for liberty. But he was past that; Rupert's presence was a tonic that nerved him to effort and confidence, but the force of the last dose was gone, and the man had sunk again to his natural irresolution.

'My lord,' she began gently, motioning him to sit, 'I have desired to speak with you, because I do not wish a gentleman of your rank to think too much evil of his Queen. Heaven has willed that my secret should be to you no secret, and therefore I may speak plainly. You may say my own shame should silence me; I speak to lessen my shame in your eyes, if I can.'

Rischenheim looked up with a dull gaze, not understanding her mood. He had expected reproaches, and met low-voiced apology.

'And yet,' she went on, 'it is because of me that the King lies dead now; and a faithful humble fellow also, caught in the net of my unhappy fortunes, has given his life for me though he didn't know it. Even while we speak it may be that a gentleman, not too old yet to learn nobility, may be killed in my quarrel; while another, whom I alone of all that know him may not praise, carries his life lightly in his hand for me. And to you, my lord, I have done the wrong of dressing a harsh deed in some cloak of excuse, making you seem to serve the King in working my punishment.'

Rischenheim's eyes fell to the ground, and he twisted his hands nervously in and out, the one about the other. I took my hand from my revolver: he would not move now.

'I don't know', she went on, now, almost dreamily, and as though she spoke more to herself than to him, or had even forgotten his presence, 'what end in Heaven's counsel my great unhappiness has served. Perhaps I, who have place above most women, must also be tried above most; and in that trial I have failed. Yet, when I weigh my misery and my temptation, to my human eyes it seems that I have not failed greatly. My heart is not yet humbled, God's work not yet done. But the guilt of blood is on my soul—even the face of my dear love I can see now only through its scarlet mist: so that if what seemed my perfect joy were now granted me, it would come spoilt and stained and blotched.'

She paused, fixing her eyes on him again; but he neither spoke nor moved.

'You knew my sin,' she said, 'the sin so great in my heart; and you knew how little my acts yielded to it. Did you think, my lord, that the sin had no punishment, that you took it in hand to add shame to my suffering? Was Heaven so kind that men must temper its indulgence by their severity? Yet I know that because I was wrong, you, being wrong, might seem to yourself not wrong, and in aiding your kinsman might plead that you served the King's honour. Thus, my lord, I was the cause in you of a deed that your heart could not welcome nor your honour praise. I thank God that you have come to no more hurt by it.'

Rischenheim began to mutter in a low thick voice, his eyes still cast down:

'Rupert persuaded me. He said the King would be very grateful, and—would give me——' His voice died away, and he sat silent again, twisting his hands.

'I know—I know,' she said. 'But you wouldn't have listened to such persuasions if my fault hadn't blinded your eyes.'

She turned suddenly to me, who had been standing all the time aloof, and stretched out her hands towards me, her eyes filled with tears.

'Yet,' said she, 'your wife knows, and still loves me, Fritz.'

'She would be no wife of mine if she didn't,' I cried. 'For I and all of mine ask no better than to die for Your Majesty.'

'She knows, and yet she loves me,' repeated the Queen. I loved to see that she seemed to find comfort in Helga's love. It is

women to whom women turn, and women whom women fear.
'But Helga writes no letters,' said the Queen.

'Why, no,' said I, and I smiled a grim smile. Well, Rudolf
Rassendyll had never wooed my wife.

She rose, saying:

'Come, let us go to the palace.'

As she rose, Rischenheim made a quick impulsive step towards
her.

'Well, my lord,' said she, turning towards him, 'will you, too,
go with me?'

'Lieutenant von Bernenstein will take care——' I began. But
I stopped. The slightest gesture of her hand silenced me.

'Will you go with me?' she asked Rischenheim again.

'Madame,' he stammered, 'madame——'

She waited. I waited also, although I had no great patience with
him. Suddenly he fell on his knee, but he did not venture to take
her hand. Of her own accord she came and stretched it out to
him, saying sadly:

'Ah, that by forgiving I could win forgiveness!'

Rischenheim caught at her hand and kissed it.

'It was not I,' I heard him mutter. 'Rupert set me on, and I
couldn't stand out against him.'

'Will you go with me to the palace?' she asked, drawing her
hand away, but smiling.

'The Count of Luzau-Rischenheim', I made bold to observe,
'knows some things that most people do not know, madame.'

She turned on me with dignity, almost with displeasure.

'The Count of Luzau-Rischenheim may be trusted to be silent,'
she said. 'We ask him to do nothing against his cousin. We ask
only his silence.'

'Aye,' said I, braving her anger, 'but what security shall we have?'

'His word of honour, my lord.' I knew that a rebuke to my
presumption lay in her calling me 'my lord,' for, save on formal
occasions, she always used to call me Fritz.

'His word of honour!' I grumbled. 'In truth, madame——'

'He's right,' said Rischenheim. 'He's right.'

'No, he's wrong,' said the Queen, smiling. 'The count will
keep his word, given to me.'

Rischenheim looked at her and seemed about to address her, but then he turned to me and said in a low tone.

'By Heaven, I will, Tarlenheim. I'll serve her in everything.'

'My lord,' said she most graciously, and yet most sadly, 'you lighten the burden on me no less by your help than because I no longer feel your honour stained through me. Come, we will go to the palace.' And she went to him, saying: 'We will go together.'

There was nothing for it but to trust him. I knew that I could not turn her.

'Then I'll see if the carriage is ready,' said I.

'Yes, do, Fritz,' said the Queen. But as I passed she stopped me for a moment, saying in a whisper: 'Show that you trust him.'

I went and held out my hand to him. He took and pressed it.

'On my honour,' he said.

Then I went out, and found Bernenstein sitting on a bench in the hall. The lieutenant was a diligent and watchful young man; he appeared to be examining his revolver with sedulous care.

'You can put that away,' said I rather peevishly—I had not fancied shaking hands with Rischenheim. 'He's not a prisoner any longer. He's one of us now.'

'The deuce he is!' cried Bernenstein, springing to his feet.

I told him briefly what had happened, and how the Queen had won Rupert's instrument to be her servant.

'I suppose he'll stick to it,' I ended; and I thought he would, though I was not eager for his help.

A light gleamed in Bernenstein's eyes, and I felt a tremble in the hand that he laid on my shoulder.

'Then there's only Bauer now,' he whispered. 'If Rischenheim's with us, only Bauer.'

I knew very well what he meant. With Rischenheim silent, Bauer was the only man, save Rupert himself, who knew the truth, the only man who threatened that great scheme, which more and more filled our thoughts and grew upon us with an increasing force of attraction as every obstacle to it seemed to be cleared out of the way. But I would not look at Bernenstein, fearing to acknowledge even with my eyes how my mind jumped with his. He was bolder, or less scrupulous—which you will.

'Yes, if we can shut Bauer's mouth——' he went on.

'The Queen's waiting for the carriage,' I interrupted snappishly.

'Ah, yes, of course, the carriage,' and he twisted me round till I was forced to look him in the face. Then he smiled and even laughed a little. 'Only Bauer now!' said he.

'And Rupert,' I remarked sourly.

'Oh, Rupert's dead bones by now,' he chuckled, and with that he went out of the hall door and announced the Queen's approach to her servants. It must be said for young Bernenstein that he was a cheerful fellow conspirator. His equanimity almost matched Rudolf's own; I could not rival it myself.

I drove to the palace with the Queen and my wife, the other two following in a second carriage. I do not know what they said to one another on the way, but Bernenstein was civil enough to his companion when I rejoined them. With us my wife was the principal speaker: she filled up, from what Rudolf had told her, the gaps in our knowledge of how he had spent his night in Strelsau, and by the time we arrived we were fully informed in every detail. The Queen said little. The impulse which had dictated her appeal to Rischenheim and carried her through it seemed to have died away; she had become again subject to fears and apprehension. I saw her uneasiness when she suddenly put out her hand and touched mine, whispering:

'He must be at the house by now.'

Our way did not lie by the house, and we came to the palace without any news of our absent chief (so I call him—as such we all, from the Queen herself, then regarded him). She did not speak of him again; but her eyes seemed to follow me about as though she were silently asking some service of me; what it was I could not understand. Bernenstein had disappeared, and the repentant count with him: knowing they were together, I was in no uneasiness; Bernenstein would see that his companion contrived no treachery. But I was puzzled by the Queen's tacit appeal. And I was myself on fire for news from the Königstrasse. It was now two hours since Rudolf Rassendyll had left us, and no word had come of him or from him. At last I could bear it no longer. The Queen was sitting with her hand in my wife's; I had been seated on the other side of the room, for I thought that they might wish to talk to one another; yet I had not seen them exchange a word. I rose abruptly and crossed the room to where they were.

'Have you need of my presence, madame, or have I your permission to be away for a time?' I asked.

'Where do you wish to go, Fritz?' the Queen asked with a little start, as though I had come suddenly across her thoughts.

'To the Königstrasse,' said I.

To my surprise she rose and caught my hand.

'God bless you, Fritz!' she cried. 'I don't think I could have endured it longer. But I wouldn't ask you to go. But go, my dear friend, go and bring me news of him. Oh, Fritz, I seemed to dream that dream again!'

My wife looked up at me with a brave smile and a trembling lip.

'Shall you go into the house, Fritz?' she asked.

'Not unless I see need, sweetheart,' said I.

She came and kissed me.

'Go if you are wanted,' she said. And she tried to smile at the Queen, as though she risked me willingly.

'I could have been such a wife, Fritz,' whispered the Queen. 'Yes, I could.'

I had nothing to say; at the moment I might not have been able to say it if I had. There is something in the helpless courage of women that makes me feel soft. We can work and fight; they sit and wait. Yet they do not flinch. Now I know that if I had to sit and think about the thing I should turn cur.

Well, I went, leaving them there together. I put on plain clothes instead of my uniform, and dropped my revolver into the pocket of my coat. Thus prepared, I slipped out and made my way on foot to the Königstrasse.

It was now long past midday. Many folk were still at their dinner and the streets were not full. Two or three people recognized me, but I passed by most unnoticed. There was no sign of stir or excitement, and the flags still floated high in the wind. Sapt had kept the secret: the men of Strelsau thought still that their King lived and was among them. I feared that Rudolf's coming would have been seen, and expected to find a crowd of people near the house. But when I reached it there were no more than ten or a dozen idle fellows lounging about. I began to stroll up and down with as careless an air as I could assume.

Soon, however, there was a change. The workmen and business-folk, their meal finished, began to come out of their houses and from the restaurants. The loafers before No. 19 spoke to many of them. Some said 'Indeed!' shook their heads, smiled and passed on: they had no time to waste in staring at the King. But many waited; lighting their cigars or cigarettes or pipes, they stood gossiping with one another, looking at their watches now and again, lest they should overstay their leisure. Thus the assembly grew to the number of a couple of hundred. I ceased my walk, for the pavement was too crowded, and hung on the out-skirts of the throng. As I loitered there, a cigar in my mouth, I felt a hand on my shoulder. Turning round, I saw the lieutenant. He was in uniform. By his side was Rischenheim.

'You're here too, are you?' said I. 'Well, nothing seems to be happening, does it?'

For No. 19 showed no sign of life. The shutters were up, the door closed; the little shop was not open for business that day.

Bernenstein shook his head with a smile. His companion took no heed of my remark; he was evidently in a state of great agita-tion, and his eyes never left the door of the house. I was about to address him, when my attention was abruptly and completely diverted by a glimpse of a head, caught across the shoulders of the bystanders.

The fellow whom I saw wore a brown wideawake hat. The hat was pulled low down over his forehead, but nevertheless beneath its rim there appeared a white bandage running round his head. I could not see the face, but the bullet-shaped skull was very familiar to me. I was sure from the first moment that the ban-daged man was Bauer. Saying nothing to Bernenstein, I began to steal round outside the crowd. As I went, I heard somebody saying that it was all nonsense; the King was not there; what should the King do in such a house? The answer was a reference to one of the first loungers; he replied that he did not know what the devil the King did there, but that the King or his double had certainly gone in, and had as certainly not yet come out again. I wished I could have made myself known to them and persuaded

N

them to go away: but my presence would have outweighed my declarations, and been taken as a sure sign that the King was in the house. So I kept on the outskirts and worked my way unobtrusively towards the bandaged head. Evidently Bauer's hurt had not been so serious as to prevent him leaving the infirmary to which the police had carried him. He was come now to await, even as I was awaiting, the issue of Rudolf's visit to the house in the Königstrasse.

He had not seen me, for he was looking at No. 19 as intently as Rischenheim. Apparently neither had caught sight of the other, or Rischenheim would have shown some embarrassment, Bauer some excitement. I wormed my way quickly towards my former servant. My mind was full of the idea of getting hold of him. I could not forget Bernenstein's remark, 'Only Bauer now!' If I could secure Bauer we were safe. Safe in what? I did not answer to myself, but the old idea was working in me. Safe in our secret and safe in our plan—in the plan on which we all, we here in the city, and those two at the hunting-lodge, had set our minds! Bauer's death, Bauer's capture, Bauer's silence, however procured, would clear the greatest hindrance from its way.

Bauer stared intently at the house; I crept cautiously up behind him. His hand was in his trousers pocket; where the curve of the elbow came there was a space between arm and body. I slipped in my left arm and hooked it firmly inside his. He turned round and saw me.

'Thus we meet again, Bauer,' said I.

He was for a moment flabbergasted, and stared stupidly at me.

'Are you also hoping to see the King?' I asked.

He began to recover himself. A slow cunning smile spread over his face.

'The King?' he asked.

'Well, he's in Strelsau, isn't he? Who gave you the wound on your head?'

Bauer moved his arm as though he meant to withdraw it from my grasp. He found himself tightly held.

'Where's that bag of mine?' I asked.

I do not know what he would have answered, for at this instant there came a sound from behind the closed door of the house.

It was as if someone ran rapidly and eagerly towards the door. Then came an oath in a shrill voice, a woman's voice, but harsh and rough. It was answered by an angry cry in a girl's intonation. Full of eagerness, I drew my arm from Bauer's and sprang forward. I heard a chuckle from him, and turned round to see his bandaged head retreating rapidly down the street. I had no time to look to him; for now I saw two men, shoulder to shoulder, making their way through the crowd, regardless of anyone in their way, and paying no attention to abuse or remonstrances. They were the lieutenant and Rischenheim. Without a moment's hesitation I set myself to push and battle a way through, thinking to join them in front. On they went, and on I went. All gave place before us in surly reluctance or frightened willingness. We three were together in the first rank of the crowd when the door of the house was flung open, and a girl ran out. Her hair was disordered, her face pale and her eyes full of alarm. There she stood on the doorstep, facing the crowd, which in an instant grew as if by magic to three times its former size, and, little knowing what she did, she cried in the eager accents of sheer terror:

'Help, help! The King! The King!'

Chapter XVII

Young Rupert and the Play-Actor

THERE rises often before my mind the picture of young Rupert, standing where Rischenheim left him, awaiting the return of his messenger and watching for some sign that should declare to Strelsau the death of its King which his own hand had wrought. His image is one that memory holds clear and distinct, though time may blur the shape of greater and better men; and the position in which he was that morning gives play enough to the imagination. Save for Rischenheim—a broken reed—and Bauer, who was gone none knew where, he stood alone against a kingdom which he had robbed of its head and a band of resolute men who would know no rest and no security so long as he lived. For protection he had only a quick brain, his courage and his secret. Yet he could not fly—he was without resources till his cousin furnished them—and at any moment his opponents might find themselves able to declare the King's death and raise the city in hue and cry after him. Such men do not repent; but it may be that he regretted the enterprise which had led him on so far and forced on him a deed so momentous; yet to those who knew him it seems more likely that the smile broadened on his firm full lips as he looked down on the unconscious city. Well, I dare say he would have been too much for me; but I wish I had been the man to find him there. He would not have had it so; for I believe that he asked no better than to cross swords again with Rudolf Rassendyll and set his fortunes on the issue.

Down below, the old woman was cooking a stew for her dinner, now and then grumbling to herself that the Count of Luzau-Rischenheim was so long away, and Bauer, the rascal, drunk in some pothouse. The kitchen door stood open, and through it could be seen the girl Rosa, busily scrubbing the tiled floor; her colour was high and her eyes bright; from time to time

188

she paused in her task, and, raising her head, seemed to listen. The time at which the King needed her was past, but the King had not come. How little the old woman knew for whom she listened! All her talk had been of Bauer—why Bauer did not come, and what could have befallen him. It was grand to hold the King's secret for him, and she would hold it with her life; for he had been kind and gracious to her, and he was her man of all the men in Strelsau. Bauer was a stumpy fellow; the Count of Hentzau was handsome, handsome as the devil; but the King was her man. And the King had trusted her; she would die before hurt should come to him.

There were wheels in the street—quick-rolling wheels. They seemed to stop a few doors away, then to roll on again past the house. The girl's head was raised; the old woman, engrossed in her stew, took no heed. The girl's straining ear caught a rapid step outside. Then it came—the knock, the sharp knock followed by five light ones. The old woman heard now: dropping her spoon into the pot she lifted the mess off the fire and turned round, saying:

'There's the rogue at last! Open the door for him, Rosa.'

Before she spoke Rosa had darted down the passage. The door opened and shut again. The old woman waddled to the threshold of the kitchen. The passage and the shop were dark behind closed shutters; but the figure by the girl's side was taller than Bauer's.

'Who's there?' cried Mother Holf sharply. 'The shop's shut today; you can't come in.'

'But I am in,' came the answer, and Rudolf stepped towards her. The girl followed a pace behind, her hands clasped and her eyes alight with excitement. 'Don't you know me?' asked Rudolf, standing opposite the old woman and smiling down on her.

There, in the dim light of the low-roofed passage, Mother Holf was fairly puzzled. She knew the story of Mr Rassendyll; she knew that he was again in Ruritania, it was no surprise to her that he should be in Strelsau; but she did not know that Rupert had killed the King, and she had not seen the King close at hand since his illness, and his beard impaired what had been a perfect likeness. In fine she could not tell whether it were indeed the King who spoke to her or his counterfeit.

'Who are you?' she asked, curt and blunt in her confusion.
The girl broke in with an amused laugh.

'Why, it's the——'

She paused. Perhaps the King's identity was a secret.
Rudolf nodded to her.

'Tell her who I am,' said he.

'Why, mother, it's the King,' whispered Rosa, laughing and
blushing. 'The King, mother.'

'Aye, if the King's alive, I'm the King,' said Rudolf.

I suppose he wanted to find out how much the old woman
knew.

She made no answer, but stared up at his face. In her bewilderment she forgot to ask how he had learnt the signal that gained
him admission.

'I've come to see the Count of Hentzau,' Rudolf continued.
'Take me to him at once.'

The old woman was across his path in a moment, all defiant,
arms akimbo.

'Nobody can see the count. He's not here,' she blurted out.

'What, can't the King see him? Not even the King?'

'King?' she cried, peering at him. 'Are you the King?'

Rosa burst out laughing.

'Mother, you must have seen the King a hundred times.' she
laughed.

'The King or his ghost—what does it matter?' said Rudolf
lightly.

The old woman drew back with an appearance of sudden
alarm.

'His ghost? Is he——?'

'His ghost!' rang out in the girl's merry laugh. 'Why, here's
the King himself, mother. You don't look much like a ghost, sir.'

Mother Holf's face was livid now, and her eyes staring fixedly.
Perhaps it shot into her brain that something had happened to
the King, and that this man had come because of it—this man
who was indeed the image, and might have been the spirit of the
King. She leant against the doorpost, her broad bosom heaving
under her scanty stuff gown. Yet still—was it not the King?

'God help us!' she muttered in fear and bewilderment.

'He helps us, never fear,' said Rudolf Rassendyll. 'Where is Count Rupert?'

The girl had caught alarm from her mother's agitation.

'He's upstairs in the attic at the top of the house, sir,' she whispered in frightened tones, with a glance that fled from her mother's terrified face to Rudolf's set eyes and steady smile.

What she said was enough for him. He slipped by the old woman and began to mount the stairs.

The two watched him, Mother Holf as though fascinated, the girl alarmed but still triumphant: she had done what the King bade her. Rudolf turned the corner of the first landing and disappeared from their sight. The old woman, swearing and muttering, stumbled back into her kitchen, put her stew on the fire, and began to stir it, her eyes set on the flames and careless of the pot. The girl watched her mother for a moment, wondering how she could think of the stew, not guessing that she turned the spoon without a thought of what she did; then she began to crawl, quickly but noiselessly, up the staircase in the track of Rudolf Rassendyll. She looked back once: the old woman stirred with a monotonous circular movement of her fat arm. Rosa, bent half-double, skimmed upstairs, till she came in sight of the King whom she was so proud to serve. He was on the top landing now, outside the door of the large attic where Rupert of Hentzau was lodged. She saw him lay his hand on the latch of the door; his other hand rested in the pocket of his coat. From the room no sound came; Rupert may have heard the step outside and stood motionless to listen. Rudolf opened the door and walked in. The girl darted breathlessly up the remaining steps, and coming to the door just as it swung back on the latch, crouched down by it, listening to what passed within, catching glimpses of forms and movements through the chinks of the crazy hinge and the crevices where the wood of the panel had sprung and left a narrow eyehole for her absorbed gazing.

Rupert of Hentzau had no thought of ghosts; the men he killed lay still where they fell, and slept where they were buried. And he had no wonder at the sight of Rudolf Rassendyll. It told him no more than that Rischenheim's errand had fallen out ill, at which he was not surprised, and that his old enemy was again in his path, at which (as I verily believe) he was more glad than sorry. As Rudolf entered, he had been half way between window and table; he came forward to the table now, and stood leaning the points of two fingers on the unpolished, dirty wood.

'Ah, the play-actor!' said he, with a gleam of his teeth and a toss of his curls, while his second hand, like Mr Rassendyll's, rested in the pocket of his coat.

Mr Rassendyll himself had confessed that in old days it went against the grain with him when Rupert called him a play-actor. He was a little older now, and his temper more difficult to stir.

'Yes, the play-actor,' he answered, smiling. 'With a shorter part this time, though.'

'What part today? Isn't it the old one, the King with a pasteboard crown?' asked Rupert, sitting down on the table. 'Faith, we shall do handsomely in Ruritania: you have a pasteboard crown, and I (humble man though I am) have given the other one a heavenly crown. What a brave show! But perhaps I tell you news?'

'No, I know what you've done.'

'I take no credit. It was more the dog's doing than mine,' said Rupert carelessly. 'However, there it is, and dead he is, and there's an end of it. What's your business, play-actor?'

At the repetition of this last word, to her so mysterious, the girl outside pressed her eyes more eagerly to the chink and strained her ears to listen more sedulously. And what did the count mean by the 'other one' and 'a heavenly crown'?

'Why not call me King?' asked Rudolf.

'They call you that in Strelsau?'

'Those that know I'm here.'

'And they are——?'

'Some few score.'

'And thus', said Rupert, waving an arm towards the window, 'the town is quiet and the flags fly.'

'You've been waiting to see them lowered?'

'A man likes to have some notice taken of what he has done,' Rupert complained. 'However, I can get them lowered when I will.'

'By telling your news? Would that be good for yourself?'

'Forgive me—not that way. Since the King has two lives, it is but in nature that he should have two deaths.'

'And when he has undergone the second?'

'I shall live at peace, my friend, on a certain source of income that I possess.' He tapped his breast-pocket with a slight defiant laugh. 'In these days,' said he, 'even queens must be careful about their letters. We live in moral times.'

'You don't share the responsibility for it,' said Rudolf, smiling.

'I make my little protest. But what's your business, play-actor?—for I think you're rather tiresome.'

Rudolf grew grave. He advanced towards the table and spoke in low, serious tones.

'My lord, you're alone in this matter now. Rischenheim is a prisoner; your rogue Bauer I encountered last night and broke his head.'

'Ah, you did?'

'You have what you know of in your hands. If you yield, on my honour I will save your life.'

'You don't desire my blood, then, most forgiving play-actor?'

'So much, that I daren't fail to offer you life,' answered Rudolf Rassendyll. 'Come, sir, your plan has failed: give up the letter.'

Rupert looked at him thoughtfully.

'You'll see me safe off if I give it you?' he asked.

'I'll prevent your death. Yes, and I'll see you safe.'

'Where to?'

'To a fortress, where a trustworthy gentleman will guard you.'

'For how long, my dear friend?'

'I hope for many years, my dear count.'

'In fact, I suppose, as long as——?'

'Heaven leaves you to the world, count. It's impossible to set you free.'

'That's the offer, then?'

'The extreme limit of indulgence,' answered Rudolf.

Rupert burst into a laugh, half of defiance, yet touched with the ring of true amusement. Then he lit a cigarette, and sat puffing and smiling.

'I should wrong you by straining your kindness so far,' said he; and in wanton insolence, seeking again to show Mr Rassendyll the

mean esteem in which he held him and the weariness his presence
was, he raised his arms and stretched them above his head, as a
man does in the fatigue of tedium. 'Heigho!' he yawned.

But he had overshot the mark this time. With a sudden swift
bound Rudolf was upon him; his hands gripped Rupert's wrists,
and with his greater strength he bent back the count's pliant
body till trunk and head lay flat on the table. Neither man spoke;
their eyes met; each heard the other's breathing and felt the
vapour of it on his face. The girl outside had seen the movement
of Rudolf's figure, but her cranny did not serve to show her the
two where they were now; she knelt on her knees in ignorant
suspense. Slowly and with patient force Rudolf began to work his
enemy's arms towards one another. Rupert had read his design in
his eyes, and resisted with tense muscles. It seemed as though his
arms must crack; but at last they moved. Inch by inch they were
driven closer; now the elbows almost touched; now the wrists
joined in reluctant contact. The sweat broke out on the count's
brow, and stood in large drops on Rudolf's. Now the wrists were
side by side, and slowly the long sinewy fingers of Rudolf's right
hand, that held one wrist already in their vice, began to creep
round the other. The grip seemed to have half numbed Rupert's
arms, and his struggles grew fainter. Round both wrists the
sinewy fingers climbed and coiled; gradually and timidly the
grasp of the other hand was relaxed and withdrawn. Would the
one hold both? With a great spasm of effort Rupert put it to the
proof. The smile that bent Mr Rassendyll's lips gave the answer.
He could hold both, with one hand he could hold both: not for
long, no, but for an instant. And then, in the instant, his left hand,
free at last, shot to the breast of the count's coat. It was the same
that he had worn at the hunting-lodge, and was ragged and torn
from the boar-hound's teeth. Rudolf tore it further open, and his
hand dashed in.

'God's curse on you!' snarled Rupert of Hentzau.

But Mr Rassendyll still smiled. Then he drew out a letter.
A glance at it showed him the Queen's seal. As he glanced Rupert
made another effort. The one hand, wearied out, gave way, and
Mr Rassendyll had no more than time to spring away, holding his
prize. The next moment he had his revolver in his hand—none

too soon, for Rupert of Hentzau's barrel faced him, and they stood thus, opposite to one another, with no more than three or four feet between the mouths of their weapons.

There is, indeed, much that may be said against Rupert of Hentzau, the truth about him wellnigh forbidding that charity of judgment which we are taught to observe towards all men. But neither I nor any man who knew him ever found in him a shrinking from danger or a fear of death. It was no feeling such as these, but rather a cool calculation of chances that now stayed his hand. Even if he were victorious in the duel, and both did not die, yet the noise of firearms would greatly decrease his chances of escape. Moreover, he was a noted swordsman, and conceived that he was Mr Rassendyll's superior in that exercise. The steel offered him at once a better prospect of victory and more hope of a safe flight. So he did not pull his trigger, but maintaining his aim the while, said:

'I'm not a street bully, and I don't excel in a rough-and-tumble. Will you fight now like a gentleman? There's a pair of blades in the case yonder.'

Mr Rassendyll, in his turn, was keenly alive to the peril that still hung over the Queen. To kill Rupert would not serve her if he himself also were shot and left dead, or so helpless that he could not destroy the letter; and while Rupert's revolver was at his heart he could not tear it up nor reach the fire that burnt on the other side of the room. Nor did he fear the result of a trial with steel, for he had kept himself in practice and improved his skill since the days when he came first to Strelsau.

'As you will,' said he. 'Provided we settle the matter here and now, the manner is the same to me.'

'Put your revolver on the table, then, and I'll lay mine beside it.'

'I beg your pardon,' smiled Rudolf, 'but you must lay yours down first.'

'I'm to trust you, it seems, but you won't trust me!'

'Precisely. You know you can trust me; you know that I can't trust you.'

A sudden flush swept over Rupert of Hentzau's face. There were moments when he saw, in the mirror of another's face or words, the estimation in which honourable men held him; and I believe that he hated Mr Rassendyll most fiercely, not for thwarting his enterprise, but because he had more power than any other man to show him that picture. His brows knit in a frown and his lips shut tight.

'Aye, but though you won't fire, you'll destroy the letter,' he sneered. 'I know your fine distinctions.'

'Again I beg your pardon. You know very well that, although all Strelsau were at the door, I wouldn't touch the letter.'

With an angry muttered oath Rupert flung his revolver on the table. Rudolf came forward and laid his by it. Then he took up both and, crossing to the mantelpiece, laid them there; between them he placed the Queen's letter. A bright blaze burnt in the stove; it needed but the slightest motion of his hand to set the letter beyond all danger. But he placed it carefully on the mantelpiece, and, with a slight smile on his face, turned to Rupert, saying:

'Now shall we resume the bout that Fritz von Tarlenheim interrupted in the forest of Zenda?'

All this while they had been speaking in subdued accents, resolution in one, anger in the other, keeping the voice to an even, deliberate lowness. The girl outside caught only a word here and there; but now suddenly the flash of steel gleamed on her eyes through the crevice of the hinge. She gave a sudden gasp, and, pressing her face closer to the opening, listened and looked. For Rupert of Hentzau had taken the swords from their case and put them on the table. With a slight bow Rudolf took one, and the two assumed their positions. Suddenly Rupert lowered his point. The frown vanished from his face, and he spoke in his usual bantering tone.

'By the way,' said he, 'perhaps we're letting our feelings run away with us. Have you more of a mind now to be King of Ruritania? If so I'm ready to be the most faithful of your subjects.'

'You honour me, count.'

'Provided, of course, that I'm one of the most favoured and the richest. Come, come, the fool is dead now; he lived like a fool and he died like a fool. The place is empty. A dead man has no rights and suffers no wrongs. Damn it, that's good law,

Rupert

isn't it? Take his place and his wife. You can pay my price then. Or are you still so virtuous? Faith, how little some men learn from the world they live in! If I had your chance——'

'Come, count, you'd be the last man to trust Rupert of Hentzau.'

'If I made it worth his while?'

'But he's a man who would take the pay and betray his associate.'

Again Rupert flushed. When he next spoke his voice was hard, cold and low.

'By God! Rudolf Rassendyll,' said he, 'I'll kill you here and now.'

'I ask no better than that you should try.'

'And then I'll proclaim that woman for what she is through all Strelsau.'

A smile came on his lips as he watched Rudolf's face.

'Guard yourself, my lord,' said Mr Rassendyll.

'Aye, for no better than—— There, man, I'm ready for you.' For Rudolf's blade had touched his in warning.

The steel jangled. The girl's pale face was at the crevice of the hinge. She heard the blades cross again and again. Then one would run up the other with a sharp grating slither. At times she caught a glimpse of a figure in quick forward lunge or rapid wary withdrawal. Her brain was almost paralysed. Ignorant of the mind and heart of young Rupert, she could not conceive that he tried to kill the King. Yet the words she had caught sounded like the words of men quarrelling, and she could not persuade herself that the gentlemen fenced only for pastime. They were not speaking now; but she heard their hard breathing and the movement of their unresting feet on the bare boards of the floor. Then a cry rang out, clear and merry with the fierce hope of triumph:

'Nearly! nearly!'

She knew the voice for Rupert of Hentzau's, and it was the King who answered calmly:

'Nearly isn't quite.'

Again she listened. They seemed to be pausing for a moment, for there was no sound, save of the hard breathing and deep-drawn pants of men who rest an instant in the midst of intense exertion. Then came again the clash and the slitherings; and one of them crossed into her view. She knew the tall figure and she saw the red hair; it was the King. Backward step by step he seemed to be driven, coming nearer and nearer to the door. At last there was no more than a foot between him and her; only the crazy panel prevented her putting out her hand to touch him. Again the voice of Rupert rang out in rich exultation:

'I have you now! Say your prayers, King Rudolf!'

'Say your prayers!' Then they fought! It was earnest, not play. And it was the King—her King—her dear King, who was in great peril of his life! For an instant she knelt, still watching. Then with a low cry of terror she turned and ran headlong down the steep stairs. Her mind could not tell her what to do, but her heart cried out that she must do something for her King. Reaching the ground floor, she ran with wide-open eyes into the kitchen. The stew was on the hob; the old woman still held the spoon, but she had ceased to stir and fallen into a chair.

'He's killing the King! He's killing the King!' cried Rosa, seizing her mother by the arm. 'Mother, what shall we do? He's killing the King!'

The old woman looked up with dull eyes and a stupid cunning smile.

'Let them alone,' she said. 'There's no King here.'

'Yes, yes. He's upstairs in the count's room. They're fighting, he and the Count of Hentzau. Mother, Count Rupert will kill him!'

'Let them alone. He the King? He's no king,' muttered the old woman again.

For an instant Rosa stood looking down on her in helpless despair. Then a light flashed into her eyes.

'I must call for help!' she cried.

The old woman seemed to spring to sudden life. She jumped up and caught her daughter by the shoulder.

'No, no,' she whispered in quick accents. 'You—you don't know. Let them alone, you fool! It's not our business. Let them alone.'

'Let me go, mother, let me go! Mother, I must help the King!'

'I'll not let you go,' said Mother Holf.

But Rosa was young and strong; her heart was fired with terror for the King's danger.

'I must go!' she cried; and she flung her mother's grasp off from her, so that the old woman was thrown back into her chair, and the spoon fell from her hand and clattered on the tiles. But Rosa turned and fled down the passage and through the shop. The bolts delayed her trembling fingers for an instant. Then she flung the door wide. A new amazement filled her eyes at the sight of the eager crowd before the house. Then her eyes fell on me where I stood beside the lieutenant and Rischenheim, and she uttered her wild cry, 'Help! The King!'

With one bound I was by her and in the house, while Bernenstein cried, 'Quicker!' from behind.

CHAPTER XVIII

The Triumph of the King

THE things that men call presages, presentiments and so forth are to my mind for the most part idle nothings: sometimes it is only that probable events cast before them a natural shadow, which superstitious fancy twists into a heaven-sent warning; oftener the same desire that gives conception works fulfilment, and the dreamer sees in the result of his own act and will a mysterious accomplishment independent of his effort. Yet when I observe thus calmly and with good sense on the matter to the Constable of Zenda, he shakes his head and answers: 'But Rudolf Rassendyll knew from the first that he would come again to Strelsau and engage young Rupert point to point. Else why did he practice with the foils so as to be a better swordsman the second time than he was the first? Mayn't God do anything that Fritz von Tarlenheim can't understand? A pretty notion, on my life!' and he goes off grumbling.

Well, be it inspiration or be it delusion—and the difference stands often on a hair's breadth—I am glad that Rudolf had it. For if a man once grows rusty, it is everything short of impossible to put the fine polish on his skill again. Mr Rassendyll had strength, will, coolness and, of course, courage. None would have availed had not his eye been in perfect familiarity with its work and his hand obeyed it as readily as the bolt slips in a well-oiled groove. As the thing stood, the lithe agility and unmatched dash of young Rupert but just missed being too much for him. He was in deadly peril when the girl Rosa ran down to bring him aid. His practised skill was able to maintain his defence. He sought to do no more, but endured Rupert's fiery attacks and wily feints in an almost motionless stillness. Almost, I say; for the slight turns of wrist that seem nothing are everything, and served here to keep his skin whole and his life in him.

There was an instant—Rudolf saw it in his eyes and dwelt on it when he lightly painted the scene for us—when there dawned on Rupert of Hentzau the knowledge that he could not break down his enemy's guard. Surprise, chagrin, amusement, or something like it, seemed blended in his look. He could not

He could not break down his enemy's guard

make out how he was caught and checked in every effort, meeting, it seemed, a barrier of iron impregnable in rest. His quick brain grasped the lesson in an instant. If his skill were not the greater, the victory would not be his, for his endurance was the less. He was younger and his frame not so closely knit; pleasure had taken its tithe from him; perhaps a good cause goes for something. Even while he almost pressed Rudolf against the panel of the door, he seemed to know that his measure of success was

full. But what the hand could not compass the head might
contrive. In quickly conceived strategy he began to give pause in
his attack, nay, he retreated a step or two. No scruples hampered
his devices, no code of honour limited the means he would
employ. Backing before his opponent, he seemed to Rudolf to
be faint-hearted; he was baffled, but seemed despairing; he was
weary, but played a more complete fatigue. Rudolf advanced,
pressing and attacking, only to meet a defence as perfect as his
own. They were in the middle of the room now, close by the
table. Rupert, as though he had eyes in the back of his head,
skirted round, avoiding it by a narrow inch. His breathing was
quick and distressed, gasp tumbling over gasp, but still his eye
was alert and his hand unerring. He had but a few moments' more
effort left in him; it was enough if he could reach his goal and
perpetrate the trick on which his mind, fertile in every base
device, was set. For it was towards the mantelpiece that his
retreat, seeming forced, in truth so deliberate, led him. There
was the letter, there lay the revolvers. The time to think of risks
was gone by; the time to boggle over what honour allowed or
forbade had never come to Rupert of Hentzau. If he could not
win by force and skill he would win by guile, and by treachery to
the test that he had himself invited. The revolvers lay on the
mantelpiece: he meant to possess himself of one, if he could gain
an instant in which to snatch it.

The device that he adopted was nicely chosen. It was too late
to call a rest or ask breathing space; Mr Rassendyll was not blind
to the advantage he had won, and chivalry would have turned to
folly had it allowed such indulgence. Rupert was hard by the
mantelpiece now. The sweat was pouring from his face, and his
breast seemed like to burst in the effort after breath; yet he had
enough strength for his purpose. He must have slackened his hold
on his weapon, for when Rudolf's blade next struck it, it flew
from his hand, twirled out of a nerveless grasp, and slid along the
floor. Rupert stood disarmed, and Rudolf motionless.

'Pick it up,' said Mr Rassendyll, never thinking there had been
a trick.

'Aye, and you'll truss me while I do it.'

'You young fool, don't you know me yet?' And Rudolf

lowered his blade, resting its point on the floor, while with his left hand he indicated Rupert's weapon. Yet something warned him: it may be there came a look in Rupert's eyes, perhaps of scorn for his enemy's simplicity, perhaps of pure triumph in the graceless knavery. Rudolf stood waiting.

'You swear you won't touch me while I pick it up?' asked Rupert, shrinking back a little, and thereby getting an inch or two nearer the mantelpiece.

'You have my promise; pick it up. I won't wait any longer.'

'You won't kill me unarmed?' cried Rupert in alarmed scandalized expostulation.

'No; but——'

The speech went unfinished, unless a sudden cry were its ending. And as he cried, Rudolf Rassendyll, dropping his sword on the ground, sprang forward. For Rupert's hand had shot out behind him and was on the butt of one of the revolvers. The whole trick flashed on Rudolf, and he sprang, flinging his long arms round Rupert. But Rupert had the revolver in his hand.

In all likelihood the two neither heard nor heeded, though it seemed to me that the creaks and groans of the old stairs were loud enough to wake the dead. For now Rosa had given the alarm: Bernenstein and I—or I and Bernenstein (for I was first, and therefore may put myself first)—had rushed up. Hard behind us came Rischenheim, and hot on his heels a score of fellows, pushing and shouldering and trampling. We in front had a fair start, and gained the stairs unimpeded; Rischenheim was caught up in the ruck and gulfed in the stormy tossing group that struggled for first footing on the steps. Yet soon they were after us, and we heard them reach the first landing as we sped up to the last. There was a confused din through all the house, and it seemed now to echo muffled and vague through the walls from the street without. I was conscious of it, although I paid no heed to anything but reaching the room where the King—where Rudolf—was. Now I was there, Bernenstein hanging to my heels. The door did not hold us a second. I was in, he after me. He slammed the door and set his back against it, just as the rush of feet flooded the highest flight of stairs. And at the moment a revolver shot rang clear and loud.

The lieutenant and I stood still, he against the door, I a pace farther into the room. The sight we saw was enough to arrest us with its strange interest. The smoke of the shot was curling about, but neither man seemed wounded. The revolver was in Rupert's hand, and its muzzle smoked. But Rupert was jammed against the wall, just by the side of the mantelpiece. With one hand Rudolf had pinned his left arm to the wainscoting higher than his head, with the other he held his right wrist. I drew slowly nearer; if Rudolf was unarmed I could fairly enforce a truce and put them on equality; yet, though Rudolf was unarmed, I did nothing. The sight of his face stopped me. He was very pale and his lips were set, but it was his eyes that caught my gaze, for they were glad and merciless. I had never seen him look thus before. I turned from him to young Hentzau's face. Rupert's teeth were biting his under lip, the sweat dropped and the veins swelled large and blue on his forehead; his eyes were set on Rudolf Rassendyll. Fascinated, I drew nearer. Then I saw what passed. Inch by inch Rupert's arm curved, the elbow bent, the hand that had pointed almost straight from him and at Mr Rassendyll pointed now away from both towards the window. But its motion did not stop; it followed the line of a circle; now it was on Rupert's arm; still it moved, and quicker now, for the power of resistance grew less. Rupert was beaten; he felt it and knew it, and I read the knowledge in his eyes. I stepped up to Rudolf Rassendyll. He heard or felt me, and turned his eyes for an instant. I do not know what my face said, but he shook his head and turned back to Rupert. The revolver, held still in the man's own hand, was at his heart. The motion ceased, the point was reached.

I looked again at Rupert. Now his face was easier; there was a slight smile on his lips; he flung back his comely head and rested thus against the wainscoting; his eyes asked a question of Rudolf Rassendyll. I turned my gaze to where the answer was to come, for Rudolf made none in words. By the swiftest of movements he shifted his grasp from Rupert's wrist and pounced on his hand. Now his forefinger rested on Rupert's, and Rupert's was on the trigger. I am no soft-heart, but I laid a hand on his shoulder. He took no heed; I dared do no more. Rupert glanced at me. I caught his look, but what could I say to him? Again my eyes were riveted on Rudolf's finger. Now it was crooked round Rupert's, seeming like a man who strangles another.

I will not say more. He smiled to the last; his proud head, which had never bent for shame, did not bend for fear. There was a sudden tightening in the pressure of that crooked forefinger, a flash, a noise. He was held up against the wall for an instant by Rudolf's hand; when that was removed he sank, a heap that looked all head and knees.

But hot on the sound of the discharge came a shout and an oath from Bernenstein. He was hurled away from the door, and through it burst Rischenheim, and the whole score after him. They were jostling one another and crying out to know what had passed and where the King was. High over all the voices, coming from the back of the throng, I heard the cry of the girl Rosa. But as soon as they were in the room, the same spell that had fastened Bernenstein and me to inactivity imposed its numbing power on them also. Only Rischenheim gave a sudden sob and ran forward to where his cousin lay. The rest stood staring. For a moment Rudolf faced them. Then, without a word, he turned his back. He put out the right hand with which he had just killed Rupert of Hentzau, and took the letter from the mantelpiece. He glanced at the envelope, then he opened the letter. The handwriting banished any last doubt he had; he tore the letter across, and again in four pieces, and yet again to smaller fragments. Then he sprinkled the morsels of paper into the blaze of fire. I believe that every eye in the room followed them and watched till they curled and crinkled into black wafery ashes. Thus at last the Queen's letter was safe.

When he had thus set the seal on his task, he turned round to us again. He paid no heed to Rischenheim, who was crouching down by the body of Rupert; but he looked at Bernenstein and me, and then at the people behind us. He waited a moment before he spoke; then his utterance was not only calm but also very slow, so that he seemed to be choosing his words carefully.

'Gentlemen,' said he, 'a full account of this matter will be rendered by myself in due time. For the present it must suffice to say that this gentleman who lies here dead sought an interview with me on private business. I came here to find him, desiring, as he professed to desire, privacy. And here he tried to kill me. The result of his attempt you see.'

I bowed low, Bernenstein did the like, and all the rest followed our example.

'A full account shall be given,' said Rudolf. 'Now let all leave me except the Count of Tarlenheim and Lieutenant von Bernenstein.'

Most unwillingly, with gaping mouths and wonder-struck eyes, the throng filed out of the door. Rischenheim rose to his feet.

'You stay, if you like,' said Rudolf, and the count again knelt by his kinsman.

Seeing the rough bedsteads by the wall of the attic, I touched Rischenheim on the shoulder and pointed to one of them. Together we lifted Rupert of Hentzau. The revolver was still in his hand, but Bernenstein disengaged it from his grasp. Then Rischenheim and I laid him down, disposing his body decently and spreading over it his riding-cloak, still spotted with the mud gathered on his midnight expedition to the hunting-lodge. His face looked much as before the shot was fired; in death, as in life, he was the handsomest fellow in all Ruritania. I wager that many tender hearts ached and many bright eyes were dimmed for him when the news of his guilt and death went forth. There are ladies still in Strelsau who wear his trinkets in an ashamed devotion that cannot forget. Well, even I, who had every good cause to hate and scorn him, set the hair smooth on his brow; while Rischenheim was sobbing like a child, and young Bernenstein rested his head on his arm as he leant on the mantelpiece and would not look at the dead. Rudolf alone seemed not to heed or think of him. His eyes had lost their unnatural look of joy, and were now calm and tranquil. He took his own revolver from the mantelpiece and put it in his pocket, laying Rupert's neatly where his had been. Then he turned to me, and said:

'Come, let us go to the Queen and tell her that the letter is beyond reach of hurt.'

Moved by some impulse, I walked to the window and put my head out. I was seen from below and a great shout greeted me.

The crowd before the doors grew every moment: the people flocking from all quarters would soon multiply it a hundredfold; for such news as had been carried from the attic by twenty wondering tongues spread like a forest fire. It would be through Strelsau in a few minutes, through the kingdom in an hour, through Europe in but little longer. Rupert was dead and the letter was safe, but what were we to tell that great concourse concerning their King? A queer feeling of helpless perplexity came over me, and found vent in a foolish laugh. Bernenstein was by my side; he also looked out, and turned again with an eager face.

'You'll have a royal progress to your palace,' said he to Rudolf Rassendyll.

Mr Rassendyll made no answer, but, coming to me, took my arm. We went out, leaving Rischenheim by the body. I did not think of him; Bernenstein probably thought that he would keep his pledge given to the Queen, for he followed us immediately and without demur. There was nobody outside the door. The house was very quiet, and the tumult from the street reached us only in a muffled roar. But when we came to the foot of the stairs we found the two women. Mother Holf stood on the threshold of the kitchen, looking amazed and terrified. Rosa was clinging to her; but as soon as Rudolf came in sight the girl sprang forward and flung herself on her knees before him, pouring out incoherent thanks to Heaven for 'his safety. He bent down and spoke to her in a whisper; she looked up with a flush of pride on her face. He seemed to hesitate a moment; he glanced at his hands, but he wore no ring save that which the Queen had given him long ago. Then he disengaged his chain and took his gold watch from his pocket. Turning it over he showed me the monogram, 'R.R.'

'Rudolfus Rex,' he whispered with a whimsical smile, and pressed the watch into the girl's hand, saying: 'Keep this to remind you of me.'

She laughed and sobbed as she caught it with one hand, while with the other she held his.

'You must let me go,' he said gently. 'I have much to do.'

I took her by the arm and induced her to rise. Rudolf, released, passed on to where the old woman stood. He spoke to her in a stern, distinct voice.

'I don't know', he said, 'how far you are a party to the plot that was hatched in your house. For the present I am content not to know, for it is no pleasure to me to detect disloyalty or to punish an old woman. But take care! The first word you speak, the first act you do against me, the King, will bring its certain and swift punishment. If you trouble me, I won't spare you. In spite of traitors, I am still King in Strelsau.'

He paused, looking hard in her face. Her lip quivered and her eyes fell.

'Yes,' he repeated, 'I am King in Strelsau. Keep your hands out of mischief and your tongue quiet.'

She made no answer. He passed on. I was following, but as I went by her the old woman clutched my arm.

'In God's name, who is he?' she whispered.

'Are you mad?' I asked, lifting my brows. 'Don't you know the King when he speaks to you? And you'd best remember what he said. He has servants who'll do his orders.'

She let me go and fell back a step. Young Bernenstein smiled at her; he at least found more pleasure than anxiety in our position. Thus, then, we left them: the old woman terrified, amazed, doubtful; the girl with ruddy cheeks and shining eyes, clasping in her two hands the keepsake that the King himself had given her.

Bernenstein had more presence of mind than I. He ran forward, got in front of both of us, and flung the door open. Then, bowing very low, he stood aside to led Rudolf pass. The street was full from end to end now, and a mighty shout of welcome rose from thousands of throats. Hats and handkerchiefs were waved in mad exultation and triumphant loyalty. The tidings of the King's escape had flashed through the city, and all were there to do him honour. They had seized some gentleman's landau and taken out the horses. The carriage stood now before the door of the house. Rudolf had waited a moment on the threshold, lifting his hat once or twice; his face was perfectly calm, and I saw no trembling in his hands. In an instant a dozen arms took gentle hold of him and impelled him forward. He mounted the carriage;

Bernenstein and I followed, with bare heads, and sat on the back
seat, facing him. The people were round as thick as bees, and it
seemed as though we could not move without crushing somebody. Yet presently the wheels turned and they began to drag us
away at a slow walk. Rudolf kept raising his hat, bowing now to
right, now to left. But once, as he turned, his eyes met ours. In
spite of what was behind and what was in front, we all three
smiled.

'I wish they'd go a little quicker,' said Rudolf in a whisper,
as he conquered his smile and turned again to acknowledge the
loyal greetings of his subjects.

But what did they know of any need for haste? They did not
know what stood on the turn of the next few hours, nor the
momentous question that pressed for instant decision. So far
from hurrying, they lengthened our ride by many pauses; they
kept us before the cathedral, while some ran and got the joy-
bells ringing; we were stopped to receive improvised bouquets
from the hands of pretty girls and impetuous handshakings from
enthusiastic loyalists. Through it all Rudolf kept his composure,
and seemed to play his part with native kingliness. I heard
Bernenstein whisper: 'By God, he must stick to it!'

At last we came in sight of the palace. Here also there was a
great stir. Many officers and soldiers were about. I saw the
chancellor's carriage standing near the portico, and a dozen other
handsome equipages were waiting till they could approach. Our
human horses drew us slowly up to the entrance. Helsing was on
the steps, and ran down to the carriage, greeting the King with
passionate fervour. The shouts of the crowd grew louder still.

But suddenly a stillness fell on them; it lasted but an instant,
and was the prelude to a deafening roar. I was looking at Rudolf,
and saw his head turn suddenly and his eyes grow bright. I
looked where his eyes had gone. There, on the top step of the
broad marble flight, stood the Queen, pale as the marble itself,
stretching out her hands towards Rudolf. The people had seen
her: she it was whom this last rapturous cheer greeted. My wife
stood close behind her, and farther back others of her ladies.
Bernenstein and I sprang out. With a last salute to the people,
Rudolf followed us. He walked up to the highest step but one,

and there fell on one knee and kissed the Queen's hand. I was by him, and when he looked up in her face I heard him say:

'All's well. He's dead, and the letter burnt.'

She raised him with her hand. Her lips moved, but it seemed as though she could find no words to speak. She put her arm through his, and thus they stood for an instant, fronting all Strelsau. Again the cheers rang out, and young Bernenstein sprang forward, waving his helmet and crying like a man possessed: 'God save the King!' I was carried away by the enthusiasm and followed his lead. All the people took up the cry with boundless fervour, and thus we all, high and low in Strelsau, that afternoon hailed Mr Rassendyll for our King. There has been no such zeal since Henry the Lion came back from his wars, a hundred and fifty years ago.

'And yet', observed old Helsing at my elbow, 'agitators say there is no enthusiasm for the House of Elphberg!' He took a pinch of snuff in scornful satisfaction.

Young Bernenstein interrupted his cheering with a short laugh, but fell to his task again in a moment. I had recovered my senses by now, and stood panting, looking down on the crowd. It was growing dusk and the faces became blurred into a white sea. Yet suddenly I seemed to discern one glaring up at me from the middle of the crowd—the pale face of a man with a bandage about his head. I caught Bernenstein's arm and whispered 'Bauer', pointing with my finger where the face was. But even as I pointed it was gone: though it seemed impossible for a man to move in that press, yet it was gone. It had come like a cynic's warning across the scene of mock triumph, and went swiftly as it had come, leaving behind it a reminder of our peril. I felt suddenly sick at heart, and almost cried out to the people to have done with their silly shouting.

At last we got away. The plea of fatigue met all visitors who made their way to the door and sought to offer their congratulations; it could not disperse the crowd that hung persistently and contentedly about, ringing us in the palace with a living fence. We still heard their jests and cheers when we were alone in the small saloon that opens on the gardens. My wife and I had come there at Rudolf's request; Bernenstein had assumed the duty of guarding the door. Evening was now falling fast, and it grew dark. The garden was quiet; the distant noise of the crowd threw its stillness into greater relief. Rudolf told us there the story of his struggle with Rupert of Hentzau in the attic of the old house, dwelling on it as lightly as he could. The Queen stood by his chair—she would not let him rise; when he finished, by telling how he burnt her letter, she stooped suddenly and kissed him on the brow. Then she looked straight across at Helga almost defiantly; but Helga ran to her and caught her in her arms.

Rudolf Rassendyll sat with his head resting on his hand. He looked up once at the two women; then he caught my eye, and beckoned me to come to him. I approached him, but for several moments he did not speak. Again he motioned to me, and, resting my hand on the arm of his chair, I bent my head close down to his. He glanced again at the Queen, seemed afraid that she would hear what he wished to say.

'Fritz,' he whispered at last, 'as soon as it's fairly dark I must get away. Bernenstein will come with me. You must stay here.'

'Where can you go?'

'To the lodge. I must meet Sapt and arrange matters with him.'

I did not understand what plan he had in his head, or what scheme he could contrive. But at the moment my mind was not directed to such matters; it was set on the sight before my eyes.

'And the Queen?' I whispered in answer to him.

Low as my voice was, she heard it. She turned to us with a sudden startled movement, still holding Helga's hand. Her eyes searched our faces, and she knew in an instant of what we had been speaking. A little longer still she stood, gazing at us. Then she suddenly sprang forward and threw herself on her knees before Rudolf, her hands uplifted and resting on his shoulders. She forgot our presence and everything in the world save her great dread of losing him again.

'Not again, Rudolf, my darling! Not again! Rudolf, I can't bear it again.'

Then she dropped her head on his knees and sobbed.

He raised his hand and gently stroked the gleaming hair. But he did not look at her. He gazed out at the garden, which grew dark and dreary in the gathering gloom. His lips were tight set and his face pale and drawn. I watched him for a moment; then I drew my wife away, and we sat down at a table some way off. From outside still came the cheers and tumult of the joyful excited crowd. Within there was no sound but the Queen's stifled sobbing. Rudolf caressed her shining hair and gazed into the night with sad set eyes.

She raised her head and looked into his face.

'You'll break my heart,' she said.

CHAPTER XIX

For our Love and her Honour!

RUPERT OF HENTZAU was dead. That was the thought which among all our perplexities came back to me, carrying with it a wonderful relief. To those who have not learnt in fighting against him the height of his audacity and the reach of his designs it may well seem incredible that his death should breed comfort at a moment when the future was still so dark and uncertain. Yet to me it was so great a thing that I could hardly bring myself to the conviction that we had done with him. True he was dead; but could he not strike a blow at us even from beyond the gulf?

Such were the half-superstitious thoughts that forced their way into my mind as I stood looking out on the crowd which obstinately encircled the front of the palace. I was alone; Rudolf was with the Queen, my wife was resting, Bernenstein had sat down to a meal for which I could find no appetite. By an effort I freed myself from my fancies and tried to concentrate my brain on the facts of our position. We were ringed round with difficulties. To solve them was beyond my power; but I knew where my wish and longing lay. I had no desire to find means by which Rudolf Rassendyll should escape unknown from Strelsau, the King, although dead, be again in death the King, and the Queen be left desolate on her mournful and solitary throne. It might be that a brain more astute than mine could bring all this to pass. My imagination would have none of it, but dwelt lovingly on the reign of him who was now King in Strelsau, declaring that to give the kingdom such a ruler would be a splendid fraud, and prove a stroke so bold as to defy detection. Against it stood only the suspicions of Mother Holf—fear or money would close her lips—and the knowledge of Bauer; Bauer's mouth could also be shut, aye, and should be before we were many days older. My reverie led me far; I saw the future years unroll before me in the

214

fair record of a great King's sovereignty. It seemed to me that by the violence and bloodshed we had passed through, Fate, for once penitent, was but righting the mistake made when Rudolf was not born a king.

For a long while I stood thus, musing and dreaming; I was roused by the sound of the door opening and closing; turning, I saw the Queen. She was alone, and came towards me with timid steps. She looked out for a moment on the square and the people, but drew back suddenly in apparent fear lest they should see her. Then she sat down and turned her face towards mine. I read in her eyes something of the conflict of emotions which possessed her; she seemed at once to deprecate my dis-approval and to ask my sympathy; she prayed me to be gentle to her fault and kind to her happiness; self-reproach shadowed her joy, but the golden gleam of it strayed through. I looked eagerly at her: this would not have been her bearing had she come from a last farewell; for the radiance was there, however much dimmed by sorrow and by fearfulness.

'Fritz,' she began softly, 'I am wicked—so wicked. Won't God punish me for my gladness?'

I fear I paid little heed to her trouble, though I can understand it well enough now.

'Gladness?' I cried in a low voice. 'Then you've persuaded him?'

She smiled at me for an instant.

'I mean you've agreed——?' I stammered.

Her eyes again sought mine, as she said in a whisper:

'Some day, not now. Oh, not now. Now would be too much. But some day, Fritz, if God will not deal too hardly with me, I—I shall be his, Fritz.'

I was intent on my vision, not on hers. I wanted him King; she did not care what he was, so that he was hers, so that he should not leave her.

'He'll take the throne?' I cried triumphantly.

'No, no, no. Not the throne. He's going away.'

'Going away!' I could not keep the dismay out of my voice.

'Yes, now. But not—not for ever. It will be long—oh, so long!—but I can bear it, if I know that at last——'

She stopped, still looking up at me with eyes that implored pardon and sympathy.

'I don't understand,' said I bluntly, and I fear gruffly also.

'You were right,' she said: 'I did persuade him. He wanted to go away again as he went before. Ought I to have let him? Yes, yes! But I couldn't. Fritz, hadn't I done enough? You don't know what I've endured. And I must endure more still. For he will go now, and the time will be very long. But at last we shall be together. There is pity in God; we shall be together at last.'

'If he goes now, how can be come back?'

'He will not come back; I shall go to him. I shall give up the throne and go to him, some day, when I can be spared from here, when I've done my—my work.'

I was aghast at this shattering of my vision, yet I could not be hard to her. I said nothing, but took her hand and pressed it.

'You wanted him to be King?' she whispered.

'With all my heart, madame,' said I.

'He wouldn't, Fritz. No, and I shouldn't dare to do that either.'

I fell back on the practical difficulties.

'But how can he go?' I asked.

'I don't know. But he knows: he has a plan.'

We fell again into silence; her eyes grew more calm and seemed to look forward in patient hope to the time when her happiness should come to her. I felt like a man suddenly robbed of the exaltation of wine and sunk to dull apathy.

'I don't see how he can go,' I said sullenly.

She did not answer me. A moment later the door again opened. Rudolf came in, followed by Bernenstein. Both wore riding-boots and cloaks. I saw on Bernenstein's face just such a look of disappointment as I knew must be on mine. Rudolf seemed calm and even happy. He walked straight up to the Queen.

'The horses will be ready in a few minutes,' he said gently. Then, turning to me, he asked: 'You know what we are going to do, Fritz?'

'Not I, sire,' I answered sulkily.

'Not I, sire!' he repeated, in a half-merry, half-sad mockery. Then he came between Bernenstein and me and passed his arms through ours. 'You two villains!' he said. 'You two unscrupulous villains! Here you are as rough as bears, because I won't be a thief. Why have I killed young Rupert and left you rogues alive?'

I felt the friendly pressure of his hand on my arm. I could not answer him. With every word from his lips and every moment of his presence my sorrow grew keener that he would not stay. Bernenstein looked across at me and shrugged his shoulders despairingly. Rudolf gave a little laugh.

'You won't forgive me for not being as great a rogue, won't you?' he asked.

Well, I found nothing to say, but I took my arm out of his and clasped his hand. He gripped mine hard.

'That's old Fritz!' he said; and he caught hold of Bernenstein's hand, which the lieutenant yielded with some reluctance. 'Now for the plan,' said he. 'Bernenstein and I set out at once for the lodge—yes, publicly, as publicly as we can. I shall ride right through the people there, showing myself to as many as will look at me, and letting it be known to everybody where I'm going. We shall get there quite early tomorrow, before it's light. There we shall find what you know. We shall find Sapt too, and he'll put the finishing touches to our plan for us. Hallo, what's that?'

There was a sudden fresh shouting from the large crowd that still lingered outside the palace. I ran to the window and saw a commotion in the midst of them. I flung the sash up. Then I heard a well-known, loud strident voice:

'Make way, you rascals, make way!'

I turned round again full of excitement.

'It's Sapt himself!' I said. 'He's riding like mad through the crowd, and your servant's just behind him.'

'My God! What's happened? Why have they left the lodge?' cried Bernenstein.

The Queen looked up in startled alarm, and, rising to her feet, came and passed her arm through Rudolf's. Thus we all stood, listening to the people good-naturedly cheering Sapt, whom they had recognized, and bantering James, whom they took for a servant of the Constable's.

The minutes seemed very long as we waited in utter perplexity,

P

almost in consternation. The same thought was in the mind of all of us, silently imparted by one to another in the glances we exchanged. What could have brought them from their guard of the great secret save its discovery? They would never have left their post while the fulfilment of their trust was possible. By some mishap, some unforeseen chance, the King's body must have been discovered. Then the King's death was known, and the news of it might any moment astonish and bewilder the city.

At last the door was flung open, and a servant announced the Constable of Zenda. Sapt was covered with dust and mud, and James, who entered close on his heels, was in no better plight. Evidently they had ridden hard and furiously; indeed they were still panting. Sapt, with a most perfunctory bow to the Queen, came straight to where Rudolf stood.

'Is he dead?' he asked, without preface.

'Yes, Rupert is dead!' answered Mr Rassendyll: 'I killed him.'

'And the letter?'

'I burnt it.'

'And Rischenheim?'

The Queen struck in.

'The Count of Luzau-Rischenheim will say and do nothing against me,' she said.

Sapt lifted his brows a little.

'Well, and Bauer?' he asked.

'Bauer's at large,' I answered.

'Hum! Well, it's only Bauer,' said the Constable, seeming tolerably well pleased. Then his eyes fell on Rudolf and Bernenstein. He stretched out his hand and pointed to their riding-boots. 'Whither away, so late at night?' he asked.

'First together to the lodge, to find you; then I alone to the frontier,' said Mr Rassendyll.

'One thing at a time. The frontier will wait. What does Your Majesty want with me at the lodge?'

'I want so to contrive that I shall be no longer Your Majesty,' said Rudolf.

Sapt flung himself in a chair and took off his gloves.

'Come, tell me what has happened today in Strelsau,' he said.

We gave a short and hurried account. He listened with few

signs of approval or disapproval; but I thought I saw a gleam in his eyes when I described how all the city had hailed Rudolf as its King, and the Queen received him as her husband before the eyes of all. Again the hope and vision, shattered by Rudolf's calm resolution, inspired me. Sapt said little, but he had the air of a man with some news in reserve. He seemed to be comparing what we told him with something already known to him but unknown to us. The little servant stood all the while in respectful silence by the door; but I could see by a glance at his alert face that he followed the whole scene with keen attention.

At the end of the story Rudolf turned to Sapt.

'And your secret—is it safe?' he asked.

'Aye, it's safe enough.'

'Nobody has seen what you had to hide?'

'No; and nobody knows that the King is dead,' answered Sapt.

'Then what brings you here?'

'Why, the same thing that was about to bring you to the lodge: the need of a meeting between yourself and me, sire.'

'But the lodge—is it left unguarded?'

'The lodge is safe enough,' said Colonel Sapt.

Unquestionably there was a secret, a new secret, hidden behind the curt words and brusque manner. I could restrain myself no longer, and sprang forward, saying:

'What is it? Tell us, Constable!'

He looked at me, then glanced at Mr Rassendyll.

'I should like to hear your plan first,' he said to Rudolf. 'How do you mean to account for your presence alive in the city today, when the King has lain dead in the hunting-lodge since last night?'

We drew closer together as Rudolf began his answer. Sapt alone lay back in his chair. The Queen also had resumed her seat; she seemed to pay little heed to what we said.

I think that she was still engrossed with the struggle and tumult in her own soul. The sin of which she accused herself, and the joy to which her whole being sprang in a greeting which would not be abashed, were at strife between themselves, but joined hands to exclude from her mind any other thought.

'In an hour I must be gone from here,' began Rudolf.

'If you wish that, it's easy,' observed Colonel Sapt.

'Come, Sapt, be reasonable,' smiled Mr Rassendyll. 'Early tomorrow we, you and I——'

'Oh, I also?' asked the Colonel.

'Yes: you, Bernenstein and I will be at the lodge.'

'That's not impossible, though I have had nearly enough riding.'

Rudolf fixed his eyes firmly on Sapt's.

'You see,' said he, 'the King reaches his hunting-lodge early in the morning.'

'I follow you, sir.'

'And what happens there, Sapt? Does he shoot himself accidentally?'

'Well, that happens sometimes.'

'Or does an assassin kill him?'

'Eh, but you've made the best assassin unavailable.'

Even at this moment I could not help smiling at the old fellow's surly wit and Rudolf's amused tolerance of it.

'Or does his faithful attendant, Herbert, shoot him?'

'What, make poor Herbert a murderer?'

'Oh, no! By accident—and then, in remorse, kill himself.'

'That's very pretty. But doctors have awkward views as to when a man can have shot himself.'

'My good Constable, doctors have palms as well as ideas. If you fill the one you supply the other.'

'I think', said Sapt, 'that both the plans are good. Suppose we choose the latter, what then?'

'Why, then, by tomorrow at midday the news flashes through Ruritania—yes, and through Europe—that the King, miraculously preserved today——'

'Praise be to God!' interjected Colonel Sapt; and young Bernenstein laughed.

'—has met a tragic end.'

'It will occasion great grief,' said Sapt.

'Meanwhile I am safe over the frontier.'

'Oh, you're quite safe?'

'Absolutely. And in the afternoon of tomorrow, you and Bernenstein will set out for Strelsau, bringing with you the body of the King.' And Rudolf, after a pause whispered: 'You must shave his face. And if the doctors want to talk about how long he's been dead, why, they have, as I say, palms.'

Sapt sat silent for a while, apparently considering the scheme. It was risky enough in all conscience, but success had made Rudolf bold, and he had learnt how slow suspicion is if a deception be bold enough. It is only likely frauds that are detected.

'Well, what do you say?' asked Mr Rassendyll. I observed that he said nothing to Sapt of what the Queen and he had determined to do afterwards.

Sapt wrinkled his forehead. I saw him glance at James, and the slightest, briefest smile showed on James's face.

'It's dangerous, of course,' pursued Rudolf. 'But I believe that when they see the King's body——'

'That's the point,' interrupted Sapt. 'They can't see the King's body.'

Rudolf looked at him with some surprise. Then speaking in a low voice, lest the Queen should hear and be distressed, he went on:

'You must prepare it, you know. Bring it here in a shell; only a few officials need see the face.'

Sapt rose to his feet and stood before Mr Rassendyll.

'The plan's a pretty one, but it breaks down at one point,' said he in a strange voice, even harsher than his was wont to be. I was on fire with excitement, for I would have staked my life now that he had some strange tidings for us. 'There is no body,' said he.

Even Mr Rassendyll's composure gave way. He sprang forward, catching Sapt by the arm.

'No body? What do you mean?' he exclaimed.

Sapt cast another glance at James, and then began in an even, mechanical voice, as though he were reciting a lesson he had learnt, or playing a part that habit made familiar:

'That poor fellow Herbert carelessly left a candle burning where the oil and the wood were kept,' he said. 'This afternoon, about six, James and I lay down for a nap after our meal. At about seven James came to my side and roused me. My room was full of smoke. The lodge was ablaze. I darted from my bed: the fire had made too much headway, we could not hope to quench it; we had but one thought——' He suddenly paused, and looked at James.

'But one thought, to save our companion,' said James gravely.

'But one thought, to save our companion. We rushed to the door of the room where he was. I opened the door and tried to enter. It was certain death. James tried, but fell back. Again I rushed in. James pulled me back: it was but another death. We had to save ourselves. We gained the open door. The lodge was a sheet of flame. We could do nothing but stand watching, till the swiftly burning wood blackened to ashes and the flames died down. As we watched we knew that all in the cottage must be dead. What could we do? At last James started off in the hope of getting help. He found a party of charcoal-burners, and they came with him. The flames had burnt down now; and we and they approached the charred ruins. Everything was in ashes. But'—he lowered his voice—'we found what seemed to be the body of Boris the hound; in another room was a charred corpse, whose hunting-horn, melted to a molten mass, told us it had been Herbert the forester. And there was another corpse, almost shapeless, utterly unrecognizable. We saw it; the charcoal-burners saw it. Then more peasants came round, drawn by the sight of the flames. None could tell who it was; only I and James knew. And we mounted our horses and have ridden here to tell the King.'

Sapt finished his lesson or his story. A sob burst from the Queen, and she hid her face in her hands. Bernenstein and I, amazed at this strange tale, scarcely understanding whether it were jest or earnest, stood staring stupidly at Sapt. Then I, overcome by the strange thing, turned half-foolish by the bizarre mingling of comedy and impressiveness in Sapt's rendering of it, plucked him by the sleeve, and asked, with something between a laugh and a gasp:

'Who had that other corpse been, Constable?'

He turned his small keen eyes on me in persistent gravity and unflinching effrontery:

'A Mr Rassendyll, a friend of the King's, who with his servant James was awaiting His Majesty's return from Strelsau. His servant here is ready to start for England to tell Mr Rassendyll's relatives the news.'

The Queen had begun to listen before now; here eyes were fixed on Sapt, and she had stretched out one arm to him, as if imploring him to read her his riddle. But a few words had in truth declared his device plainly enough in all its simplicity. Rudolf Rassendyll was dead, his body burnt to a cinder, and the King was alive, whole and on his throne in Strelsau. Thus had Sapt caught from James the servant the infection of his madness, and had fulfilled in action the strange imagination which the little man had unfolded to him in order to pass their idle hours at the lodge.

Suddenly Mr Rassendyll spoke in clear short tones:

'This is all a lie, Sapt,' said he, and his lips curled in contemptuous amusement.

'It's no lie that the lodge is burnt and the bodies in it, and that half a hundred of the peasants know it, and that no man could tell the body for the King's. As for the rest, it is a lie. But I think the truth in it is enough to serve.'

The two men stood facing one another with defiant eyes. Rudolf had caught the meaning of the great and audacious trick which Sapt and his companion had played. It was impossible now to bring the King's body to Strelsau; it seemed no less impossible to declare that the man burnt in the lodge was the King. Thus Sapt had forced Rudolf's hand; he had been inspired by the same vision as we, and endowed with more unshrinking boldness. But when I saw how Rudolf looked at him, I did not know but that they would go from the Queen's presence set on a deadly quarrel. Mr Rassendyll, however, mastered his temper.

'You're all bent on having me a rascal,' he said coldly. 'Fritz and Bernenstein here urge me; you, Sapt, try to force me. James there is in the plot, for all I know.'

'I suggested it, sir,' said James, not defiantly or with disrespect, but as in simple dutiful obedience to his master's implied question.

'As I thought—all of you! Well, I won't be forced. I see now that there's no way out of this affair, save one. That one I'll follow.'

We none of us spoke, but waited till he should be pleased to continue.

'Of the Queen's letter I need say nothing, and will say nothing,' he pursued. 'But I will tell them that I'm not the King, but Rudolf Rassendyll; and that I played the King only in order to serve the Queen and punish Rupert of Hentzau. That will serve, and it will cut this net of Sapt's from about my limbs.'

He spoke firmly and coldly, so that when I looked at him I was amazed to see how his lips twitched and that his forehead was moist with sweat. Then I understood what a sudden, swift and fearful struggle he had suffered, and how the great temptation had wrung and tortured him before he, victorious, had set the thing behind him. I went to him and clasped his hand: this action of mine seemed to soften him.

'Sapt, Sapt,' he said, 'you almost made a rogue of me!'

Sapt did not respond to his gentler mood. He had been pacing angrily up and down the room. Now he stopped abruptly before Rudolf and pointed with his finger at the Queen.

'I make a rogue of you!' he exclaimed. 'And what do you make of our Queen, whom we all serve? What does this truth that you'll tell make of her? Haven't I heard how she greeted you before all Strelsau as her husband and her love? Will they believe that she didn't know her husband? Aye, you may show yourself, you may say they didn't know you. Will they believe she didn't? Was the King's ring on your finger? Where is it? And how comes Mr Rassendyll to be at Fritz von Tarlenheim's for hours with the Queen, when the King is at his hunting-lodge? A King has died already, and two men besides, to save a word against her. And you—you'll be the man to set every tongue in Strelsau talking, and every finger pointing in suspicion at her!'

Rudolf made no answer. When Sapt had first uttered the Queen's name, he had drawn near and let his hand fall over the back of her chair. She put hers up to meet it, and so they remained. But I saw that Rudolf's face had gone very pale.

'And we, your friends?' pursued Sapt. 'For we've stood by you as we've stood by the Queen, by God we have: Fritz and young Bernenstein here, and I. If this truth's told, who'll believe that we were loyal to the King, that we didn't know, that we weren't accomplices in the tricking of the King—maybe in his murder? Ah, Rudolf Rassendyll, God preserve me from a conscience that won't let me be true to the woman I love or to the friends who love me!'

I had never seen the old fellow so moved; he carried me with him, as he carried Bernenstein. I know now that we were too ready to be convinced; rather that, borne along by our passionate desire, we needed no convincing at all. His excited appeal seemed to us an argument. At least the danger to the Queen on which he dwelt was real and true and great.

Then a sudden change came over him. He caught Rudolf's hand and spoke to him again in a low broken voice, an unwonted softness transforming his harsh tones.

'Lad,' he said, 'don't say "No!" Here's the finest lady alive sick for her lover, and the finest country in the world sick for its true King, and the best friends—aye, by Heaven, the best friends —man ever had, sick to call you master. I know nothing about your conscience, but this I know: the King's dead, and the place is empty; and I don't see what Almighty God sent you here for unless it was to fill it. Come, lad—for our love and her honour! While he was alive I'd have killed you sooner than let you take it. He's dead. Now—for our love and her honour, lad!'

I do not know what thoughts passed in Mr Rassendyll's mind. His face was set and rigid. He made no sign when Sapt finished, but stood as he was, motionless, for a long while. Then he slowly bent his head and looked down into the Queen's eyes. For a while she sat looking back into his. Then carried away by the wild hope of immediate joy, and by her love for him, and her pride in the place he was offered, she sprang up and threw herself at his feet crying:

'Yes, yes! For my sake, Rudolf—for my sake!'

'Are you too against me, my Queen?' he murmured, caressing her ruddy hair.

Chapter XX

The Decision of Heaven

WE WERE half mad that night, Sapt and Bernenstein and I. The thing seemed to have got into our blood and to have become part of ourselves. For us it was inevitable—nay, it was done. Sapt busied himself in preparing the account of the fire at the hunting-lodge; it was to be communicated to the journals, and it told with much circumstantiality how Rudolf Rassendyll had come to visit the King, with James his servant, and, the King being summoned unexpectedly to the capital, had been awaiting His Majesty's return when he met his fate. There was a short history of Rudolf, a glancing reference to his family, a dignified expression of condolence with his relatives, to whom the King was sending messages of deepest regret by the hands of Mr Rassendyll's servant. At another table young Bernenstein was drawing up, under the Constable's direction, a narrative of Rupert of Hentzau's attempt on the King's life and the King's courage in defending himself. The count, eager to return (so it ran), had persuaded the King to meet him by declaring that he held a State document of great importance and of a most secret nature; the King, with his habitual fearlessness, had gone alone, but only to refuse with scorn Count Rupert's terms. Enraged at this unfavourable reception, the audacious criminal had made a sudden attack on the King, with what issue all knew. He had met his own death, while the King, perceiving from a glance at the document that it compromised well-known persons, had, with the nobility which marked him, destroyed it unread before the eyes of those who were rushing in to his rescue. I supplied suggestions and improvements; and engrossed in con-triving how to blind curious eyes, we forgot the real and per-manent difficulties of the thing we had resolved upon. For us they did not exist: Sapt met every objection by declaring that

226

the thing had been done once and could be done again. Bernenstein and I were not behind him in confidence. We would guard the secret with brain and hand and life, even as we had guarded and kept the secret of the Queen's letter, which would now go with Rupert of Hentzau to his grave. Bauer we could catch and silence: nay, who would listen to such a tale from such a man? Rischenheim was ours; the old woman would keep her doubts between her teeth for her own sake. To his own land and his own people Rudolf must be dead, while the King of Ruritania would stand before all Europe, recognized, unquestioned, unassailed. True he must marry the Queen again; Sapt was ready with the means, and would hear nothing of the difficulty and risk in finding a hand to perform the necessary ceremony. If we quailed in our courage, we had but to look at the alternative, and find recompense for the perils of what we meant to undertake by a consideration of the desperate risk involved in abandoning it. Persuaded that the substitution of Rudolf for the King was the only thing which would serve our turn, we asked no longer whether it was possible, but sought only the means to make it safe and yet more safe.

But Rudolf himself had not spoken. Sapt's appeal and the Queen's imploring cry had shaken but not overcome him; he had wavered, but he was not won. Yet there was no talk of impossibility or peril in his mouth, any more than in ours: those were not what gave him pause. The score on which he hesitated was whether the thing should be done, not whether it could; our appeals were not to brace a failing courage, but to cajole a sturdy sense of honour which found the imposture distasteful so soon as it seemed to serve a personal end. To save the King he had played the King in old days, but he did not love to play the King when the profit of it was to be his own. Hence he was unmoved till his care for the fair fame of the Queen and the love of his friends joined to buffet his resolution. Then he faltered; but he had not fallen. Yet Colonel Sapt did all as though he had given his assent, and watched the last hours in which his flight from Strelsau was possible go quickly by with more than equanimity. Why hurry Rudolf's resolve? Every moment shut him closer in the trap of an inevitable choice. With every hour

that he was called the King it became more impossible for him
to bear any other name all his days. Therefore Sapt let Mr
Rassendyll doubt and struggle, while he himself wrote his story
and laid his long-headed plans. And now and then James the
little servant came in and went out, sedate and smug, but with a
quiet satisfaction gleaming in his eyes. He had made a story
for a pastime, and it was being translated into history. He at
least would bear his part in it unflinchingly.

Before now the Queen had left us, persuaded to lie down and
try to rest till the matter should be settled. Stilled by Rudolf's
gentle rebuke, she had urged him no more in words, but there
was an entreaty in her eyes stronger than any spoken prayer,
and a piteousness in the lingering of her hand in his harder to
resist than ten thousand sad petitions. At last he had led her
from the room and commended her to Helga's care. Then,
returning to us, he stood silent a little while. We also were
silent, Sapt sitting and looking up at him with his brows knit
and his teeth restlessly chewing the moustache on his lip.

'Well, lad?' he said at last, briefly putting the great question.

Rudolf walked to the window and seemed to lose himself for
a moment in the contemplation of the quiet night. There were
no more than a few stragglers in the street now; the moon shone
white and clear on the empty square.

'I should like to walk up and down outside and think it over,'
he said, turning to us, and, as Bernenstein sprang up to accompany him, he added, 'No. Alone.'

'Yes, do,' said old Sapt, with a glance at the clock, whose
hands were now hard on two o'clock. 'Take your time, lad,
take your time.'

Rudolf looked at him and broke into a smile.

'I'm not your dupe, old Sapt,' said he, shaking his head.
'Trust me, if I decide to get away, I'll get away, be it what
o'clock it will.'

'Yes, confound you!' grinned Colonel Sapt.

So he left us, and then came that long time of scheming and
planning and most persistent eye-shutting, in which occupa-
tions an hour wore its life away. Rudolf had not passed out of
the porch, and we supposed that he had betaken himself to the

gardens, there to fight his battle. Old Sapt, having done his work, suddenly turned talkative.

'That moon there,' he said, pointing his square thick fore-finger at the window, 'is a mighty untrustworthy lady. I've known her wake a villain's conscience before now.'

'I've known her send a lover's to sleep,' laughed young Bernenstein, rising from his table, stretching himself and lighting a cigar.

'Aye, she's apt to take a man out of what he is,' pursued old Sapt. 'Set a quiet man near her, and he dreams of battle; an ambitious fellow, after ten minutes of her, will ask nothing better than to muse all his life away. I don't trust her, Fritz; I wish the night were dark.'

'What will she do to Rudolf Rassendyll?' I asked, falling in with the old fellow's whimsical mood.

'He will see the Queen's face in hers,' cried Bernenstein.

'He may see God's,' said Sapt; and he shook himself as though an unwelcome thought had found its way to his mind and lips.

A pause fell on us, born of the colonel's last remark. We looked one another in the face. At last Sapt brought his hand down on the table with a bang.

'I'll not go back!' he said sullenly, almost fiercely.

'Nor I,' said Bernenstein, drawing himself up. 'Nor you, Tarlenheim?'

'No, I also go on,' I answered. Then again there was a moment's silence.

'She may make a man soft as a sponge,' reflected Sapt, start-ing again, 'or hard as a bar of steel. I should feel safer if the night were dark. I've looked at her often from my tent and from bare ground, and I know her. She got me a decoration, and once she came near to making me turn tail. Have nothing to do with her, young Bernenstein.'

'I'll keep my eyes for beauties nearer at hand,' said Bernen-stein, whose volatile temper soon threw off a serious mood.

'There's a chance for you, now Rupert of Hentzau's gone,' said Sapt grimly.

As he spoke there was a knock at the door. When it opened, James entered.

'The Count of Luzau-Rischenheim begs to be allowed to speak with the King,' said James.

'We expect His Majesty every moment. Beg the count to enter,' Sapt answered; and, when Rischenheim came in, he went on, motioning the count to a chair: 'We are talking, my lord, of the influence of the moon on the careers of men.'

'What are you going to do? What have you decided?' burst out Rischenheim impatiently.

'We decide nothing,' answered Sapt.

'Then what has Mr—what has the King decided?'

'The King decides nothing, my lord. *She* decides,' and the old fellow pointed again through the window towards the moon. 'At this moment she makes or unmakes a king; but I can't tell you which. What of your cousin?'

'You know that my cousin's dead.'

'Yes, I know that. What of him, though?'

'Sir,' said Rischenheim with some dignity, 'since he is dead, let him rest in peace. It is not for us to judge him.'

'He may well wish it were. For, by Heaven, I believe I should let the rogue off,' said Colonel Sapt, 'and I don't think his Judge will.'

'God forgive him, I loved him,' said Rischenheim. 'Yes, and many have loved him. His servants loved him, sir.'

'Friend Bauer, for example?'

'Yes, Bauer loved him. Where is Bauer?'

'I hope he is gone to hell with his loved master,' grunted Sapt, but he had the grace to lower his voice and shield his mouth with his hand, so that Rischenheim did not hear.

'We don't know where he is,' I answered.

'I am come', said Rischenheim, 'to put my services in all respects at the Queen's disposal.'

'And at the King's?' asked Sapt.

'At the King's? But the King is dead.'

'Therefore "Long live the King!"' struck in young Bernenstein.

'If there should be a King——' began Sapt.

'You'll do that?' interrupted Rischenheim in breathless agitation.

'She is deciding,' said Colonel Sapt, and again he pointed to the moon.

'But she's a plaguy long time about it,' remarked Lieutenant von Bernenstein.

Rischenheim sat silent for a moment. His face was pale, and when he spoke his voice trembled. But his words were resolute enough.

'I gave my word of honour to the Queen, and even in that I will serve her if she commands me.'

Bernenstein sprang forward and caught him by the hand.

'That's what I like,' said he, 'and damn the moon, colonel!'

His sentence was hardly out of his mouth when the door opened, and to our astonishment the Queen entered. Helga was just behind; her clasped hands and frightened eyes seemed to protest that their coming was against her will. The Queen was clad in a long white robe, and her hair hung on her shoulders, being but loosely bound with a riband. Her air showed great agitation, and without any greeting or notice of the rest she walked quickly across the room to me.

'The dream, Fritz!' she said. 'It has come again. Helga persuaded me to lie down, and I was very tired, so at last I fell asleep. Then it came. I saw him, Fritz—I saw him as plainly as I see you. They all called him King, as they did today; but they did not cheer. They were quiet, and they looked at him with sad faces. I could not hear what they said; they spoke in hushed voices. I heard nothing more than "The King, the King ", and he seemed to hear not even that. He lay still; he was lying on something, something covered with hanging stuff, I couldn't see what it was; yes, quite still. His face was so pale, and he didn't hear them say "The King". Fritz, Fritz, he looked as if he were dead! Where is he? Where have you let him go?'

She turned from me and her eyes flashed over the rest.

'Where is he? Why aren't you with him?' she demanded with a sudden change of tone. 'Why aren't you around him? You should be between him and danger, ready to give your lives for his. Indeed, gentlemen, you take your duty lightly'.

It might be that there was little reason in her words. There appeared to be no danger threatening him; and after all he was not our King, much as we desired to make him such. Yet we did not think of any such matter. We were abashed before her reproof and took her indignation as deserved. We hung our heads, and Sapt's shame betrayed itself in the dogged sullenness of his answer.

'He has chosen to go walking, madame, and to go alone. He ordered us—I say, he ordered us not to come. Surely we are right to obey him?'

The sarcastic inflection of his voice conveyed his opinion of the Queen's extravagance.

'Obey him? Yes. You couldn't go with him if he forbade you. But you should follow him, you should keep him in sight.'

This much she spoke in proud tones and with a disdainful manner, but then came a sudden return to her former bearing. She held out her hands towards me, wailing:

'Fritz, where is he? Is he safe? Find him for me, Fritz, find him.'

'I'll find him for you if he's above ground, madame,' I cried, for her appeal touched me to the heart.

'He's no farther off than the gardens,' grumbled old Sapt, still resentful of the Queen's reproof and scornful of the woman's agitation. He was also out of temper with Rudolf himself, because the moon took so long in deciding whether she would make or unmake a king.

'The gardens!' she cried. 'Then let us look for him. Oh, you've let him walk in the gardens alone?'

'What should harm the fellow?' muttered Sapt.

She did not hear him, for she had swept out of the room. Helga went with her, and we all followed, Sapt behind the rest of us, still very surly. I heard him grumbling away as we ran downstairs and, having passed along the great corridor, came to the small saloon that opened on the gardens. There were no servants about, but we encountered a night-watchman, and Bernenstein snatched the lantern from the astonished man's hand.

Save for the dim light thus furnished, the room was dark. But outside the windows the moon streamed brightly down on the broad gravel walk, on the formal flower-beds and the great trees in the gardens. The Queen made straight for the window. I followed her, and, having flung the window open, stood by her. The air was sweet, and the breeze struck with grateful coolness on my face. I saw that Sapt had come near and stood on the other side of the Queen. My wife and the rest were behind, looking out where our shoulders left space.

There, in the bright moonlight, on the far side of the broad terrace, close by the line of tall trees that fringed its edge, we saw Rudolf Rassendyll pacing slowly up and down, with his hands behind his back and his eyes fixed on the arbiter of his fate, on her who was to make him a king or send him a fugitive from Strelsau.

'There he is, madame,' said Sapt. 'Safe enough!'

The Queen did not answer. Sapt said no more, and of the rest of us none spoke. We stood watching him as he struggled with his great issue: a greater surely has seldom fallen to the lot of any man born in a private station. Yet I could read little of it on the face that the rays of white light displayed so clearly, although they turned his healthy tints to a dull grey, and gave unnatural sharpness to his features against the deep background of black foliage.

I heard the Queen's quick breathing, but there was scarcely another sound. I saw her clutch her gown and pull it away a little from her throat; save for that, none in the group moved. The lantern's light was too dim to force notice from Mr Rassendyll. Unconscious of our presence, he wrestled with fate that night in the gardens.

Suddenly the faintest exclamation came from Sapt. He put his hand back and beckoned to Bernenstein. The young man handed his lantern to the Constable, who set it close to the side of the window-frame. The Queen, absolutely engrossed in her lover, saw nothing, but I perceived what had caught Sapt's attention. There were scores on the paint and indentations in the wood, just at the edge of the panel and near the lock. I glanced at Sapt, who nodded his head. It looked very much as though somebody had tried to force the door that night, employing a knife which had dented the woodwork and scratched the paint. The least thing was enough to alarm us, standing where

Q

we stood, and the Constable's face was full of suspicion. Who
had sought an entrance? It could be no trained and practised
housebreaker: he would have had better tools.

But now our attention was again diverted. Rudolf stopped
short. He still looked for a moment at the sky, then his glance
dropped to the ground at his feet. A second later he jerked his
head—it was bare, and I saw the dark-red hair stir with the
movement—like a man who has settled something which caused
him a puzzle. In an instant we knew, by the quick intuition of
contagious emotion, that the question had found its answer. He
was by now king or a fugitive. The Lady of the Skies had given
her decision. The thrill ran through us; I felt the Queen draw
herself together at my side; I felt the muscles of Rischenheim's
arm which rested against my shoulder grow rigid and taut.
Sapt's face was full of eagerness and he gnawed his moustache
savagely. We gathered closer to one another. At last we could
bear the suspense no longer. With one look at the Queen and
another at me, Sapt stepped on to the gravel. He would go and
learn the answer: thus the unendurable strain that had stretched
us like tortured men on a rack would be relieved. The Queen
did not answer his glance, nor even seem to see that he had
moved. Her eyes were still all for Mr Rassendyll, her thoughts
buried in his; for her happiness was in his hands and lay poised
on the issue of that decision whose momentousness held him for
a moment motionless on the path. Often I seem to see him as he
stood there, tall, straight and stately, the King a man's fancy
paints when he reads of great monarchs who flourished long ago
in the springtime of the world.

Sapt's step crunched on the gravel. Rudolf heard it and turned
his head. He saw Sapt, and he saw me also behind Sapt. He
smiled composedly and brightly, but he did not move from
where he was. He held out both hands towards the Constable
and caught him in their double grasp, still smiling down in his
face. I was no nearer to reading his decision, though I saw that
he had reached a resolution that was immovable and gave peace
to his soul. If he meant to go on he would go on now, go on to
the end, without a backward look or a falter of his foot; if he had
chosen the other way, he would depart without a murmur or a

hesitation. The Queen's quick breathing had ceased; she seemed like a statue; but Rischenheim moved impatiently, as though he could no longer endure the waiting.

Sapt's voice came harsh and grating.

'Well?' he cried. 'Which is it to be? Backwards or forward?'

Rudolf pressed his hands and looked into his eyes. The answer asked but a word from him. The Queen caught my arm; her rigid limbs seemed to give way, and she would have fallen if I had not supported her. At the same instant a man sprang out of the dark line of tall trees, directly behind Mr Rassendyll. Bernenstein uttered a loud startled cry, and rushed forward, pushing the Queen herself violently out of his path. His hand flew to his side, and he ripped the heavy cavalry sword that belonged to his uniform of the Cuirassiers of the Guard from its sheath. I saw it flash in the moonlight, but its flash was quenched in a brighter short blaze. A shot rang out through the quiet gardens. Mr Rassendyll did not loose his hold of Sapt's hands, but he sank slowly on to his knees. Sapt seemed paralysed. Again Bernenstein cried out. It was a name this time.

'Bauer! By God, Bauer!' he cried.

In an instant he was across the path and by the trees. The assassin fired again, but now he missed. We saw the great sword flash high above Bernenstein's head and heard it whistle through the air. It crashed on the crown of Bauer's head, and he fell like a log to the ground with his skull split. The Queen's hold on me relaxed; she sank into Rischenheim's arms. I ran forward and knelt by Mr Rassendyll. He still held Sapt's hands, and by their help buoyed himself up. But when he saw me he let go of them and sank back against me, his head resting on my chest. He moved his lips, but seemed unable to speak. He was shot through the back. Bauer had avenged the master whom he loved, and was gone to meet him.

There was a sudden stir from inside the palace. Shutters were flung back and windows thrown open. The group we made stood clean-cut, plainly visible, in the moonlight. A moment later there was a rush of eager feet, and we were surrounded by officers and servants. Bernenstein stood by me now, leaning on his sword: Sapt had not uttered a word; his face was distorted with horror and bitterness. Rudolf's eyes were closed and his head lay back against me.

'A man has shot the King,' said I in bald, stupid explanation.

All at once I found James, Mr Rassendyll's servant, by me.

'I have sent for doctors, my lord,' he said. 'Come, let us carry him in.'

He, Sapt and I lifted Rudolf and bore him across the gravel terrace and into the little saloon. We passed the Queen. She was leaning on Rischenheim's arm and held my wife's hand. We laid Rudolf down on a couch. Outside I heard Bernenstein say: 'Pick up that fellow and carry him somewhere out of sight.' Then he also came in, followed by a crowd. He sent them all to the door, and we were left alone, waiting for the surgeon. The Queen came up, Rischenheim still supporting her.

'Rudolf, Rudolf!' she whispered very softly.

He opened his eyes, and his lips bent in a smile. She flung herself on her knees, and kissed his hand passionately.

'The surgeon will be here directly,' said I.

Rudolf's eyes had been on the Queen. As I spoke he looked up at me, smiled again and shook his head. I turned away.

When the surgeon came Sapt and I assisted him in his examination. The Queen had been led away, and we were alone. The examination was very short. Then we carried Rudolf to a bed: the nearest chanced to be in Bernenstein's room; there we laid him, and there all that could be done for him was done. All this time we had asked no questions of the surgeon, and he had given no information. We knew too well to ask: we had all seen men die before now, and the look on the face was familiar to us. Two or three more doctors, the most eminent in Strelsau, came now, having been hastily summoned. It was their right to be called; but, for all the good they were, they might have been left to sleep the night out in their beds. They drew together in a little group at the end of the room and talked for a few minutes in low tones. James lifted his master's head and gave him a drink of water. Rudolf swallowed it with difficulty. Then I saw him feebly press James's hand, for the little man's face was full of sorrow. As his master smiled the servant mustered a smile in answer.

I crossed over to the doctors.

'Well, gentlemen?' I asked.

They looked at one another, then the greatest of them said gravely:

'The King may live an hour, Count Fritz. Should you not send for a priest?'

I went straight back to Rudolf Rassendyll. His eyes greeted me and questioned me. He was a man, and I played no silly tricks with him. I bent down and said:

'An hour, they think, Rudolf.'

He made one restless movement, whether of pain or protest I do not know. Then he spoke, very low, slowly and with difficulty.

'Then they can go,' he said; and when I spoke of a priest he shook his head.

I went back to them and asked if anything more could be done. The answer was, 'Nothing'; but I could not prevail further than to get all save one sent into an adjoining room; he who remained seated himself at a table some way off. Rudolf's eyes closed again; old Sapt, who had not once spoken since the shot was fired, raised a haggard face to mine.

'We'd better fetch her to him,' he said hoarsely. I nodded my head.

Sapt went while I stayed by him. Bernenstein came to him, bent down and kissed his hand. The young fellow, who had borne himself with such reckless courage and dash throughout the affair, was quite unmanned now, and the tears were rolling down his face. I could have been much in the same plight, but I would not before Mr Rassendyll. He smiled at Bernenstein. Then he said to me:

'Is she coming, Fritz?'

'Yes, she's coming, sire,' I answered.

He noticed the style of my address; a faint amused gleam shot into his languid eyes.

'Well, for an hour, then,' he murmured, and lay back on his pillows.

She came, dry-eyed, calm and queenly. We all drew back, and she knelt down by his bed, holding his hand in her two hands. Presently the hand stirred; she let it go; then, knowing well what he wanted, she raised it herself and placed it on her head, while she bowed her face to the bed. His hand wandered for the last time over the gleaming hair that he loved so well. She rose, passed her arm about his shoulders and kissed his lips. Her face rested close to his, and he seemed to speak to her, but we could not have heard the words even if we would. So they remained for a long while.

The doctor came and felt his pulse, retreating afterwards with close-shut lips. We drew a little nearer, for we knew that he would not be long with us now. Suddenly strength seemed to come upon him. He raised himself in his bed, and spoke in distinct tones:

'God has decided,' he said. 'I've tried to do the right thing through it all. Sapt, and Bernenstein, and you, old Fritz, shake my hand. No, don't kiss it. We've done with pretence now.'

We shook his hand as he bade us. Then he took the Queen's hand. Again she knew his mind, and moved it to his lips.

'In life and in death, my sweet Queen,' he murmured. And thus he fell asleep.

CHAPTER XXI

The Coming of the Dream

THERE is little need, and I have little heart, to dwell on what followed the death of Mr Rassendyll. The plans we had laid to secure his tenure of the throne, in case he had accepted it, served well in the event of his death. Bauer's lips were for ever sealed; the old woman was too scared and appalled to hint even to her gossips at the suspicions she entertained. Rischenheim was loyal to the pledge he had given to the Queen. The ashes of the hunting-lodge held their secret fast, and none suspected when the charred body which was called Rudolf Rassendyll's was laid to quiet rest in the graveyard of the town of Zenda, hard by the tomb of Herbert the forester. For we had from the first rejected any idea of bringing the King's body to Strelsau and setting it in the place of Mr Rassendyll's. The difficulties of such an undertaking were almost insuperable; in our hearts we did not desire to conquer them. As a King Rudolf Rassendyll had died, as a King let him lie. As a King he lay in his palace at Strelsau, while the news of his murder at the hands of a confederate of Rupert of Hentzau went forth to startle and appal the world. At a mighty price our task had been made easy; many might have doubted the living, none questioned the dead; suspicions which might have gathered round a throne died away at the gate of the vault. The King was dead. Who would ask if it were in truth the King who lay in state in the great hall of the palace, or whether the humble grave at Zenda held the bones of the last male Elphberg? In the silence of the grave all murmurs and questionings were hushed.

Throughout the day people had been passing and repassing through the great hall. There, on a stately bier, surmounted by a crown and the drooping folds of the royal banner, lay Rudolf Rassendyll. The highest officers guarded him; in the cathedral the archbishop said a mass for his soul. He had lain there three days; the evening of the third had come, and early on the morrow he was to be buried. There is a little gallery in the hall, that looks down on the spot where the bier stood; here was I on this evening, and with me Queen Flavia. We were alone together, and together we saw beneath us the calm face of the dead man. He was clad in the white uniform in which he had been crowned; the riband of the Red Rose was across his breast. His hand held a true red rose, fresh and fragrant; Flavia herself had set it there, that even in death he might not miss the chosen token of her love. I had not spoken to her, nor she to me, since we came there. We watched the pomp round him, and the rows of people that came to bring a wreath for him or to look upon his face. I saw a girl come and kneel long at the bier's foot. She rose and went away sobbing, leaving a little circlet of flowers. It was Rosa Holf. I saw women come and go weeping, and men bite their lips as they passed by. Rischenheim came, pale-faced and troubled; and while all came and went, there, immovable, with drawn sword, in military stiffness, old Sapt stood at the head of the bier, his eyes set steadily in front of him, and his body never stirring from hour to hour through the long day.

A distant faint hum of voices reached us. The Queen laid her hand on my arm.

'It is the dream, Fritz,' she said. 'Hark! They speak of the King; they speak in low voices and with grief, but they call him King. It's what I saw in the dream. But he does not hear nor heed. No, he can't hear nor heed even when I call him my King.'

A sudden impulse came on me, and I turned to her, asking:

'What had he decided, madame? Would he have been King?'

She started a little.

'He didn't tell me,' she answered, 'and I didn't think of it while he spoke to me.'

'Of what then did he speak, madame?'

'Only of his love—of nothing but his love, Fritz,' she answered.

Well, I take it that when a man comes to die, love is more to him than a kingdom: it may be, if we could see truly, that it is more to him even while he lives.

'Of nothing but his great love for me, Fritz,' she said again. 'And my love brought him to his death.'

'He wouldn't have had it otherwise,' said I.

'No,' she whispered; and she leant over the parapet of the gallery, stretching out her arms to him. But he lay still and quiet, not hearing and not heeding when she murmured, 'My King! My King!' It was even as it had been in the dream.

That night James, the servant, took leave of his dead master and of us. He carried to England by word of mouth—for we dared write nothing down—the truth concerning the King of Ruritania and Mr Rassendyll. It was to be told to the Earl of Burlesdon, Rudolf's brother, under a pledge of secrecy; and to this day the earl is the only man besides ourselves who knows the story. His errand done, James returned in order to enter the Queen's service, in which he still is; and he told us that when Lord Burlesdon had heard the story he sat silent for a great while, and then said:

'He did well. Some day I will visit his grave. Tell Her Majesty that there is still a Rassendyll, if she has need of one.'

The offer was such as should come from a man of Rudolf's name, yet I trust that the Queen needs no further service than such as it is our humble duty and dear delight to render her. It is our part to strive to lighten the burden that she bears, and by our love to assuage her undying grief. For she reigns now in Ruritania alone, the last of all the Elphbergs; and her only joy is to talk of Mr Rassendyll with those few who knew him, her only hope that she may some day be with him again.

In great pomp we laid him to his rest in the vault of the kings of Ruritania in the cathedral of Strelsau. There he lies among the princes of the House of Elphberg. I think that if there be indeed any consciousness among the dead, or any knowledge of what passes in the world they have left, they should be proud to call him brother. There rises in memory of him a stately monument, and people point it out to one another as the memorial of King Rudolf. I go often to the spot, and recall in thought all that passed when he came the first time to Zenda, and again on his second coming. For I mourn him as a man mourns a trusted leader and a loved comrade, and I should have asked no better than to be allowed to serve him all my days. Yet I serve the Queen, and in that I do most truly serve her lover.

Times change for all of us. The roaring flood of youth goes by, and the stream of life sinks to a quiet flow. Sapt is an old man now: soon my sons will be grown up, men enough themselves to serve Queen Flavia. Yet the memory of Rudolf Rassendyll is fresh to me as on the day he died, and the vision of the death of Rupert of Hentzau dances often before my eyes. It may be that some day the whole story shall be told, and men shall judge of it for themselves. To me it seems now as though all had ended well. I must not be misunderstood: my heart is still sore for the loss of him. But we saved the Queen's fair fame, and to Rudolf himself the fatal stroke came as a relief from a choice too difficult: on the one side lay what impaired his own honour, on the other what threatened hers. As I think on this my anger at his death is less, though my grief cannot be. To this day I know not how he chose; no, and I don't know how he should have chosen. Yet he had chosen, for his face was calm and clear.

Come, I have thought so much of him that I will go now and stand before his monument, taking with me my last-born son, a little lad of ten. He is not too young to desire to serve the Queen, and not too young to learn to love and reverence him who sleeps there in the vault and was in his life the noblest gentleman I have known.

I will take the boy with me and tell him what I may of brave King Rudolf, how he fought and how he loved, and how he held the Queen's honour and his own above all things in this world. The boy is not too young to learn such lessons from the life of Mr Rassendyll. And while we stand there I will turn again into his native tongue—for, alas, the young rogue loves his toy soldiers better than his Latin!—the inscription that the Queen wrote with her own hand, directing that it should be inscribed in that stately tongue over the tomb in which her life lies buried: 'To Rudolf, who reigned lately in this city, and reigns for ever in her heart.—QUEEN FLAVIA.'

I told him the meaning, and he spelt the big words over in his childish voice; at first he stumbled, but the second time he had it right, and recited with a little touch of awe in his fresh young tones:

'RUDOLFO

Qui in hac civitate nuper regnavit
In corde ipsius in aeternum regnat

FLAVIA REGINA.'

I felt his hand tremble in mine, and he looked up in my face. 'God save the Queen, father,' said he.